WHO REALLY INVENTED THE AUTOMOBILE

SKULDUGGERY AT THE CROSSROADS

Gurney, whose name as the extender of Steam to
economic uses will take a higher place in the gratitude
of posterity than Watt, the applier of it to physical. . .--
Richard Broun

FOR OTHER BOOKS BY DR. BEASLEY REPRODUCE AND SEND THIS PAGE TO DAVUS PUBLISHING, 150 NORFOLK ST. S., SIMCOE, ON. N3Y2W2 CANADA or P O BOX 1101, BUFFALO, N.Y. 14213-7101 UNITED STATES or ASK YOUR BOOKSTORE. [Libraries call Coutts 800-263-1686] PLEASE INCLUDE $3 FOR POSTAGE AND HANDLING FOR ORDERS FROM 1-3; $4 FOR 4-7; $6 FOR 8-10. FOR LARGER ORDERS CALL DAVUS 519 426 2077.

PLEASE SEND ME   (1) ....COPIES OF WHO REALLY INVENTED THE AUTOMOBILE for $17.95 (Cdn) $13.95 (U. S.) "Only automobile enthusiasts whose interests begin after World War II will not find this an engrossing book. It is excellent." Charles W. Bishop.
(2)...........COPIES OF THE GRAND CONSPIRACY; A NEW YORK LIBRARY MYSTERY FOR $10.95 (U.S.). & 14.95 (Cdn.) Rudyard Mack on the trail of political kidnapping and international crime syndicates.
(3)........ COPIES OF THE JENNY; A NEW YORK LIBRARY DETECTIVE NOVEL AT $7.95(U.S.).& $9.95 (Cdn) Library detective Mack solves case of biggest stamp theft in U.S. history. "Held me rivetted"--*ROTARY ON STAMPS;* "a fascinating tale,"--*STONEY CREEK NEWS.* "fun reading,"--*GLOBAL STAMP NEWS.* "The solution is as surprising as it is ingenious."--*THE SIMCOE REFORMER.* "It gets Gold for the "whodunnit" plot and the exciting, don't-put-me-down read that it is."--*CANADIAN STAMP NEWS.* "The writing is fast paced, ... a pleasant diversion on a hot summer afternoon."--*THE CANADIAN PHILATELIST.*
.(4)......... COPIES OF HAMILTON ROMANCE; a Hamilton-Toronto Nexus $19.95 Cdn., $14.95 U.S. (Romance and society after World War II. A sesquicentennial edition.) "A good read... funny and sad, just like life itself, as it traces the tale of young love... when everything seemed so different, yet things weren't really so different."--STONEY CREEK NEWS.: "thoughtful and often humorous... an enjoyable, rebellious, anti-establishment rant,...deserves a wide audience" *VIEW*
(5)..........COPIES OF CHOCOLATE FOR THE POOR; a story of rape in 1805 $13.95 Cdn. $11.95 U.S.. (Berkshires in 1805; a father accused of raping his daughter) "Held me spellbound," Angela Ariss, Children's Rights Advocate. "Gripping story...interesting cast of colourful characters...well written novel...Beasley paints pictures with short phrases."VIEW. "The political intrigues are brought to life vividly....Beasley allows us to see, and more importantly to feel, some of the forces that enmesh a man only too easily and drive him to acts otherwise incomprehensible." HAMILTON SPECTATOR.
(6)............ COPIES OF THAT OTHER GOD, A NOVEL $18.95 (U.S. and Cdn) American mystic brings people through telepathic communion into the universal subconscious to a realization of the God of humanity. "Compelling, really interesting, exciting...a cry for peace at a time of anarchy," *BRANTFORD EXPOSITOR;* "Absorbing....Gripping style, detailed observation, poetic images. Vital, entertaining, apocalyptic," Peter Rankin, NYC. "Compelling story [of] the saving values deep within the human spirit," *HUMAN QUEST.*
(7).............COPIES OF THROUGH PAPHLAGONIA WITH A DONKEY; A JOURNEY THROUGH THE TURKISH ISFENDYARS [illus.] $9.95 U.S. $11.95 Cdn. "Charmingly written,"--*EXPLORERS JOURNAL;* "Now that I have concluded my fourth re-reading, I have become...a thorough-going dweller in Paphlagonia and an ardent partisan of Bobby, the donkey"--*LOCAL 1930 NEWSLETTER;* "Insightful for students of cross-cultural communication."--*INTERNATIONAL JOURNAL OF INTERNATIONAL RELATIONS.*
(8)............ .COPIES OF THE CANADIAN DON QUIXOTE; THE LIFE AND WORKS OF MAJOR JOHN RICHARDSON, CANADA'S FIRST NOVELIST $6.95 Cdn.; $5.50 U.S. "Definitive "; "Not only a good read but the fulfillment of 'an aching void'." *BRICK;* "Very useful... mass of new information," *TORONTO GLOBE & MAIL.* "A roaring good adventure yarn about a highly eccentric dreamer," *LIBRARY JOURNAL.* "Brings to life the early history of this country," *KINGSTON WHIG STANDARD;*

NAME:
ADDRESS:

ENCLOSED PLEASE FIND A CHEQUE TO DAVUS PUBLISHING FOR $....................

WHO *REALLY* INVENTED THE AUTOMOBILE

by

DAVID BEASLEY

DAVUS PUBLISHING
SIMCOE ONTARIO
Davus sum, non Oedipus

This edition is a revised and enlarged edition of THE SUPPRESSION OF THE AUTOMOBILE; SKULDUGGERY AT THE CROSSROADS published by Greenwood Press, Westport, CT. in hard cover in 1988.

Beasley, David, 1931-
    Who really invented the automobile: skulduggery at the crossroads

Rev. ed.
First ed. published under title: The suppression of the automobile.
Includes bibliographical references and index.
ISBN 0-915317-08-7

        1. Automobile industry and trade--History. 2. Automobiles, Steam--
History. 3. Railroads--History.
I. Title: The suppression of the automobile.

HD9710.A2B42 1996   338.4'6292'09   C96-900803-1

DAVUS PUBLISHING

Canadian & American orders
150 Norfolk St. S.
Simcoe, On N3Y 2W2

American orders
P O Box 1101
Buffalo, N. Y. 14213-
7101

Contents

Illustrations

Tables

Preface

This detective story winds through a maze of clues over the span of a century. To give it the depth of a theory I had the guidance of the late Professor David M. Gordon. He showed me how to recreate the facts of the crime in a logical manner. I am grateful for his suggestions, encouragement, and concern for the subject.

I thank those people who helped me along the route of detection, in particular Mr. and Mrs. Peter Gurney and Lord Congleton for their hospitality and aid. Monsieur G. Dalimier kindly opened the papers of the Paris House of Rothschild to me. I thank Mr. G. Knight and Miss Y. Moss for their help with the London Rothschild papers. Archivists and librarians at the Bibliotheque Nationale, Archives Nationales, the British Libraries, various county and college archives in England, and the New York Public Library were very helpful.

I dedicate this book with great respect to my good friend the late Art Shields, indefatigable labor reporter and author of the autobiography *My Shaping-Up Years* and *On the Battle Lines, 1919-1939.*

Introduction

When asked to give a date for the invention of the automobile, most people will say that it originated in the early years of the twentieth century and that its discovery reflected some important technical breakthrough. In reality the automobile has a much longer history. It was developed to "perfection" by 1829, ran on the roads of Great Britain, and was suppressed by the British government.

Between this early date and the early twentieth century when the automobile was manufactured in several countries, there were two key moments in its history: the battle between the steam carriage and the railway in the 1830s and 1840s in Great Britain, and the battle between the steam automobile and the petroleum automobile in the 1880s and 1890s in France and Germany. In the first instance, the railway won a decisive victory; in the second instance, the petroleum automobile was victorious and throughout the twentieth century has been called the automobile.

In order to understand the automobile's development, we have to account for these two moments in its history. Two general economic approaches help provide an explanation. The first is through neoclassical economic theory. Neoclassical economics looks on invention as exogenous to the economy until it is introduced into the production process by an entrepreneur who finds the invention more cost-efficient or labor-saving than the technology in use. The diffusion of the invention in the economy depends on the extent of consumer demand for it or for its products. If the invention, through continuous innovation, remains competitive with other inventions that are introduced into the production process, it will continue to contribute to the economy. This neoclassical approach leads one to look for specific variables as factors affecting adoption of technology, such as the cost of producing the steam carriage relative to the cost of competing technology, its relative profit performance, consumer demand for it, and its capacity as a labor-saving or cost-saving function in producing economic wealth.

Three neoclassical economists developed these variables as explanations of invention. Joseph Schumpeter emphasized the moment of introduction of the invention as the choice of the entrepreneur who felt it would stimulate or regenerate a faltering economy. Such a moment happened on the downward curve of the long-range business cycle—at which time the entrepreneur would choose among a combination of innovations to create a new technology that met the demands of the consumer.

J. R. Hicks described "induced invention" as the introduction of new technology into the economy induced by a change in the relative share of factors. For example, if the price of labor rose relative to the price of capital and consequently the workers began to receive a larger share of the national revenue than the capitalists, the capitalists would introduce a labor-saving innovation to the production process. The production function in the neoclassical economic model would shift, and a new position of equilibrium would result. The variable one looks for in this case is the labor-saving or cost-saving function of the invention.

The third neoclassical economist, Jacob Schmookler, stressed the profitability of an industry as an attraction to inventors to create innovations for it, arguing that "capital goods invention tends to be distributed among industries . . . in accordance with inventive profits, and that expectations concerning the latter are probably governed by sales of capital goods to the particular industries involved, not by the state of the economy as a whole."[1] Inventions appear, therefore, in response to an assumption that the market demand is growing for products that may be produced by a particular industry.

As for testing the inventive potential of the average industry, Schmookler drew attention to the role of cost differentials in determining which product technologies among supplying firms are tapped to improve the production technology. He reasoned that the invention that costs the least will be used. Therefore, the important variables in his view were the profit advantages of an industry and the least-cost factor of an invention.

An alternative economic approach draws on the Marxian economic perspective—with its attention not only to the effects of competition and costs on the organization of production, but also to the political-economic forces that shape the environment within which production is organized. The Marxian perspective draws our attention to the demand for and supply of innovations as well as to the balance of inter- and intraclass power affecting the likelihood that cost-reducing innovations will, in fact, be applied.

The Marxian approach suggests, therefore, that we allow for the possibility of differentiating between what David M. Gordon calls "quantitative efficiency" and "qualitative efficiency." An invention or technical innovation that allows the production of more output with the same amount of input, or the same output at lower input cost, may be said to have improved the quantitative efficiency of production. Such inventions may be more or less qualitatively efficient, however, depending on their reinforcement or erosion of the controlling power of the dominant economic groups in a given social formation.[2]

I argue in this book that the Marxian approach is more illuminating as an explanation of the development of the automobile. I argue specifically that, in the first instance, the steam carriage was economically advantageous but failed because it was repressed. It was repressed because the political-economic groups supporting the railway were more powerful than those supporting the steam carriage. They supported the railway because they had monopoly control over it. The mineral industries they wished to develop were closely tied to railway development, and the railway as a carrier of heavy freight fitted in with their plans to develop England as a free trading economy.

In the second instance, the argument is more complicated. The use of petrol for the automobile may have been more advantageous than steam in the later version of the steam carriage, but its principal advantages lay in the likelihood that a specific complex of French financial and industrial interests, with strong international connections to sources of petroleum, would be able to control the full range of industries whose development would be spurred by the development of the petroleum automobile.

This argument requires a complex set of steps. It is not enough simply to examine the character and relative costs of different inventions. In order to allow for the possibility that factors identified by the Marxian argument may in fact have been decisive, one needs to develop a reasonable understanding of the broader climate and the specific economic interest groups with differential interests in various technologies.

I pursue these aspects of the argument in the following way: I introduce the steam carriage of Goldsworthy Gurney as a unique invention, demonstrate its viability as a commercial enterprise, explore the manner of its suppression, and explain the political-economic motivations of those groups which repressed it as against those which supported it.

In order to compare the steam carriage with the railway in this first moment of its development, I must examine each of the necessary elements of an invention—technical features, access to capital backing, evidence of relative marketability, and comparative costs. I review the evidence on each of these elements in turn. I conclude that certain interest groups preferred the railway because it was, from their vantage point, qualitatively efficient.

I further explore the connections between financial interest groups and the choice of technique, setting the stage for the later development of the petroleum automobile by reviewing the relative power and problems of different groups of financiers and merchants in Belgium, France, and England, the major economies competing for position in the Western European economy in the middle of the century. This analysis lays the groundwork for conclusions about the economic groups that promoted development of the railway in Europe, the growth of commercial nationalist rebellion against English domination, and the emerging struggle over markets for petroleum.

I conclude with an analysis of the invention and diffusion of the petroleum automobile, accounting for the final triumph of the petroleum automobile over the steam automobile in this second critical moment in the automobile's development. I show that, once again, the political-economic concerns of different economic interest groups in different countries shaped their evaluation of the advantages of the railway and the automobile and resulted in the final introduction of the automobile, fueled by petroleum, as an essential technique in twentieth-century capitalist production.

1

The Existence of the Steam Carriage

THE INVENTION ITSELF

The several survey histories of the automobile usually refer to Cugnot in France, Evans in Maryland, Symington in Scotland, Murdock in Cornwall followed by a dozen names from the 1820s and 1830s who tried and failed to make the steam carriage practicable. Goldsworthy Gurney is always mentioned and even excoriated in some works from the mid-nineteenth century. The truth is that Goldsworthy Gurney produced a workable steam carriage in 1827 and "perfected" it by 1829.

With hindsight it is difficult to see how anyone but Gurney could have invented the steam carriage. He was a medical doctor, a chemist, and a student of the steam engine from his schooldays in Cornwall where he frequented the home of Davies Gilbert (or "Giddy," as he was also known) and became a close friend of Richard Trevithick, already known for his invention of the high pressure steam engine which Giddy pronounced superior to James Watt's condensing steam engine. (Indeed, it was four times as powerful and rapidly replaced all Boulton and Watt engines in Cornwall mines.) The young boy and the famous engineer corresponded throughout Gurney's student years so that Gurney knew of all Trevithick's improvements in the steam engine. In his testimony before a parliamentary committee in 1834, Gurney recalled witnessing Trevithick's first experiment with a steam carriage in 1804.[3] The carriage steamed down a declivity but remained stuck in the hollow, its wheels spinning round until the steam was dissipated. Wheels inexplicably seemed unable to move a carriage along the ground surface, although they could do so quite readily on rails, as Trevithick demonstrated convincingly the same year with a steam locomotive at Merthyr Tydvil in Wales and at Euston Square in London in 1813. As a result, engineers firmly believed that there was a lack of sufficient friction for carriages to be self-propelled on level ground.

Gurney came to London as a young doctor in 1820 and, aside from building up a profitable practice, lectured on chemical science at the Surrey Institute. His lecture courses, which he published in 1823 as *A Course of Lectures on Chemical Science*, were so original and intellectually stimulating that they were attended by many prominent scientists and engineers. Here he laid the scientific groundwork for the steam carriage in three discoveries: (I) the chemical components required in steam to generate motive power, (2) the steam jet to raise that power to high levels, and (3) the principle of the separator which made his carriage boiler distinctive and superior to all the boilers devised by his rival steam carriage builders. He stated in these lectures that "elementary power was capable of being applied to propel carriages along common roads with great political advantage," and that "the floating knowledge of the day placed the object within our reach." Only one of his prominent listeners, Dr. William Hyde Wollaston, the chemist, supported him.

Chemical Components

Gurney's experimentation with different gases that could be managed with the equipment of the day led him to discover that ammonial gas, like steam, was absorbable in water under reduced temperature and pressure and when heated could be given out again with considerable force. In combination with other absorbable gases, it became manageable within an apparatus which he perfected by May 1825. Thus was laid the basis of his steam engine.

The Steam Jet

Gurney's idea for the steam jet had been brewing in his head since his youth. In those early years he had written to Trevithick about Trevithick's experiment in which he held the chimney of a burning argand lamp below the vapor issuing from the spout of a tea kettle in order to dissolve the vapor in the warm air. Trevithick tried to bring the waste steam from his locomotive into contact with the ascending hot air from the fire in the funnel, but the steam disappeared only when the temperature of the air in the flue was sufficiently high. Trevithick, finding on the whole that the smoke billowed forth as before, turned up the eduction pipe, allowing the waste steam to escape and setting an example that others followed. Gurney recognized the need for "the blow pipe" (as

2

he called it in lecture XIII) if enough power were ever to be generated to move a carriage swiftly. His daughter Anna recalled that as a young girl she would watch her father's experiment in the classroom with the oxyhydrogen blowpipe which filled the place with a "wonderful light," and again after he had given up his practice and his lecturing to spend all his time on the steam carriage.

We occupied rooms which were probably intended for Sir William Adams, a celebrated oculist, for whom this building was erected, as an eye infirmary, in Albany Street, Regent's Park. From a window of my room I looked into the yard where my father was constructing his steam carriage. The intense combination caused by the steam blast, and the consequent increase of high pressure steam force acting on the jet, created such a tremendous current or draught of air up the chimney that it was something terrific to see or hear. The workmen would sometimes throw things into the fire as the carriage passed round the yard--large pieces of slate or sheet iron--which would dart up the chimney like a shot, falling occasionally nearer to the men than was safe, and my father would have to check their enthusiasm. The roaring sound, too, sometimes was astounding. Many difficulties had to be overcome, which occupied the years before "1827". The noise had to be got rid of, or it would have frightened the horses, and the heat had to be insulated, or it might have burnt the whole vehicle. [4]

Gurney tried to harness this powerful force with centrifugal fans moving horizontally within a box and conveying the blast through a tube to the fire-place where the heat would evaporate the steam, but he could not control its great noise. In 1824 he introduced it to steamboats where noise was not the issue it would be on roadways. The idea quickly spread to France and America. He showed the steam jet to Timothy Hackworth, manager of the Stockton and Darlington railway, who adapted it to the railway locomotive, in particular the Royal George in 1827. Without the jet, locomotives moved at about four miles per hour, but with it there seemed no limit to the speed that might be reached. Its application took the locomotive out of competition with the horse drawn rail carriages into a world of unlimited possibilities.

The jet blast was adaptable to railways without further experiment because the noise factor was not important. Gurney eventually found that the jet noise could be silenced by passing the waste steam from the engines into a cylinder. There the steam, acting by expansion, produced a blowing effect, which, when directed through the orifice of the vertical jet in the center of the chimney, drew after it a corresponding portion of atmospheric air. The importance of this action, aside from the tremendous velocity of air shooting from the chimney, was the drawing of the waste steam and the atmospheric air over the fire—thus annihilating noise and evaporating the steam at once.

The increase or decrease of draught was regulated by altering the size of the opening through which it was ejected. As a result, the fire was enlivened or dampened according to the required speed of the engine.

The Separator

The separator, the third principle closely connected with the jet and the chemical composition of the steam, was the key element differentiating Gurney's steam carriages from those of his rivals.

The circulation of water within a vessel was activated by a change in specific gravity caused by heat with a rapidity proportional to the intensity of the heat. When particles of water in contact with a heated surface became lighter and rose, colder portions of water descended by virtue of greater specific gravity. As the heated water rose as steam, the movement was swift and a large amount of water was carried up with it only to return in a circular movement. In a vessel with tube outlets, the steam carried some water with it when it escaped. The water, landing on the side of the hot tubes and suddenly becoming hot, formed steam and blew open the tubes.

Gurney arranged for the water rising with the steam to pass through a separate vessel in a distinct descending current away from the heating surface in order that the steam would be drawn off dry for the engines. Rather than exposing a large flat surface of iron plates to the fire as some experimenters did, Gurney constructed a series of tubes of less than 4 inches in diameter. If by accident one of the tubes exploded, there would be only a small break and the speed of the carriage would be scarcely impaired.

Gurney's main objective for a boiler was lightness. With each subsequent carriage he reduced the weight--from 4 tons down to 35 hundredweight--and maintained the same power. He found that two factors allowed him to construct a generator with an increasingly smaller surface for raising steam (l) heating surfaces passed free heat through them with a facility in an inverse proportion to their thickness, (2) and simultaneously, heat was given out by combustion with an intensity of the same proportion as the quantity of oxygen given to it within a given time.

To keep a continuous and unimpeded motion, two engines were applied to the same boiler and rotated so that one engine was always in full force while the other was passing the centre.

All engineers contended that it was impossible for steam carriage wheels to move the carriage forward because the periphery of the wheels had not sufficient hold of the ground to make an

4

available fulcrum. Their error was the result of a fundamental misunderstanding, the resolution of which Gurney said was "important in the history of the invention."

The steam in the ordinary stationary engines is thrown full upon the cylinder by large openings [he said] and by that means it acts suddenly upon the piston of the engine; this, by the laws of percussion, strikes or starts the wheel round before sufficient bite is obtained to move the carriage; but if the steam be slowly let on, then sufficient hold is obtained and the carriage will advance.[5]

Through many experiments on the hills about London, Gurney learned to apply the steam in a manner called "wire drawing" which caused the hind wheels to bite the ground. He found that the bite of one wheel was sufficient, and he kept it attached to the axle while the other wheel ran free but could be united with the crank by means of a socket whenever its friction power was needed. Either of these hind wheels could be fastened to the axle to turn around with it by means of a round plate fixed on a hexagonal part at either end of the axle. A similar plate was fastened to the nave of each wheel, screw bolts passed between the two plates, and the bolts were secured with nuts. When the engine caused the axle to revolve, the wheels revolved. One stroke of the piston corresponded to one revolution of the wheels.

Aside from climbing hills, wire drawing was used to check speed downhill by passing steam onto the opposite side of the piston. In addition, it was used to stop the carriage suddenly. An additional brake was provided by shoe-drags which were attached to a spindle passing through a hollow cylinder whose handle was managed by the driver of the carriage to force one or both drags tight onto the road and raise the wheels slightly. A carriage traveling at twenty miles an hour stopped in a yard or two.

Owing to the scarcity of efficient engineers, Gurney had to become his own engineer and was appreciative of any advice that proved useful. It was Watt's manufactory in Birmingham, for example, which suggested a simple contrivance to give the driver better control over the machine on rough stones.

Throughout his years of experimentation, from 1823 to 1830, Gurney had no serious accident from the failure of machinery. Tubes often broke open, and steam and water gushed out until he perfected the giving off of dry steam. Moreover, the escaping hot water could not scald anyone because under Gurney's system of pressure, the escaping water expanded and became aeriform immediately, and was so changed in temperature, it produced cold.

Control of the engine was Gurney's primary goal as he prepared the carriage for public sale. In his last large carriage he made the valve, which regulated the steam, dependent on the weight of the driver, so that if the driver rose or was thrown off his seat, the valve shut and stopped the carriage. But speed also interested him. In 1831 he built a carriage weighing 5 hundredweight for two to three people with the goal of attaining high speeds. This small runabout reflected Gurney's awareness of the desire in this age of romanticism for independence and freedom of movement. Commercial prospects may have been at the back of his mind, but they did not come to the fore until the invention was perfected.

THE ROAD TO BATH

Gurney and his financial supporters agreed to drive the steam carriage to Bath, about ninety miles from London, and back. Their memorandum is an important document in the history of transportation.

Suffolk Place
July 14, 1829
Present
Mr. Hanning in the Chair
Mr. Gurney
Dr. Mackie
Mr. Thiselton

Mr. Gurney reported that the Steam Carriage was now ready to perform an extended journey—whereupon it was unanimously agreed that Mr. Gurney should make immediate arrangements for taking the Carriage to Bath—the expense attending the journey as also that of Mr. Gurney from London to Bath to make the previous necessary arrangements—to be defrayed out of the first proceeds of the Patents.

Mr. Gurney also reported that he had made important improvements not included in the present Patents—whereupon it was resolved that additional Patents be taken and to secure the same—in England, Scotland, Ireland and France—and the expense of taking out the same be defrayed by the Patentees in proportions equal to their respective interest therein.

> W. Hanning
> Goldth Gurney
> Patrick Mackie
> Charles A. Thiselton[6]

Gurney altered the design from a single carriage to two vehicles. The first with engine and crew was attached to the second by a rod; the second which had no engine, carried the passengers and supply of fuel, that is, coke and water.

Not only would passengers feel safer away from the engine, the new design might interest the military which was looking for ways

Mr. Gurney's Steam Carriage on the High Road between London and Bath, July, 1829.

(From a Pen and Ink Sketch.)

7

of transporting troops quickly. Colonel Sir Charles Dance, who took an active interest in his investment, invited Sir J. Willoughby Gordon and other high-ranking officers to view Gurney's new steam carriage at Dance's residence near Watford, just outside London, on July 11. Willoughby reported on what he observed to Sir Herbert Taylor, Secretary to the Duke of York, Commander-in-Chief of the Army at the Horse Guards.

...instead of being drawn forwards by power in front, this machine is pushed forwards from behind by means of power impressed upon the axle of the hind wheels.... The length of the machine is the same as that of a four-wheel carriage without the pole, about ten feet, so that when a carriage with passengers shall be affixed to it, the whole length of the two carriages taken together will not exceed the length of one four-wheeled carriage with one pair of horses.... The noise of the steam-carriage, with the passenger carriage attached to it, is not so great as the noise of a traveling carriage with two horses. There is very little or no smoke from the burning of coke. The eight wheels of the two carriages cause less dust than would a carriage with four wheels and two horses.... The expense at which this apparatus can be plied upon the road is stated not to amount to three pence per mile.... [7]

In the dead of night on July 27, 1829, Gurney drove the carriage to Cranford Bridge Inn on the western limits of London. Shortly after four the next morning an excited party began the great experiment. To avoid crowds, Gurney made no announcement of his journey and planned to stop at those inns which were outside towns along the route.

Goldsworthy Gurney, James Stone, and another engineer, Tom Bailey, who stoked the fuel, rode the steam carriage, which was about 30 hundredweight (cwt) when loaded with sufficient coke and water to carry them for six to eight miles. Attached behind was a carriage carrying Thomas Gurney, Colonel James Viney, Captain William Augustus Dobbyn, and two engineers from Gurney's manufactory who perched on the dickey. Accompanying this self-propelled group were two horse drawn vehicles. The first, a phaeton drawn by two horses, carried William Hanning, Sir Charles Dance, and Dance's monied friends, William Bulnois and Davis; the second, a post carriage carrying coke lest fuel not be found at some of the way stations, was driven by two post-boys with David Dady, Gurney's factory manager, and Thomas Martin, an assistant engineer.

At first the phaeton preceded the steam carriage, but at a speed of 14 mph on the level road the steam carriage left it far behind. As for the post carriage, its horses were in a lather trying to keep up, and it had to be pulled by two pairs of horses after they left Maidenhead, the first stop for coke and water.

The party continued rapidly until at Longford it encountered a narrow wooden bridge erected temporarily while the regular bridge was being rebuilt. Because the road leading up to the bridge was piled high with bricks, Gurney failed to see the mail coach from Bristol racing along the bridge until he was at the foot of it. Dance, who was in the phaeton in advance of the steam carriage, cried out to the coach driver to pull up, but he was ignored. The carriages became entangled, the mail coach's lead horses bolted and broke their mail traces, and Gurney veered the steam carriage into a pile of bricks as he had no time to stop.

The mail passed but pulled up down the road, and the coachman, the guard, and some passengers returned to offer their help. Gurney, however, reversed the engine and brought the carriage back onto the road. Only one of the driving irons attached to a rear wheel was broken. The steam carriage continued with the driving power of one wheel to Reading, where the party waited impatiently for the iron to be mended.

Leaving orders for the post-carriage to bring the iron onto the next station, the party pushed ahead at half-past ten (though not without grave concern at encountering the loose gravel and hills near Marlborough Forest) with power in only one wheel. On a steep hill beyond Newbury the carriage wheel slipped round on the ground. One of the men was about to fetch a horse to pull it, when two of the engineers by putting their shoulders to the carriage gave it the impetus to reach the top of the hill. From then on they were confident in the bite of just one wheel.

Today the road leading out of the woods into Marlborough plummets between high hedges, and no doubt it was as steeply narrow in 1829. The engineers apprehensively prepared a drag chain to be thrown over the side of the carriage and an extra hand drag on the wheels to be worked by the driver. To their delight and surprise, when they cut off the steam, the friction of the engine alone was found to be sufficient to slow their descent. From here the rolling land sweeps the mechanized traveler southward to the town of Devizes.

In the first lap of the journey from Cranford to Reading, Dance counted the vehicles they overtook on the road: "21 carts, 7 wagons, 2 post-chaises, 4 mail-coaches, 7 stage-coaches, 1 dray with 2 horses, a drove of cart horses, 3 gigs and 6 horses." Immensely pleased by their achievement, the men in the carriages took the dogleg through Devizes as the sun sank behind the horizon, and they continued on to Melksham, a town of gray stone houses only eight miles from Bath. One drawback was that at certain places the party, for lack of coke, had to buy coal which gave off smoke. At Devizes the coke was so bad it would not burn. Consequently, Gurney used coal, and sparks flew up the chimney giving "the appearance of a beautiful firework" in the darkening evening.

Melksham, a center for rubber, rope, flour, and dairy industries with a large weaving industry in neighboring Trowbridge, was in a festive mood from the second day of a fair attended by thousands. The steam carriage stopped at the Canal Bridge at the eastern end of town to take on water. It was 8:00 P.M. as Gurney slowly guided the steam carriage onto the main street through the heavy crowds of agricultural laborers and "manufacturers" in the district. As it reached the height of the slight ascent opposite the George pub, the carriage came under attack.

A mob shouting insults brought the carriage to a standstill. Unemployed and impoverished in the depression following the financial crisis of 1826, the men of Melksham took out their frustrations on the mechanical apparatus: "Down with machinery! Knock it to pieces!" They threw rocks and flints at the gentlemen who had come out of their carriages to form files on either side of the steam carriage to prevent people from climbing onto it. Gurney was cut on the head, the stoker, Bailey, was knocked senseless into the road, and Martin was severely hurt.

Picking up steam, the carriage dashed out of town followed by a stone throwing group for a mile and a half to the village of Shaw where Gurney steered the carriage into the high-walled stone yard of the local brewer. The wounded Bailey was immediately taken to Bath for medical treatment. Two constables guarded the carriage during the night and accompanied it to Bath the following day.

After a rest of three days in Bath during which the broken rod was restored to the carriage and damage suffered from the stoning was repaired, Gurney drove the carriage about the center of town, found the machine worked perfectly, and ran 9 mph with the engine at half-power.

In the middle of a Sunday night to avoid the citizenry, the party accompanied the steam carriage dragged by horses through Melksham to a mile beyond it, a tedious and painfully slow operation. At 6:30 A.M., Gurney got up the steam, laid on the full power of the engine, and left the fearful manufacturing area far behind. As the party approached a steep hill leading into Devizes, the drivers of the mail coach and a private coach descending the hill stopped at the bottom to watch the ascent. Having both wheels connected to the axle, the steam carriage with the barouche in tow easily climbed the hill at 7 mph to the cheers of the spectators.

The inhabitants at Devizes where the party took in coke and water showed them much friendliness, and some of them rode at top speed behind them to within three miles of Marlborough. But on cresting one of the hills before Marlborough, the party spotted a large crowd on the steepest hill, one which stagecoaches usually required six horses to climb.

"The engineers felt great apprehension of an attack," wrote David Dady,

and in order to get up the hill as fast as possible, a strong fire was got up previous to reaching the town. . . . We moved the carriage on steadily, until it came within a short distance of the steepest part, where the people were collected; the full steam was now laid on the engines; the carriage instantly yielded to the power and went up with rapidity at a rate of not less than eight miles per hour. . . . This success gave us great glee.[8]

They discovered the Marlborough crowd to be "the most respectable people. . . assembled from curiosity."

Gurney and his party proceeded at 12 mph, passed through a heavy downpour, and arrived drenched at a welcoming committee outside Reading whose mayor and distinguished citizens accompanied them on horse back and carriages through the town. Convinced of the steam carriage's great prospects, the party pulled into Cranford Inn at a quarter to five in the afternoon.

Gurney learned two lessons from this experiment. First, he recognized that clinkers, if allowed to gather in the fireplace, slowed his speed. By removing them as they formed on the return trip, he kept up a fast speed and shortened the journey by four hours. Second, the stops for fuel accounted for a quarter of the traveling time. When water was needed, the eight gentlemen and six engineers and attendants formed a line over a hedge to a pond in a field and passed buckets from one to another until the tank was filled. A better method would have to be devised.

Two weeks after the trip to Bath, Gurney took his steam carriage to the Hounslow Barrack Yard at the request of the Duke of Wellington to demonstrate its powers to an assemblage of scientific and military dignitaries. The steam carriage drew Wellington's carriage around the yard, and then with Gurney and two engineers on the engine, it pulled a wagon of twenty-seven soldiers over a roadway of rough loose sand and gravel, first at 10 mph and later at 17 mph to show its speed. The carriage must have won the onlookers' approval as a few days later a long letter written by John Herapath addressed to "His Grace the Duke of Wellington on the utility, advantages and national importance of Mr. Gurney's Steam Carriage" appeared in the London *Times*. Herapath described the steam carriage's haulage powers and speed in detail. He concluded that since friction from the road was the same at all velocities, the steam carriage might travel 30, 40, 50 mph, and more.

11

Railway engineers, however, were alarmed. They planned to use Gurney's steam jet to make their locomotives competitive with his steam carriage. The Rainhill trials in October 1829 on the Liverpool and Manchester Railroad represented a frantic public relations effort by the Lancashire group of merchants financing the railways to offset Gurney's London to Bath achievement three months before. That only one of the four competing locomotives, Stephenson's *Rocket*, did not fall apart at jet steam speed indicates how unprepared they were.

Gurney claimed that he gave the steam jet to Timothy Hackworth for his *Sans Pareil* before the Rainhill trials.[9] But Hackworth claimed that the *Sans Pareil* was his second engine to have the blast pipe and that his *Royal George*, which began working in October 1827, was the first. (This was not to the point. Gurney had shown him an earlier form of the jet in 1827). Articles to this effect appeared in London journals in the 1850s by persons boosting Hackworth's claim to the invention of the steam jet, which really was the single element that made modern transport possible. A report on the *Royal George*'s performance by Robert Stephenson in 1827 placed its top speed at 11 mph versus 4 mph by competing locomotives, and it consumed two-thirds to three-fourths the fuel of its competitors. Consequently, it must have had an earlier form of steam jet like the one used by steamships, but it was the introduction of Gurney's jet affixed to the eduction pipe of the engine of the *Sans Pareil* which caused it to travel at swift speeds in 1829.

Hackworth also claimed that in the night before the Rainhill trials Stephenson sent men to study the jet on Hackworth's *Sans Pareil* and reproduce it for his engine, the *Rocket*, which allowed it to attain a speed of 35 miles an hour and win for Stephenson the L 500 prize.

TECHNICAL FEASIBILITY AND COMPARATIVE COSTS OF STAGECOACH TO STEAM CARRIAGE

Friction

Gurney corrected a general misconception about friction. A steam carriage encountered friction, not from the road, but from the workmanship in the carriage: the worse the workmanship, the greater the friction.

Resistance was the term for impediment to transit, but it was not found on the road. Rather, it was encountered on rails where at that time it amounted to 4 pounds per ton as a result of "extraneous matter."

Traction as a force was encountered when going uphill. Since horses had extreme difficulty and railway engines could not ascend a slight incline, engineers thought that gravitation would have the same effect on the steam carriage. Actually, the steam carriage met far less traction on the upgrade. The traction force required to draw a ton on a common road was, on the average, 1/12th the weight of the engine, whereas to draw a ton on a level railway required a traction force of 8 pounds, or 1/240th the engine's weight. Thus, on a level railway, locomotives encountered less traction than steam carriages by a ratio of I to 20. But to ascend a rise on the road (say one foot in twelve at the steepest), the steam carriage needed additional traction equal to 1/12th its weight to overcome the increase in gravitational force, thus doubling the traction power used on the level. For the railway the traction required to climb the same grade would be 1/240 x 1/12 = 21/240, or twenty-one times the traction force required on the level. The steam carriage could climb the steepest hill by doubling its power, whereas the railway engine needed twenty-one times its power.

A New Concept of Horsepower

The discussion on traction power gave Gurney the opportunity to correct the misconception of engineers about horsepower, which equated 200 pounds moving at 2 mph with one horsepower.

A horse can concentrate its power, Gurney explained, only by the principle of vitality. The amount of power expended by a horse over ordinary roads is 1/24 to 1/30 its whole weight. A horse weighing 1200 pounds requires 50 pounds of power to move at 2 mph. Thus, if a horse could exert power without moving its body, it would have 250 pounds of actual power at 2 mph. At 4 mph it needs to exert 100 pounds more power, making 300 pounds. At 6 mph it requires 150 pounds more power. But when it pulls a coach, it gives out in one hour the same vitality it ordinarily expends in eight hours. Therefore, a steam engine doing the work of a four-horse coach for eight hours is said to have 32 horsepower.

The problem with this concept arose when measuring the power exerted by a steam carriage against a stagecoach over a period of time. Whereas the stagecoach changed horses on the hour, employing about fifty horses on a journey, the steam carriage exerted no more than the power of four horses continuously throughout the journey.

Doubling the horsepower in a steam engine was a matter of changing the size of the cylinder. The length of stroke and the area of the piston gave power in proportion to the pressure of steam on it. For instance, a 6-inch cylinder has an area of 36 circular inches. By using steam pressure of 50 pounds per inch, the steam carriage would exert 1,806 pounds on the piston. In order to double this pressure, the diameter of the 6-inch cylinder would have to be increased to 8 inches to make the area of the piston (8 x 8) 64 circular inches. With the same steam pressure of 50 pounds per inch, there would be 3,200 pounds of pressure on the piston, and thus the power of the steam carriage would be doubled. (Gurney advised that the size of the cylinder used in a steam carriage should be adequate to overcome the resistance by pressure within a range of 20 to 80 pounds per inch.)

With the larger cylinder, therefore, there would be double the quantity of steam and the need for a larger boiler to contain it. Thus, the weight of the boiler determined the amount of horsepower of an engine. A boiler of 350 to 400 pounds was equivalent to 1 horsepower. A 6-inch cylinder, which had sufficient power to do the work of two horses on the road, required a boiler weighing 500 to 600 pounds.

The point Gurney made was that the size of the boiler determined, not the intensity, but the quantity of power generated within an hour. Horsepower could be doubled with the same steam pressure per inch but not without a larger cylinder and thus a larger boiler. Of course, a larger boiler required a bigger steam carriage.

Since the size of a boiler can be estimated by the amount of water it holds, Gurney suggested that horsepower be measured by the evaporation of the water. The evaporation of 9 gallons of water in an hour should be equivalent to 1 horsepower. For instance, a road trustee collecting a toll according to horsepower could determine that a steam carriage with a 6-inch cylinder and a boiler of 600 pounds carrying 18 gallons of water had 2 horsepower (by dividing 9 into 18).

Gurney estimated that his boilers had a life span of three years and required cleaning once a fortnight or every three weeks depending on the amount of lime in the water.

Related to this new understanding of horsepower was the question of speed. A steam carriage could increase its speed at no additional cost by letting more steam pressure onto the piston, whereas a stage coach required more effort from its horses to move faster, which cost more because the horses were exhausted sooner. Such an intangible as speed, however, could not be taken into account in the comparison of costs between the two modes of transport.

A Cost Comparison between the Stagecoach
and the Steam Carriage

Goldsworthy Gurney gave the most conservative and reliable estimate on relative costs to the House of Commons Select Committee on Steam Carriages of 1831:

Mr. Gurney
5 August, 1831
Mr. Goldsworthy Gurney called in; and Examined.
Will you give in the Statement that you were directed to produce on the last Examination?—I will.
[*The Witness delivered in the same.*]

Calculation as to the relative Expenses betwixt Horse and Steam Power for Locomotion.

In order to estimate the comparative expense between *Horse* and *Steam Power* for drawing Carriages on common roads, I will take the relative expense on 100 miles of ground for working a common stage coach *by steam* and *by horses*.

The first cost, wear and tear of the coach drawn, in every respect is the same in both cases.

The expense of men to manage is about the same also. In one case there is a coachman and guard; in the other, an engineer and director.

Government duty and *turnpike tolls* must also be considered the same.

It remains then to show the difference in the expense of Power only; viz. betwixt the expense of Horses and the expense of Steam. First in the outlay, on 100 miles of ground. To work a coach well with horses 100 miles up and 100 miles down once a day, will require 100 horses. A horse a mile is the present calculation for doing the work. If these horses be taken at £20 or £30 per horse, or say £25, it will amount to £2,500. *Three* Steam Carriages will do the same work, and the expense of these will be about £500 each, or £1,500 for the three. A saving will consequently be effected in the first outlay of £1,000 in capital.

The wear and tear of horses may be estimated at about £5 each per annum on the 100 horses; viz. £500 per annum.

The wear and tear of the three Steam towing Carriages will not exceed £100 each per annum; £300 for the three; saving in wear and tear, £200.

The expense of shoeing, keep, provision, attendance, harness, etc., is per day somewhere about 3s. each, or £15 upon the 100 horses.

The expense of fuel for two carriages, one up and the other down, doing the same work, will be that of 100 bushels of coke at 6d. per bushel; say £2.10.

Or if we take 1s. *per mile* per horse power, it will be about the same. The expense of fuel for the Steam Carriage will be, on an average throughout England, about 3d. In some coal districts it will not exceed 1d. per mile; while in other situations it will amount to 6d.

15

I have not taken into this estimate the expense of stables, which is considerable when compared with sheds for coke and water.

From these data I conclude the Carriage may be worked by *Steam* at one-fifth the expense of horses. [see Table 1].

Table 1
Gurney's Estimate of Comparative Costs of Maintaining Horse Carriages and Steam Carriages

ABSTRACT:

HORSE POWER	L.	s.	d.	STEAM POWER	L.	s.	d.
Outlay for horses	2,500	-	-	Outlay for Steam Carriages	1,500	-	-
				Balance of saving n the outlay in favour of Steam Power	1,000	-	-
Wear and tear of Horses, per annum	500	-	-	Wear and tear of Steam towing Carriages	300	-	-
				Balance, saving in tear and wear in favour of Steam Power	200	-	-
Shoeing, keep, attendance, provision, harness etc. per day for 100 Horses	15	-	-	Fuel for Steam Carriages, half bushel per mile travelled, at 6d. per bushel -	2	10	
				Balance, saving	12.10		

The military engineer John Herapath figured the relative costs in more detail, such as estimating that one ostler was needed for a stagecoach every twelve miles at a cost of 18 shillings per week for each ostler. He concluded that the introduction of the steam carriage would save 14 shillings out of every guinea spent on stage coaching.

Maceroni was equally sanguine. He calculated that the costs of the daily running of a stagecoach relative to a steam carriage on 100 miles for 313 working days in the year amounted to £10,166.16 for the stagecoach and £3,721.16 for the steam carriage, making a difference annually in favor of the steam carriage of £6,445. When he did his calculations in 1834 the stagecoach paid a government duty of 3d per mile amounting to £391.5 per coach per year, whereas the steam carriage was exempted from paying duty by act of Parliament.[10]

As the railway also was exempted from paying duty, the tax did not figure in the calculations of the relative costs of railway to steam carriage.

2. Artist's view of Gurney's 1827 model and labeled to commemorate the London to Bath trip which was, however, made with an engine and drag. It was captioned: The Guide or Engineer is seated in front, having a lever rod from the two guide wheels to turn & direct the Carriage & another at his right hand connecting with the main Steam Pipe by which he regulates the motion of the Vehicle—the hind part of the Coach contains the machinery for producing the Steam, on a novel & secure principle, which is conveyed by Pipes to the Cylinders beneath & by its action on the hind wheels sets the Carriage in motion. The Tank which contains about 60 Gallons of water, is placed under the body of the Coach & is its full length and breadth. The Chimneys are fixed on the top of the hind boot & as Coke is used for fuel, there will be no smoke, while any hot or rarified air produced will be dispelled by the action of the Vehicle. At different stations on a journey the Coach receives fresh supplies of fuel & water. The full length of the Carriage is from 15 to 20 feet & its weight about 2 Tons. The rate of travelling is intended to be from 8 to 10 miles per hour. The present Steam Carriage carries 6 inside & 12 outside Passengers. The front boot contains the Luggage. It has been constructed by Mr. Goldsworthy Gurney, the Inventor & Patentee. (Courtesy of the Science Museum, London, England, c. 1829.)

2

The Company Itself

The first entrepreneur to contract for a share of Gurney's patent was a retired official of the East India Company. John Ward engaged for the sole right to run Gurney's carriages on the London to Liverpool road in late 1825. William Augustus Dobbyn of Wells, Somerset, made an agreement with Goldsworthy and his brother Thomas Gurney on September 10, 1827, by the terms of which Gurney would supply eight steam carriages under a fourteen-year lease to be run only on the Bristol to London road at a duty of I penny per mile. Later the road to Bath was included. The premium on mileage duty was about £1,800 in cash. The premium on the road from London to Bath to Bristol was £4,500 in advance for building the carriages, which Dobbyn paid Gurney.

William Hanning made his first payment to Gurney on November 26, 1827—£700—as an advance on an intended contract for carriages to run from London through Plymouth to Exeter. Gurney depicted Hanning as the mainstay behind the development of the invention. Hanning, a great agriculturist with a very large fortune, demonstrated his interest in inland transportation by constructing a new road between London and Exeter in partnership with Lord Heathfield and establishing a line of stagecoaches on it.

George Henry Ellis, representing Hanning, and William Portal, Gurney's solicitor, drew up an agreement in which Hanning purchased eight and one half shares out of twenty-four which represented the whole of the proceeds of a "proposed" company. The proceeds were "all profits, patents, further patents on steam boilers or any other mode of propelling or forcing carriages, boats or vessels to travel by the force of steam on railroads, common roads or water and which may be applicable to other works or machinery."[11] Hanning was to pay Gurney £6,000 and a bonus of £2,000 when a steam carriage was brought to such perfection that it could run as a common stage for a whole year on any turnpike road. Only 200 pounds was placed at Gurney's disposal (which Hanning prepaid Gurney on July 25, 1828, the contract being

18

signed on August 21, 1828), and additional sums were to be paid by the patentees in proportion to their several shares.

A banking concern in Whitehall—Messrs. Cockburn and Company— agreed to handle the funds for the venture, and one of the bank's officers, Charles Thiselton, became a prospective patentee. Hanning advanced sums of money to the Cockburn Bank on behalf of Goldsworthy Gurney, who also was a prospective patentee, with the intention of purchasing Gurney's patent shares at £4,000 and under the impression that these sums would stand in their final settlement of account. In this way, Gurney, having pledged to complete his invention in contracts with the other prospective patentees and with contractors for the steam carriages he was expected to construct, would be dependent on Hanning's financial aid to fulfill those contracts.

Gurney immediately encountered two disadvantages. One was the patent law. If an invention were publicly on view, it had to be patented to prevent it from being pirated, but work in progress could not be patented. Therefore, Gurney had to take out a series of patents at successive stages of his experiments in order to take the carriage on trial runs in nearby Regent's Park. Each patent cost 360 pounds. He procured patents on May 14, 1825, October 21, 1825, October 14, 1827, and July 8, 1829.

The other disadvantage was the law against limited corporations in England. Capitalists joining in an enterprise were liable to the whole of their wealth should the enterprise fail. Some capitalists in Parliament advocated the practice of limited liability but it did not become a right until 1855. Limited partnership, on the other hand, went unrecognized in England until the twentieth century by which time it had become an anachronism. Joint stock companies could be chartered by parliamentary edict, however (as was done by railway and canal companies), or were set up by capitalists who remained anonymous behind a board of directors that had no property. Alternatively, a patentee had the power to vest his patent in not more than five other persons, a group too small to meet the costs of building a large enterprise and to combat the opposition arising from interested parties, whether in Parliament or the courts.

The other patentees forming the "proposed" company never paid any sums because a company could not be legally formed without involving them in liabilities to which they objected. Thus, Hanning advanced Gurney money on behalf of the other patentees at their request, the sums being chargeable by their consent to the first proceeds obtained under the patent. Altogether, according to Ellis, Hanning invested from L6,000 to £10,000 in the project. However, he did not formally complete the purchase of his share in the patent because he feared that if he did complete it he could not turn it to his advantage without getting involved in the actual manufacture of steam carriages and thus become subject to the Bankruptcy Laws.

Aside from Hanning, the "prospective" patentees were James Stone, Gurney's chief engineer who managed the steam engines and superintended most of Gurney's experiments from the commencement in 1823; Charles Thiselton of the Cockburn Bank; Patrick Mackie, a London medical doctor; James Viney, colonel in the Royal Regiment of Artillery (soon to become a major-general and to be knighted); and Goldsworthy Gurney. They represented distinct spheres of interest: agriculture, engineering, banking, medicine, and the military. Hanning bought out Stone's share for L1,000 very early.

The patentees set their solicitors to work devising an agreement that would allow them to avoid the obligations of a company with unlimited liability and called on an arbitrator, Jonathan Pollock.

Gurney had a major disagreement with Hanning over the legitimacy of the company, which Gurney considered as reality, not "prospective." Gurney regarded all of Hanning's payments since June 1828, save a few hundred pounds, as having been made solely on behalf of the company for the manufactory. Hanning, still fearful of liability, disagreed, but Ellis persuaded him to accept the advice of the arbitrator which had the following results. By an agreement entered into on May 29, 1829, the parties interested in Gurney's patents would take his manufactory premises and stock in trade on Clarence Street from June 24 at valuation to be made by valuers agreeable to Gurney and to the others. This valuation would be paid in four equal installments—June 30, September 29, December 25,1829, and March 30, 1830. All parties to the agreement held equal voting power, and, if any contracting was done by one without the agreement of the others, that person was required to forfeit his right to the patents. James Stone was appointed the valuer.

On June 23, the patentees agreed that Hanning pay Gurney L50 a week for carrying on the manufactory. Hanning would be reimbursed from the first proceeds of the invention by each patentee according to his proportionate share. This, at least, resolved the matter of expenses at the manufactory for the future, but the question of whether Hanning's payments for the past year were personal advances to Gurney or on behalf of the company was left to Pollock's final decision on the nature of the company. (The advances amounted to over L3,500.)

Pollock, after holding numerous discussions on all issues, gave his award in November 1829: that the sum of L6,666.13.4 charged against the patentees for costs thus far should be credited to them less an amount claimed by Gurney, but that the patentees should take liabilities on themselves. The patents contracted with parties other than the five patentees were declared valid—that is, the road contracts for Ward, Bulnois, Dobbyn, Dance, and also Hanning, who had contracted for the London-Plymouth Exeter road and the Exeter-Bristol road. Viney, under pressure from Hanning, gave up his one-sixth share (L6,000), which was assumed by Dance. Viney's contract included a clause specifying his sole right to the Gloucester-Cheltenham road.

Gurney was not pleased with Pollock's award, however, and wrote to Hanning in November 1829:

Being without funds I had no alternative but to suspend the manufactory on Saturday night and have now only two or three men to keep the place open. I have received your letter yesterday enclosing a cheque for 100, which I shall hold until I see you, for with Mr. Pollock's award before me I cannot recommence proceedings without a clear understanding from the Patentees. His award does not seem to have settled any one point. It appears we are to form a co-partnership, a thing we wish to avoid and that the patentees are not indebted anything to me for my exertions or money before the 21 of April. No man can suppose that I can sacrifice my time and money for the benefit of others which is the property of my children. The step I have been driven to may have a temporary mischievous effect which is soon remedied but having been forced so far, all matters must now be settled before I can recommence. I have done the utmost in my power and the carriage is perfect. Time will remove the effect of any competition which at this moment may affect some minds and the value of my carriage will prove itself just as well six months hence as at present. I know its value and feel that under all circumstances my determination is founded on strict justice. I feel that towards the patentees which will never allow me to involve personal responsibility on their account. I do not feel this towards you. For (illegible) our ideas and measures have been mutually the same and I therefore—if you will consent to act independent of them on the new patent, will join you heart and hand and with the full force of my abilities and perseverance which they in connection with themselves have gone a great way to destroy, and that so soon as you come up and arrangements made. If not I must wait the settlement of the Patentees. I trust you will not for a moment think I have acted hastily; but on reflection perceive that I had no alternative. The only act of the Patentees as a body is the license lately granted; if you act under the new patent this may also be found to give it strength.
(P.S.) I have opened my letter to inform you that one part of my view in this letter is justified. I am just informed that Hancock's boiler has bursted. This is as I supposed. It happened to me with them some years since.[12]

As the postscript illustrates, Gurney did not fear his competitors, in this case Walter Hancock, inasmuch as they lacked his grasp of the fundamentals. But he was sickened by the bickering, overcautious, and even obstructionist behavior of the patentees. Hanning responded by joining with Dr. Mackie and Thiselton in an agreement in which the partners (as they were now called) should have voting strength in proportion to their shares. Furthermore, none should share in the profits until he had paid to the other partners his proportion of all advances made by them on the partnership account. Finally, on January 23, 1830, wording agreeable to the parties was signed, and Hanning's account against monies owed him by the other patentees was settled.

By the end of 1829 Hanning had paid Gurney £4,860.16.10 and had advanced Gurney £1,545.9.0 on behalf of the patentees. In addition, Gurney's share of the patent cost paid for by Hanning was £519. The amounts due Hanning from the three other patentees for the patent costs were:

Col. Viney's share	£254
Dr. Mackie's share	126
Thiselton's share	64

The total advanced by Hanning, therefore, came to L5,743.16.10. Hanning advanced £134 on the new English, Scots, and Irish patents, £135 on the Dutch, and £265 on the French patents. Hanning also paid for the repairs at Bath and for legal services at Melksham.

The actual expenses of the manufactory, according to David Dady, Gurney's "confidential manager" from 1825 to 1832, varied between £30 and £100 a week. Wages averaged about £40 weekly and sometimes £50. The premises on Albany Street rented for £700 a year, taxes added another £300, and fixed capital investment was £8,000. Dady figured that £4,000 had been spent on tools, lathes, and separate smithies from 1825 through 1830. Expenses at the close of 1830 totaled between £16,000 and 17,000. Consequently, Gurney may be seen as the main source of capital for his own invention.

Uniting "with extraordinary talent and great perseverance the most amiable qualities of mind and temper" (to quote Dance), Gurney was finally exasperated with his overcautious partners. In February 1830 he accepted an offer from William Crawshay of the Hirwain Iron Works to try his steam carriage on a new railroad at Hirwain Common, near Merthyr Tydvil in Wales, where the first locomotive, incidentally, was run by Trevithick in 1804.

The steam carriage was pulled by a pair of horses to Cyfartha where it was fitted with cast iron wheels and transferred the following day to the Hirwain railway, three miles long on a dead level. Pulling five carriages, four containing loads of pig-iron and one with seats for over 100 people, the engine traveled the three miles in thirty-three minutes and returned in thirty-two minutes.

In subsequent experiments the engine, on being loaded to 40 cwt, drew 33.9 tons at a speed of 2.5 mph.

Crawshay was convinced that Gurney's boiler was superior to any other as he found that the engine pulled thirty to thirty-five times its own weight at 3 to 4 mph. He bought the engine and ran it from January 1831 to January 1832. During that time it conveyed 42,300 tons of coal, iron-stone, and iron on the Hirwain railroad at a cost of £44.17.0 for 299 tons of coal consumed and a total expense of L112.9.0, or 1 farthing per ton per mile.

An ensuing depression in the iron trade forced Crawshay to give up the Hirwain works which prevented further introduction of Gurney's engine into Wales.[13]

Hanning engaged Goldsworthy Gurney to build eight carriages for the Western Roads with a promise to pay 6d per mile duty to the patent and to establish the carriages on the road as soon as they were built. Gurney built a testing station at Finchley and put his brother, Samuel, in charge of it. As the carriages ran progressively smoother and faster, easily overtaking the express mail coach, Hanning enthusiastically began negotiating contracts with innkeepers on the Western Road and making preparations for stations.

This particular contract was worth £200 per carriage annually to Gurney. A carriage traveling 100 miles per day would bring in 100 sixpence amounting to £700 per annum. But his expectations for that area of the country were greater. Captain Dobbyn in Bath would need twenty carriages and the west of England would require more than fifty. Gurney figured on a return of £1,000 per carriage. If he could build cheaper, he would, but the manufacturing profit was limited to 25 percent. Thus, if the manufacturing profit were £250, the remainder of the £1,000 would be made up by the mileage duty paid by the contractor to the patent for the exclusive right of the road.

3

Chronology of Failure

To demonstrate that the steam carriage mechanism could withstand the day-to-day grind of a regular passenger service, Colonel Dance and a Cheltenham stockbroker, William Lee, ordered a steam carriage from Gurney for passenger service on the Gloucester-Cheltenham road.

The steam carriage ran the nine miles of flat road between Cheltenham and Gloucester several times a day, amounting to over sixty miles on the average day over a period of four months. After a trial run on February 1, 1831 , passenger service began on February 21. The service was regular and took between fifty and sixty minutes. On June 23 the Cheltenham road trustees, intent on seeing the steam carriage fail, instructed their surveyor to strew large stones over the road in order to stop it. This was in a season, according to Alexander Gordon, a marine engineer who helped promote the steam carriage, when there were written instructions not to lay any new covering on the road.

The steam carriage continued to travel over the rough patch about four miles out of Gloucester four or five times a day. On the fourth day, June 23, 1831, the loose stones, augmented to a height of 18 inches, badly weakened the axle of the steam carriage on its third trip. The axle broke on the return journey about two miles from Cheltenham. The stones presented a hazard to other traffic as well. Horses on the stage coach broke their harness, and the mail coach could not get through.

Dance had the axle repaired and intended to continue when he was confronted with the imposition of high tolls. Although he had planned to extend the service in both directions to Bristol and Birmingham, he now abandoned the project.

Dance's failure was a blow to Gurney's company, but, almost simultaneously, it suffered a sharper blow from its experiment in Scotland. On January 3, 1831, Ward had contracted with the Gurney Steam Carriage Company, which now comprised Dance, Thiselton, Gurney, and Hanning (Mackie had been bought out by

24

Hanning.) The company would rescind Ward's previous agreement of 1825 if Ward made three payments of £5,000 each: for the Scottish patent six weeks after Dance's carriages commenced running on the Cheltenham-Gloucester road; within three months of signing the contract; and at the end of nine months. The final two payments were guaranteed by "the most respectable House in Edinburgh."

The Edinburgh Banking House proposed buying the Scotch patent from Ward for 32,000. The patent ran for seven years under which Gurney would receive from Ward 4 1/2d on a duty of 6d per mile. If Gurney should reduce mileage duty to 2d to other licensees, Ward's duty would be reduced by 25 percent, that is, 3 1/2d per mile. Six carriages were to be run right away on the Glasgow-Edinburgh road.

Ward negotiated for 2,000 to extend the contract to the Liverpool-London road which he had contracted for in 1825 but on which he had paid nothing as the carriages had not been perfected. Since twelve to twenty carriages were projected for running on the London-Manchester-Liverpool road, Gurney stood to gain a large fortune.

Gurney had taken Ward's steam carriage by sea to Leith and driven to Edinburgh. On March 1 as he drove with distinguished company to Glasgow, the carriage broke down near the halfway house to which it was towed by horses. Leakages were repaired, and the carriage continued to within two miles of Glasgow when it stopped. Realizing that the carriage had been damaged on the ship, Gurney ordered the carriage packed up to await his decision either to repair it in Scotland or to send it back to London, and he returned to London. Although the engineer took off parts of the machinery, especially that which was connected with the safety valve, and Gurney had forbidden its use, the carriage was taken out in June and run about the Cavalry Barracks in Glasgow. As two boys got on the carriage, the boiler burst, shattering the vehicle and severely injuring them. The accident, widely reported in the newspapers, damaged Gurney's reputation.

Hanning refused to advance more money. Of the eight carriages he had ordered, three were almost completed and the frames of the remaining five were laid. With his manufactory shut, Gurney continued to pay the rent and taxes and could only watch as his workers took the knowledge they had gained under him to the more than thirty steam carriage companies that had begun to form after the London-Bath trip.

In the spring of 1832 Gurney auctioned off his fixed capital. His carriages were sold in pieces; for instance, a pair of engines and a carriage frame sold for L11. The loss was borne solely by Gurney. In addition, his company's contracting and licensing for the great roads of Great Britain and Ireland had to be suspended. In 1834

Gurney gave the statement of his direct and indirect losses as shown in Table 2.[14]

Table 2
Gurney's Losses

Direct Loss of Money Paid out of Pocket:	in L
Paid six years' rent and taxes, at L 1,000 per annum	6,000
Paid for four patents and specifications	1,200
Paid wages	15,000
Loss by forced sale on tools, lathes and fittings-up of manufactory	6,000
Paid for materials, over and above that accounted for the loss in forced sale	8,000
Direct Loss	36,200
Received from sale of patents, contracts, etc.	20,000
Money paid out of pocket from private funds over and above what had been received from others	16,200
Indirect Loss	
Sales of the Scotch patent and contract for road from Edinburgh to Liverpool	17,000
Loss by precedence of railways for five years, from fair expected mileage duty on those great roads	15,000
By fair expected mileage duty from contracts entered into	50,000
By fair expected mileage duty on the remaining great roads	150,000
	232,000

Gurney also lost ten years of income from his medical profession, in which he had earned £1,000 a year, and from his lecturing in chemistry, which netted him another 400 annually, amounting to L14,000. He had no chance of regaining his medical practice after an absence of ten years, and since his steam carriage was discredited in the eyes of the public, no one would hire him as an engineer. Moreover, Gurney had expected his steam carriage to take over the mail service, which paid 3d per mile to mail contractors, or over L200,000 annually.

The great promise of the Gloucester-Cheltenham commuter service, however, encouraged a group of Scottish entrepreneurs to try to form a successful steam carriage company. Whether John Scott Russell, the proprietor of the Steam Carriage Company of Scotland, took over Gurney's carriages as the Radical M.P. Robert Wallace claimed, or whether Russell invented them as he claimed is a minor point. The Grove House Engine Works at Edinburgh built six steam carriages for Russell in 1833-1834 which were added to two he had purchased presumably from Ward. The carriages were worked constantly for over eight months, and except for minor alterations they were found to be in perfect condition. In March 1834 they began running between Glasgow and Paisley.

The steam carriages pulled carts carrying water and charcoal which fed the engines for eight to ten miles. These were detached at stations on the route, and carts with fresh supplies were attached in a matter of seconds. In June when the company began a commuting service between Glasgow and Paisley by the hour, its engineers had improved the carriages to where the boiler and machinery weighed a ton and drew two vehicles, one carrying water and fuel, and the second, twenty-eight passengers from 14 to 16 mph (very like Gurney's drag and carriage). But in early July the carriages encountered a mile of bad causeway.

[The Trustees] having found the carriages more than competent to the task of ploughing through the stratum of broken stones, previously laid down, they employed a large number of men, on the following day, to lay down another stratum of equal thickness on top of the former, rendering the road scarcely passable to any heavy load. Finding this expedient also ineffectual, we learnt yesterday that horses and carts and a number of men had been engaged during the whole of the night, in laying down loads of broken stones, to such a depth, that they were obliged to cut away the bottom of the toll-gate, in order to allow it to close over the mass.[15]

Then on July 29 with success in view, the company suffered a fatal accident. John Scott Russell who became famous as a marine engineer, spoke of it thirty-nine years later:

. . . they succeeded in driving everybody off the road except us, for there was another way to Paisley, only a good deal roundabout . . . but we had to have one new set of wheels every day, and we had a large establishment making new wheels, which we put on every morning. At last one wheel broke down at 4 o'clock, before it was time to go home and have a new one, and the breaking down of that wheel let the boot fall down to the ground, and the ground tore the bottom of the boiler, and produced an explosion which injured many passengers.... I do not think any of them died upon the spot, but several of them afterwards died, I am sorry to say, of their wounds. The matter then became more serious. I need not say to you that the expense which we went to during that month was something quite out of proportion to any reasonable earnings. The public stuck to us, and crowded our carriages, and they paid us any sum we pleased to ask them, but the war of life and death was too much, and in the end we were discouraged and gave it up.[16]

Five passengers died. The Scottish Court of Sessions suspended steam carriage operations temporarily. The company sued the trustees of the turnpike road between Glasgow and Paisley for L30,000 in damages.

27

3. The explosion of Scott Russell's steam carriage at Paisley on July 29, 1834 (drawn from eyewitness accounts). The illustrator neglected to show the stones piled high over the road which caused the carriage wheel to collapse. Twelve passengers in the coach were thrown onto the road, some fatally injured, whereas those riding in the tender drawn behind it went unscathed. The list of injured demonstrated that the steam carriage had become popular with the professional traveler: a merchant from Gallowgate; a merchant from Leicester whose leg had to be amputated; an army captain from Ireland who died from a contusion of the spine; a traveler from Messrs. White, Urquart and Company of Glasgow who died from a severe head wound. (Courtesy of *Histoire de la locomotion terrestre*, Paris, 1935-36.)

Within two years Goldsworthy Gurney unexpectedly turned public enthusiasm for steam carriages into public demand for steam carriage shares.

A prospectus issued by the Plymouth and Devonport Steam Carriage Company on March 23, 1836, offered 500 shares at £5 each to attain a desired capital of £2,500. Local capitalists graced its roster of directors and trustees, Gurney was its consulting engineer, and Thomas Woolcombe was its secretary. "From the interest excited here," Woolcombe wrote to Gurney in Cornwall, "we can't give you more than one hundred shares to disperse in your neighborhood . . . forty-eight hours after the prospectus is out all will be full." He was referring to a second prospectus that was to be issued in April calling for £5,000 in 1,000 shares at £5 each."[17]

Woolcombe, who later became a director of Devon railroads, was planning to employ steam carriages as feeders to the railways being constructed in the region. In London and the north of England, the railway capitalists had taken over the Pickford Carriers and the Chaplin Coaching establishment as carriers of passengers and parcels to the train stations or as links between lines. Thus, they forced all competing coach lines into bankruptcy and rewarded William Chaplin, owner of the coaching establishment who had sold his coaches to them, with the chairmanship of the South Western railway line. The disappearance of stage coach lines caused long delays, many inconveniences, and public fury--exemplified by this letter from a commuter to the London-Birmingham railroad: "You have deprived us of all our accustomed conveyances and have given us in exchange neither economy, nor civility, nor even increased rapidity. All the coaches have been taken off our roads although we live 16 miles from the nearest station and 40 miles from London."[18]

Railway promoters in South England, learning from that experience, promoted shares in the railroad and steam carriage companies together. Woolcombe mentioned to Gurney in 1836: "Just heard from the Secretary to the Railway that upwards of 14,000 £50 shares are applied for."[19]

In July Gurney testified to a parliamentary committee that he had granted licenses to large capitalists. "Within the last two months applications have been made to me, to the extent of thirty or forty, and I have now entered into Contracts with influential and powerful parties, and have engaged to build them carriages."[20] Mysteriously, nothing more was heard of the proposed Plymouth and Devonport Steam Carriage Company.

During these years Gurney worked in cooperation with Sir George Cayley, the inventor of the aeroplane. Gurney helped Cayley build air engines, while Cayley financed Gurney's steam carriages and used Gurney's tubular boilers to propel his steam balloons.[21]

One of Cayley's mechanics, T. Wadeson, whose brilliance with machinery Cayley and Gurney valued highly, tinkered on his own with the new steam carriage which he had helped to develop and drove it out of London on the road to Hounslow without informing Gurney about what he intended to do. Avoiding a boy in the street, he crashed into a store and died shortly afterward from blood poisoning caused by minor cuts. This was in 1840, a watershed year, for it marked the last time the public of that generation was to hear of Gurney's steam carriages

4

Was There a Market?

In accounting for the failure of the steam carriage, we might expect to find that there was insufficient public demand to establish a market for its sale. The evidence, however, contradicts this assumption.

During the months of Dance's commuter service between Cheltenham and Gloucester, steam carriages gained in popularity. The poorer classes in particular benefited from their cheapness, speed, and relative comfort, according to James Stone, despite "gross misstatements industriously and extensively circulated with a view to deter passengers from choosing the new mode of conveyance." The fare was only 1 shilling, whereas the stagecoach with four horses charged 2 shillings.

The daily accounts of the company kept by James Stone from its commencement on February 21 to its termination on June 22, 1831, showed that the number of passengers each trip rarely exceeded ten, the outstanding exception being at the time of the Gloucester election on May 10 when six trips tallied 9, 24, 12, 13, 38, and 8 passengers, respectively. On 396 journeys covering 3,644 miles there were 2,666 paying passengers (nonpaying were not counted).

There are no accounts extant of the operations of the Steam Carriage Company of Scotland. The public supported it with enthusiasm: "Wednesday morning and all day yesterday afternoon they swarmed like bees around the office and hung upon the carriages in clusters, it being impossible some times to prevent 30 of them from taking seats though regular accommodation is 26."[22]

Some of the carriages were sold to John Macneill, acting engineer for the London, Holyhead, and Liverpool Steamcoach and Road Company. The 1833 prospectus of the company proposed to reconstruct and improve a portion of the road between London and Birmingham to make it fitter for steam travel. The consulting engineer was the famous road and canal builder Thomas Telford.

31

In building the Menai bridge over the straits between Anglesey Island and the mainland and sections of the Holyhead road in Wales for the government, Telford had worked closely with Sir Henry Parnell, chairman of the London and Holyhead Road Committee, whose interest in steam carriages arose because they promised a means of swift communication between London and Dublin. Parnell's notebook of the time details travel on the Holyhead road for each month of every year from 1834 through 1841, enumerating the pairs of horses used, the cost of the tolls, and the passengers carried. Arranging for Liverpool steam packets to ply between Holyhead and Dublin, he proposed to his parliamentary committee that a light, four-wheeled steam carriage traveling at an average of 11 mph could make the following schedule: London to Birmingham in ten hours, arriving at Birmingham at 6:00 A.M., and onto Holyhead in 15 1/2 hours arriving at 9:30 P.M.; by steam packet for six hours arriving at Houth at 4:15 A.M., by steam carriage to Dublin in 55 minutes, arriving Dublin at 5:10 A.M.; "Back--leave Dublin at 5 A.M., in 9 1/2 hours at Holyhead at 2 1/2 P.M.; at Birmingham in 16 hours at 6 A.M. Drying boiler 7 P.M. In London in 11 hours at 6 A.M."[23]

Parnell's dreams as revealed by his notebook scribblings depended on Telford's actions. Aging and in ill health, Telford nevertheless persuaded his notable engineering friends such as Bryon Donkin, Colonel (later General) Pasley, Joshua Field, and Timothy Bramah to accompany him on an experimental trip from London to Birmingham on a steam carriage. The trial run on November 1, 1833, was made with a carriage constructed after Dance's patent by the engineers, Henry Maudslay and Joshua Field, and paid for by Telford and his friends. The carriage developed boiler trouble and broke down at Stony Stratford because, as Gurney explained, the builders neglected to employ a separator. Yet the engineers signed a strong statement of support for the steam carriage and its promising future, which was copied in all the papers.

Telford confided tersely to his diary: "Ist Nov. Travelled by steam carriage from St. Albans to Stoney Stratford, found it had not sufficient power."[24] Nevertheless, Macneill had notices printed, drew up a prospectus, and began selecting a provisional committee. The company appointed a secretary, A. M. Robertson, who began to meet with the road trustees. Robertson reported in January 1834: ". . . the St. Albans Trustees have given their unanimous assent to our Plans without troubling me to make a speech."[25] The proprietors of the Highgate Archway Company met the following week to approve the building of the granite roadway and vowed support for the bill on the subject, which Sir Henry Parnell would introduce to Parliament.

John Macneill enthusiastically wrote to Telford in early February 1834: "Many of the coach proprietors have said they will take shares and the Innkeepers are to have a meeting early next week to support us. I sold 50 shares on my way home today."[26] Parnell scribbled in his notebook: "Print Mr. Neil's (i.e. Macneill's) report. Get Copy of his Survey for Steam Carriage Co. To use Mr. Neil's carriage." Despite its early promise Parnell's company was not formed.

The efforts of the capitalists who encouraged Francis Maceroni to establish steam carriage companies with his carriages were similarly revealing. They knew that these companies could be commercially successful, but they lacked the means to bring them to fruition. Maceroni's steam carriages attracted attention in the press in the early 1830s when he drove them about London.

When his partner, John Squire, who had been Gurney's carpenter, warned they would lose their Belgian and French patents if Maceroni did not run carriages in Belgium and France before October 1834, Maceroni dispatched two steam carriages with Colonel d'Asda, an Italian speculator, and the Wearn brothers, formerly in Gurney's employ. In Belgium d'Asda drove between Antwerp and Brussels for four months and had much coverage in the European press. In January 1835 he was welcomed to Paris by Louis Philippe and drove between the city and Versailles for two months, after which he sold the carriages and pocketed Maceroni's share of £1,200. Maceroni, bankrupted, watched his factories stripped of tools and steam engines, and went to prison until his creditors collected the proceeds, while his wife and daughters found refuge in the kitchen of his former servant. He raised money by writing articles and pamphlets on scientific subjects, on his *Memoirs* which Lord Henry Brougham reviewed at Maceroni's request, and by begging from Brougham.

In 1838 Maceroni negotiated with three separate groups to provide them with steam carriages. He finally made a deal with Ernst Wolff, "the first rate sharebroker in England, and, indeed in Europe" who authorized the largest bankers in Europe to receive subscriptions of £5 to £100 for two weeks, in which time he expected to raise £10,000 "voluntarily." The subscribers were to receive one-quarter of the profits of the company to be formed and first choice of a limited number of shares at par. Maceroni was promised one-quarter share of the profits.[27]

Maceroni agonized over the slowness of the company to reach the magic mark of L12,000 in shares at which time he was promised his first payment of £2,500. Starving, he complained of having to walk twenty miles daily to superintend the building of the carriages by J. T. Beale in his factory in East Greenwich. By the end of May 1840 the first carriage was running. By the new year, 1841, Maceroni complained that the company had drawn him into "utter helplessness and destitution." The very week Maceroni was to receive the first payment of £2,500 as patentee the Maceroni Common Road Steam Conveyance Company disbanded.

Maceroni complained that three successive steam carriage companies were "allowed to go to sleep. This last shared the same fate, although it may be seen, from the subjoined report of the manufacturing Engineer that the new carriage did all that can be desired."[28] He agreed to form another company in October 1841 which failed by the end of the year. He advertised the sale of his "unique steam-boiler," the patent for which had seven years to run, but he could not sell it or his carriage which still stood at Beale's factory in 1843.

An indication of the profitability of the passenger services which did operate may be gleaned from the Gloucester-Cheltenham steam carriage service. During the four months of its operation, it brought in £202.4.6 minus £78 for coke, one-third of which was used in experimentation. After four months, the engine showed no wear and tear. The boiler tubes were cleaned once monthly so that the upkeep was cheap. The director and engineer who ran the carriage received £2 each per week, which amounted to £80 for twenty weeks.[29] Thus:

Working Expenses			Revenue
Coke	L 52		L 202.4.6
Wages	80		
	132		less 132
			70.4.6 profit (35%)

In addition, the cost of building the steam carriage was £250 which would have been worked off through depreciation allowance over ten years. The cost of replacing the boiler after three years and repairing the small fractures in the boiler tubes, which happened very occasionally, would have been small amounts in the long-term account.

Fear of a lack of profit was not the problem, as Walter Hancock illustrated (Table 3) in his account of his daily profit from running a passenger service with two carriages in the City of London for some years in the 1830s.[30]

Table 3
Hancock's Daily Profit
One day's work or one hundred miles

Expenditure		Revenue	
Coke, 1s. per mile	5.0.0	50 passengers 1 1/2 each	
Repairs, wear and tear	4.0.0	per mile	31.5.0
Oil, hemp etc.	0.10.0	1 ton of goods 1d per cwt	
2 engineers, 2 steersmen,		per mile	9.6.8
2 stokers, 1 guard	2.0.0		40.11.8
Rent of stations and offices			
--wages of attendants	3.0.0	Deduct 10% for	
Tolls	1.10.0	light loads	8.2.4
Fund for renewal of			32.9.4
carriage at L2 each	4.0.0		
Contingencies	2.0.0		
	22.0.0		
Daily Profit	10.9.0		
	32.9.4		

The revenue generated by these steam carriages indicated that there was a demand for them in the marketplace. Recognizing that profits could be made, entrepreneurs floated numerous steam carriage companies, and "inventors," from gentlemen of leisure to naval engineers, produced their unique steam carriages to meet the demand.

GURNEY'S IMPROVED STEAM CARRIAGE.

4. Above Colonel Sir Charles Dance, Goldsworthy Gurney, Francis Maceroni; center, Gurney's improved steam carriage, Sept. 1829 after London-Bath and Hounslow demonstrations; bottom, George Stephenson, Lord Wharncliffe, Timothy Hackworth.

5

Was Gurney Beaten by His Competitors?

In trying to account for the failure of the steam carriage, we must also consider whether Gurney's steam carriage competitors had constructed machines that were technically better than his and operated commercially successful passenger services that attracted capital investment away from Gurney's company.

TECHNICAL COMPARISONS

Contemporary accounts suggest that most steam carriages that performed well were fashioned after Gurney's design. Only three steam carriages of different design rivalled Gurney's in technical perfection.

One of these three was the Scott Russell carriage used in Scotland. The carriage design was fashioned after Gurney's model, but the most important element, the boiler, was not tubular but a conventional plate boiler. If Gurney's tubular boiler had been used, the explosion would have destroyed just one small tube, causing no damage when the boiler struck the ground.

The second of the three carriages came from the workshop of William H. James, the son of William James who did the original railway surveys before he was replaced by George Stephenson. W. H. James sold his patent for a steam boiler to Stephenson in 1821 and went to South America where he worked with Richard Trevithick, became interested in steam carriages, and in 1829 drove his own steam carriage at 15 mph on the roads about London. In 1832 James patented a change-speed gear, but on encountering high road tolls he emigrated to America and formed a steam carriage company in New York City.[31]

The third steam carriage to rival Gurney's was built by the stolid mechanic Walter Hancock, who claimed to have invented the steam carriage.

When a parliamentary committee asked William Poole, the keeper of the patents, to give the date patents were granted for steam carriages, he had exact dates for every patent except Walter Hancock's. He set Hancock's vaguely as in 1825, when Gurney had taken out his first two patents which favored his claim as the first in the field. Poole was not alone in forwarding Hancock for consideration as the inventor of the steam carriage; certain members of Parliament presented petitions from Hancock following petitions or proposed legislation introduced by Gurney's supporters. In addition, John Farey, an engineer who had written a book on steam engines and was a consultant to railway interests, was a strong advocate of Hancock's steam carriage in preference to Gurney's. Farey had drawn the specifications for Gurney's earliest carriages and then had drawn Hancock's. Another promoter of Hancock was Joseph Clinton Robertson, the editor of the *Mechanics' Magazine* from 1823 to 1852. This influential organ belittled the achievements of Gurney and Dance and subtly maintained a bias against steam carriages. Yet, at the same time, it lauded Hancock's experiments in the streets of London.

Gurney testified that Hancock turned his attention to locomotives on roads only after Gurney drove him repeatedly around Regent's Park and took the carriage up Highgate Hill in 1827. Correcting Poole, Gurney gave the correct date for Hancock's patent: May 30, 1827. In a letter to the *Mechanics' Magazine* Hancock denied that he had taken rides with Gurney; rather, he took only one ride.[32]

As for Hancock's boiler, the best judgment on its practicability was presented to a committee in July 1834 by Dionysius Lardner, a prolific writer on inland transportation.[33] The difference between Gurney's and Hancock's boilers, he said, was the same as that between rope and tape. Whereas Gurney had round threads or cords to hold water, Hancock had thin plates with the consequence that Hancock's boilers produced less power and his grate bars were burned out after two or three trips. Because of the water circulation in Gurney's boiler, it was not injured by high temperatures, but Hancock's had portions without water and could burst. Moreover, Hancock had no separator and he did not understand the principle of the jet blast; rather, he used a fanner to keep up his fire at the expense of much power.

The efforts of some of the other early developers of the steam carriage should be noted, although many of them, as Gurney said, hurt the reputation of the steam carriage by the badly constructed machines they exhibited. They contributed to the public interest in road travel, however, and they began to attract capital investment on a wide scale.

In Manchester, Richard Roberts, whom Alexander Gordon called "decidedly one of the best mechanics in Europe," experimented with a steam carriage that blew up when loaded with fifty persons because its boiler had large chambers. the sides of which gave way from steam pressure when the water failed to fill them. Another carriage with a large plate boiler in the shape of a bottle invented by Timothy Burstall and John Hill exploded, killing a boy and wounding two men. John Braithwaite, who built engines for the railroads, developed a tubular boiler that was the basis for a fire engine used in London. It was destroyed by a rioting mob in the early 1830s before the public began to appreciate the virtues of steam carriages.

There were also steam carriages which, grossly inappropriate, gave cartoonists a funny subject, such as Dr. Church's carriage which was widely advertised as intended for the London-Birmingham road. "The whole machine is so large and unwieldy," wrote Robertson to Telford, "that Macneill thinks it will never be able to run quicker than four miles an hour. It is calculated to carry 150 passengers."[34]

By contrast, Gurney declared his steam carriage "perfect" by the end of the Cheltenham experiment in 1831. By then his carriages had run over 15,000 miles. "I believe success rests on certain points specified in my patents," said Gurney. "Every attempt to work without these have failed."[35] "If Mr. Gurney's patent was thrown open tomorrow," John Macneill said in support, "there would be many new steam carriages commenced that are not now thought of."[36]

RELATIVE COMMERCIAL SUCCESS

Since almost all the steam carriages, including those built by Maceroni, remained in the experimental stage, there were only two steam carriage companies with successful passenger services which could have competed with the Gurney Steam Carriage Company: Russell's and Hancock's companies. These two companies, however, operated in areas remote from Gurney's intended routes and could not have drained away capital from Gurney. Moreover, Russell's commuting service between Paisley and Glasgow was financed by Scottish capitalists. Hancock's carriages ran in London, and he claimed he had no financial backing.

After Gurney's company in Devon failed to develop, after Parnell met an impasse in Parliament in his attempt to obtain a charter for his steam carriage company and for a granite road from

London to Birmingham, and when the many promoters of steam carriage companies negotiating with Maceroni saw their speculative bubbles burst, the various interests tried to come together to form one company.

Robert Torrens, the political economist, argued in Parliament on the efficacy of the steam carriage for carrying produce from the countryside to the cities. He thereby united Liberals, Radicals, and some Conservative landed interests, known as the Country Party, behind the steam carriage, which soon became a *cause célèbre* for agriculturists. A parliamentary committee investigating the "distressed condition" of the countryside was not allowed by the indifferent commercial class to make an official report to Parliament on the wretched state of the farmers. But the report was published by a commercial house in an act of defiance.[37]

The country gentry broadened its political base by forming the Central Agricultural Society in December 1835 from the Central Landed Interest Society and the National Institution of Locomotion, with over sixty chapters in England, Scotland, and Wales, for the promotion of the mechanization of agriculture.

The National Institution for Locomotion originated in 1833 from the efforts of a handful of men from Dumfries. Among them were Alexander Gordon whose lectures on the steam carriage at the Mechanics' Institute in October 1832 drew thousands of listeners, and Richard Broun, secretary to the Committee of Baronets for Privileges, whose arguments for a national political economy earned him a reputation as the founder of " a new school . . . which immediately will prostrate those of Malthus and Ricardo." The objective of the institution was to "benefit the laboring classes by benefitting their employers." By accelerating inland commercial intercourse with the steam carriage, cheap corn could be raised to feed the starving thousands and domestic agriculture could remain protected. Moreover, "new extensive and permanent fields of human industry" would be opened up.

With an introduction to Lord Brougham from Brougham's old school friend, the Reverend Henry Duncan, "the father of the Savings Bank," and a Dumfriesshireman, Gordon and Broun sought to influence legislators to adopt a national plan for steam carriages under the government. W. R. Keith Douglas, Sir Andrew Agnew, M.P., Hope Johnston, M.P., and other notables were interested in Gordon as "a Dumfriesshire man," and supported his project for nationalizing steam carriage travel together with the Post Office.

Broun and Gordon calculated that, after paying all costs of introducing steam carriages and reducing fares to one-half the present coach fare, profit would amount to 50 percent. "If Government thus will borrow L10,000,000 to introduce the project, it will eventually reap for state purposes about L5,000,000 annually which will admit of the reduction of taxation without its present accompanying evil curtailment of expenditure: and that in a way which will be attended by the most important political consequences."[38]

The government could not overlook the impressive array of names, noblemen and gentry, listed on the prospectus of the National Institution of Locomotion, particularly as Parnell and Telford were involved in a similar project. The fact that Coutts and Company, one of the most respected London banking firms, acted as banker for the National Institution of Locomotion and that its senior partner, Sir Coutts Trotter, was prominent on its committee, gave notice to Parliament that the steam carriage was not to be taken lightly. The Marquess of Sligo, Earl of Kerry, Sir George Cayley, Sir Charles Lefevre, and W. B. Baring, Esq., were among its early supporters; their names indicated that the monied agricultural class intended to promote the steam carriage.

But the Central Agricultural Society soon encountered difficulties from within its organization. In the "Captain Swing" rioting in the early 1830s, bands of agricultural laborers destroyed the threshing machines that had put them out of work. "Captain Swing," whose identity was never revealed, was said to be their leader. The large landholders hanged or transported whoever was caught smashing the new machinery, but the farmers sympathized with the laborers because they did not want to be forced by the pressure of competition to buy machines when the labor surplus made the hiring of laborers cheaper. The major disagreement, however, was over the Corn Laws. Broun, the Radicals and Reformers, most merchants, and some agriculturalists considered the Corn Laws irrelevant to a domestic economy developed by machinery. Broun did cry out that the government's gradual repeal of protective tariffs was ruining English and Irish industries, but he thought that agricultural industries could thrive with the help of machinery only under free trade, which by fostering competition encouraged the greater use of machinery. The majority of landowners, on the other hand, regarded the Corn Laws as their only protection against the growing power of the industrialists. This division of opinion led to the dissolution of the Society.

Some of its members persuaded Lord Althorp, now in private life, to organize the Royal Agricultural Society and to take over its responsibilities for encouraging innovations in animal husbandry and agriculture. At the same time, the protectionists in the Society, alarmed by the extraordinary advances in public relations made by the Anti-Corn Law League begun by Lancashire manufacturers in 1835, threw out Broun and renamed themselves the Society for the Protection of Agriculture.[39] In the three years of its existence, the Central Agricultural Society had encouraged a handful of inventions and improvements in the soil, brought about changes in a few restrictive laws, and advanced the steam carriage not one whit. Therefore, the invitation for all steam carriage interests to unite in one company, which the Society had sponsored, did not have the political support it appeared to have. Despite the willingness of all the steam carriage interests, except Walter Hancock, to cooperate, it is not surprising that the company failed to materialize.

When a parliamentary committee asked Gurney about his competitors, especially Hancock, Gurney replied that he did not regard them as serious about the development of the steam carriage as they made no attempt to attract capital for a grand undertaking.

Hancock's relationship to the railway interests has been questioned.[40] In 1838 he published a book, *Narrative of Twelve Years' Experiments (1824-1836) Demonstrative of the Practicability and Advantage of Employing Steam-Carriages on Common Roads....* which, written in the third person, recounted problems he encountered from a hostile public and unscrupulous capitalists, but not from tolls and railway interests. He closed his book with a personal note that he was applying his latest boiler to the locomotive engine for the railway "from which I confidently anticipate very considerable advantages to arise." This sentiment coming from an advocate of steam carriages was extraordinary.

Railway capitalists may have encouraged Hancock to drive about London because by remaining there he offered no competition to their rail lines. This supposition gains credence from the fact that Parliament passed the Metropolis Act in 1829 to equate tolls for steam carriages with horsedrawn carriages within city boundaries. In the same year it passed the Newcastle and Carlisle Act, which in effect gave the railroad companies a monopoly of the railway lines.

Hancock's antagonism to Gurney's carriages and the discrediting of Gurney by Hancock's journalistic supporters who also supported railways lead us to examine the railway interests and their relationship to the steam carriage.

6

Opposition of the Railroad Interests

Railways were made entirely of wood until the mid-eighteenth century because, until the adoption of coked coal for smelting iron-stone, iron was too expensive and thus mechanical invention was slow. But when the landlords in Parliament transferred mineral royalty rights from the Crown to the lord of the manor, the landed class at the collieries quickly made agreements with coal merchants of the port cities, and an incentive to quicken delivery was found.

When steam was introduced to railways in 1821 (on the Stockton-Darlington line), railway promoters were given a great advantage by the many surveys made throughout the country by William James. Quaker industrialists at Yarmouth, Leeds, and Norwich were awakened to the need for better transport from factory to port.

The Pease family, which made its fortune in woolen manufacturing, and the Backhouses, who were linen-drapers, led the opposition to the Darlington nobility (who wished to preserve the land for fox-hunting). They pushed the Stockton-Darlington Railway Bill through Parliament against a combination of the landed gentry, turnpike road trustees, coach proprietors, and some farmers who feared their fields would be cut up so as to make their farms uncultivatable. Similarly, John Moss, oil refiner, sugar merchant, and banker, successfully led his Liverpool associates against landed nobility and canal interests in Parliament to lay the Manchester-Liverpool line.

Opposition from great landowners was bought off with money settlements and shares of stock, or circumvented by rerouting the lines. Opposition from lesser interests was overlooked, or, in the case of canal interests, they were engaged in parliamentary battle until after some years of resistance they were beaten in committees and by House vote. Gradually, railway shares replaced canal securities.

5. The railway train in England in 1831, from a German lithograph. (Courtesy of John Grand-Carteret, *Voiture de demain*, Paris, 1898.)

An advantage that railway companies held over canal companies, which were prevented by law from trading on their own canals, came from the Newcastle and Carlisle Act of 1829 which the Lancashire capitalists initiated. Until this time horses had the right of way over locomotives when both were used in rail traffic, but under the act railway companies charged tolls for the use of their lines by coaches and carriages, and, with the sudden great speed of their locomotives from the steam jet, they chased all other traffic off the rails. Hence, the railway proprietors and the locomotive owners being one and the same, they monopolized the railways.

This monopoly favored Robert Stephenson's railway locomotives exclusively, since Robert and his father, George, were the principal engineers for the Lancashire railway capitalists, and Henry Pease, one of the primary promoters of the railway, financed Robert Stephenson's locomotive factory at Newcastle. As Colonel Dance complained to the Duke of Wellington, the monopoly did not allow Gurney to introduce his tubular boilers on railways and never would if it interfered with "Stephenson's arrangements."[41]

The railway capitalists' man in Parliament was Lord Wharncliffe from Yorkshire. He chaired the Lords' Committee for all of the early and important private railway bills that had to pass the House of Lords to become law. Wharncliffe, whose prestige with the Lords was enhanced by the King's reliance on his recommendations as to who should be his advisers, masterminded the passage of the second bill for the Birmingham-London railway in 1832. He also chaired the committees for the Cheltenham and

Great Western Union Railway Bill and the Cheltenham-Birmingham Bill in 1836 which had been on the planning boards for some years. The plan was to extend the Cheltenham-Gloucester railway (previously a horse railway) to the Cheltenham-Birmingham-Stroud, where it would be connected to Bristol and the Great Western, and open up the manufacturing districts near Stroud to improved communications, "essential now that the manufacturers of cloth in the north have the advantage of similar communications."

The railway bankers were grateful to Wharncliffe, as evidenced by George Carr Glyn whose private bank in London served the banking interests of Lancashire and Yorkshire: "I was yesterday afternoon in our parliament and went for miles by the first locomotive engine ever in use in London. I propose naming it the 'Wharncliffe.'"[42] With such financial and political powers, the railway companies took over the canals and either closed them or charged exorbitant rates to canal traffic.

In the 1850s, the first Earl of Redesdale, who had succeeded Wharncliffe as leader of the Lords, was addressed on the subject of railway and canal combination by Thomas Grahame, who, as the principal defender of canal interests in Parliament, was Alexander Gordon's ally against railways. Grahame asked Redesdale to ensure that further acts permitting railways to take over canals would have a proviso that Parliament could relieve the evils inflicted on the public (such as railways mulcting local inhabitants who had to travel by canal in order to support railway operations elsewhere). Redesdale blandly replied that one could not lay down general terms.[43]

As for the attitude of railway capitalists to steam carriage promoters, the first clear indication of competition between them emerged in the 1833 to 1838 period during the construction of the London-Birmingham railway, when the promoters of the London, Holyhead, Liverpool Steam-coach and Road Company tried to run a passenger service on the same route. Railway officials advised large stockholders in railways who were interested in the new steam carriage to stay clear of such doubtful projects. "I know not what success the projected Steam Coach Company may have in raising subscriptions but I am quite sure the money subscribed must be ultimately so much lost," wrote Richard Creed, secretary for the London-Birmingham railway. "Projects of this sort will of course be entertained, for there is a fascination about them to ingenious men which makes them reluctant to examine the tests by which their practical utility must be eventually determined.... perfect machinery with a larger outlay is preferable to imperfect machinery with a smaller outlay."[44]

Creed resented Thomas Telford for promoting the steam carriage: "The old race of Civil Engineers fear that Railways are destroying their fame and occupation. They talk against us, and their listeners have not the means from deficiency of information on the subject discussed, to judge whether the speakers are to be relied upon. At all events their confidence is shaken."[45]

"Because of his association with so many canal projects," wrote Telford's biographer, "railway promoters looked upon Telford as their arch-enemy and did their utmost to discredit his opinions."[46] Telford's argument against railroads was the paramount objection for all who opposed them: railroads meant the monopolization of transportation by a commercial group whose stranglehold over the carriage of produce from farm to market gave it control of pricing and distribution to the detriment of the farmers.

For the first time the London banking houses and London merchants overcame their reluctance to invest in railway shares. Led by the banker George Carr Glyn, they joined with Birmingham manufacturers to finance the Birmingham-London rail regardless of cost. When it opened in September 1838, the expense amounted to about 4.5 million pounds. Wharncliffe had used his influence in the Lords to win support for the bill, and Robert Stephenson, George Stephenson's son who added a first-rate education and engineering experience in South America to the inventive, indomitable qualities he inherited from his father, pushed the work to the finish on the ground.

As Parnell prepared clauses for his bill for the new granite road (such as "to allow of agreement with Steam Company for use of the road"), his opposition had already been alerted to its dangers. "The only objection that we have ever felt against Sir H. Parnell's working in this matter," editorialized the *Bankers' Circular*,

is that he has saddled the British public with an expense of seven or eight thousand pounds to pay for a good road for his own countrymen. This project of a new Steam Carriage Road . . . is a proof of a determination to give steam carriage on common roads a fair trial. The plan never can, we conclude, be executed, because the passing of steam-engines on a line close to the turnpike road would be fraught with so much danger to the lives and property of His Majesty's subjects . . . . We allude to the fact only to show the strong determination which exists in a very influential quarter to apply steam-carriages on hard common roads to the uses of the public. In this regard it is of importance for railroad speculators to consider its bearing upon their property.[47]

The value of this property had grown dramatically.

Beginning in 1825-1826, Parliament had authorized the construction of eighteen railways and in each successive year five more until 1836 when it granted statutory powers to twenty-nine, and in 1837 to fifteen. Meanwhile, dozens more were being promoted, for instance, thirty-five railways in 1835 at a capitalization of over £34 million. The sudden acceleration of capital flow to railways therefore seems to have taken place in 1836. By January 1839 Parliament had passed 107 railway bills with a total capital in joint stock of £41,610,814 and the power to raise by loan of Ll6,177,630, for a total of £57,788,444. By 1843 when England stood on the threshold of the great railway mania, £66 million had been raised for railways on a nominal capital of £82.8 million. Perhaps the best indication of railway growth during this period is the increase in income derived from the duty on passengers—from £6,852 in 1835 to £72,216 in 1840.[48]

Since Lancashire merchants had the greatest investment in the nation's international trade through which they had influenced its foreign policy for a century or more, the Crown, the apparatus of government, the ministries, and trade boards were bound closely to them and, as a consequence, favored railway development. The class most affected by these ties was the city gentry. By entering the professions and Parliament and through its kinship with the aristocracy, this gentry had become quite separate from the country gentry. Prepared to do the professional bidding of the commercial entrepreneurs, the city gentry welcomed a rise in interest rates and the greater demand of government for funds to pursue its wars on behalf of industry.

The groups to whom these financial interests gave employment on railway construction added their voices against the steam carriage—that is, railway engineers, surveyors, and the mechanics who worked in the subsidiary industries to which the railway gave birth. With the backing of this combination of economic interests, the railway capitalists pushed their private bills for rail lines through the Select Committees of the House of Lords with increasing ease.

The Lancashire group used this legislative power to suppress the steam carriage, but, owing to political support for the steam carriage from landed interests, it acted in a veiled way until the railway interests were entrenched. The Lancashire group may also have manipulated the early opposition of the road trustees to the steam carriage. Alexander Gordon told a Commons Committee in 1834: "Impressions had gone abroad amongst the landed interest, that it was contrary to their advantage that the steam carriage should be introduced, and amongst road trustees also, who are of course immediately connected with the land and with agricultural pursuits; and these altogether combined to form a very serious opposition to the introduction of steam carriages on turnpike roads."[49]

Those aggrieved directly were the stagecoach proprietors. Whereas the stagecoach required eighteen horses at 2/6 each per day to travel the nine-mile road six times daily (say 45 shillings), the steam carriage between Cheltenham and Gloucester paid 9/3

47

for coke each day and was, therefore, five times as cheap. Since the steam carriage charged one-half the fare of the stagecoach and made the trip in one-half the time, the men who ran the coaches and managed the stables, as well as the stable boys, felt threatened by unemployment.

On the other hand, when Gurney argued that a horse consumes as much as eight people and that its replacement by the steam carriage would provide food for the rapidly increasing population, he alarmed the landlords. Sir William Molesworth, a Philosophical Radical, expressed their fears (though not on their behalf) when speaking in support of the steam carriage in debate in the House of Commons: steam carriages, by replacing horsedrawn carriages, would drastically reduce the need for horses, which would cause the demand for oats to fall and ruin the farmers whose rents would have to be reduced, thus lowering income for the landed agricultural interests.

There is no evidence that the stagecoach companies were involved in strewing rocks over the roadway to stop Dance's steam carriage near Cheltenham. Not only were they more inconvenienced than the steam carriage by the obstructed roadway, but also they lacked the political power needed to persuade the road trustees that they could commit such an act with impunity.

The landlords may have had the power in the local community to flout the law, but whatever economic harm they feared from the steam carriage, the effect was too far in the future to cause them on their own initiative to retaliate against the steam carriage in this manner. Rather, the sabotage appeared to be a reaction to a demonstration of the steam carriage's hauling power because it happened one week later. In mid-June, James Stone replaced the hind wheels of 5-foot circumference with 3-foot wheels, attached a wagon loaded with cast iron, and drove the steam carriage at high speed. At the conclusion of the demonstration he offered the spectators a ride back to Gloucester; twenty-six climbed onto the carriage. By driving the ten extra tons with only one wheel attached to the engine up the rise in the approach to Gloucester (1 inch in 20 inches), Stone successfully demonstrated that the wheel did not slip.

The enthusiastic response from the agriculturists who wanted licenses caused Dance to beg Gurney to postpone for a week the meeting of the company's patentees which he had called in London to combat the high road tolls. This enthusiasm made the road trustees intensify their opposition to the steam carriage. A toll collector warned one of Dance's engineers that if the loose stones did not stop the carriage, the trustees would get a "tickler down from parliament."

Dance wrote the Cheltenham road trustees on June 20, 1831, to point out the advantages to be derived from steam travel, especially that passenger traffic would be increased, which would be to their profit. He reminded them that the King and leaders of the country supported the introduction of the steam carriages.

At a meeting of the Gloucester road trustees on June 25, 1831, Dance's carriage was condemned as a "public nuisance." Present were William Cother, Esq., a farmer with property along the turnpike; James "Jemmy " Wood, owner of the Gloucester City Old Bank and the community leader by virtue of being one of the wealthiest men in the kingdom; John Chadborn, Wood's solicitor; Thomas Smith an attorney; William Ellis Viner, an attorney; William Goodrich, gameskeeper; Charles Church, manufacturer of rope and sacking; Thomas John Baker, justice of the peace and antiquarian; Joseph Rea, horsedealer; Frederick Woodcock; and four members of the landed gentry: James H. Byles, John Michael Saunders, James Woodbridge Walters, and David Walters. Several of them were introduced into the Minute Ledger as meeting the qualifications of the 1798 Road Trustees Act, that is, they held "no place of profit" under the act, were not personally interested, received at least L40 yearly in rents or owned a personal estate of L800, or were heirs to lands with a clear annual value of L80. [50]

At the next meeting on August 6, after the steam carriage had been forced off the road, only one of these community leaders showed himself: John Chadborn. As chairman, he conducted the meeting alone: "He stated his Belief that the proprietors of the Steam Carriage referred to at the meeting of the Trustees on the 25th June last had discontinued the use of that Carriage."

The composition of the trustees was such that none would welcome the steam carriage, and some such as Joseph Rea, the horsedealer, were hostile to it. Doubtless, the landowners did fear a drop in rents from a fall in the price of oats, and they could have been panicked into requesting private laws against steam carriages. But of these trustees, Jemmy Wood was the leader and Chadborn, his legal servant. Both knew that Wood's Gloucester City Old Bank was near bankruptcy and depended for support on the good graces of Lubbock and Company, one of the close inner circle of London private bankers, on which it drew. Jemmy Wood's closest relative was Matthew Wood, a London alderman, who, as an insider, was well acquainted with government policy.

A connection with Jemmy Wood and Lord Wharncliffe, the promoter of railways in Parliament, can be traced through Matthew Wood, who was not really related but was adopted as an heir by Jemmy and his spinster sister because of his liberal politics. Matthew Wood rose through apprenticeship in the drug trade to merchandising in the hop trade which made him rich. He was elected Lord Mayor of London twice, represented London City in the House of Commons from 1817, and was made a baronet by the Melbourne administration in 1837. His second son, William Page Wood, who was admitted to the bar in 1827 and made L1000 a year by 1829, "was much employed in railway work before parliamentary committees from 1828 to 1841... and it was out of one of his cases that the clause known as the 'Wharncliffe clause' originated." He was an impassioned advocate for the Stephensons as, of course, was Wharncliffe, whose family was one of the three Grand Allies, colliery owners, who gave George Stephenson his first opportunity by putting him in charge of steam-driven machinery in their Yorkshire collieries.

The London Woods dealt more closely with Chadborn than with Jemmy, who was then in his seventies and was inclined to leave matters in Chadborn's hands. On Jemmy's death, Chadborn altered Jemmy's Will so that he and Matthew Wood figured largely to receive Jemmy's great fortune. Chadborn was found out by the courts, however, and hanged himself in his coachhouse in early August 1839. When Matthew Wood died in 1843, his son, William, refused to accept that portion of money that his father had gotten from Jemmy Wood, because, he said, "it savoured too much of gambling."[51]

Therefore, to blame the private acts that set high tolls for steam carriages on road trustees and landowners fearing a fall in rents is to overlook the profound and long-term interests of the railways. Nathaniel Ogle, whose steam carriage company was unsupported by investors because of high tolls in the early 1830s, found that at one trust, Warrington, the clause setting high rates for steam carriages in its turnpike law was obtained by the proprietors of the contiguous railway between Liverpool and Manchester. Alarmed by steam carriages, the railway proprietors, he said "oppose every attempt either directly or indirectly to their being established upon the common roads as the future interest of their outlay depends on it."[52]

This argument of the complicity of road trustees with railways does not discount the likelihood that in some cases financially hard-pressed trustees could have made the overtures. The debt of the turnpike trusts was increased annually by the trustees' procedure of converting unpaid interest into principal. That is, they would issue bonds bearing interest for the amount of interest due, thus augmenting the bonded debt and increasing the sum of interest due. There developed the system of leasing tollgates to lessees who, under pressure of paying rent, extorted money from the public. In common agreement, they lowered the bidding price for the leases and raised the tolls over the legal amount to the public. The steam carriage promoters were, therefore, confronting a thoroughly corrupted system.

With the advances of the railway, road trustees and stagecoach proprietors quickly realized that railways were a greater menace than steam carriages. By 1835 the evils of the railway monopoly were foreseen by a conjunction of forces—landowners, occupiers, canal and navigation proprietors, coach, wagon, and van masters, steam navigation and steam carriage proprietors, innkeepers, creditors of turnpike trusts, and others—who warned in a General Anti-Railway Petition to the Commons that railways "bring to ruin a great majority of all tradesmen in every town of the United Kingdom for the benefit of the metropolis alone—force numerous proprietors to quit their family mansions—and throw out of cultivation not less than 100,000 acres of valuable soil—besides annihilating the prosperity of the whole carrying body by land and water." [53]

The sabotage of Russell's steam carriages by the trustees of the Paisley road in 1834 demonstrated the ruthlessness of the railway opposition. In May 1834 the Steam Carriage Company promoters negotiated a moderate toll with the trustees of the Shotti road and of the Bathgate and Airdrie roads, but met opposition on the Paisley road. "The whole arose (i.e., the piling of stones on the road) from their insisting on our paying six times the amount of the tolls of the other coaches and our merely agreeing to offer the same rate of toll which they paid," wrote Downey, one of the promoters, about the trustees of the Paisley road. "Gentlemen of the Glasgow-Paisley district are among that sort (that broke down Sir Charles Dance's carriage) and wish to follow the example which was set them by Cheltenham and Gloucester."[54]

The Lancashire railway group opposed Ward's steam carriage because Ward was about to run a passenger service from Edinburgh to Liverpool, Birmingham, and London. Although Russell gave no indication that he planned to expand his short commuter service to take over Ward's route, it was apparent that the Scottish financial interests that were behind Ward were now behind Russell and that landed interests, including the Duke of Buccleigh who invested L10,000, were backing Russell's company. It follows that the Birmingham-London Railway Company opposed Russell's carriage as strongly as it opposed Parnell, Telford, and Gordon's attempt to run steam carriages along the same route. But finding the steam carriage promoters in Scotland better organized and more determined than in Cheltenham, the Lancashire group risked sabotage and the lives of passengers to force the steam carriages off the road.

Once the road trustees were led (to their subsequent regret) into filing private bills raising road tolls against steam carriages in a panic of legislation, as if orchestrated throughout the whole of England, the railway capitalists enjoyed what amounted to a restraining order against steam carriage companies until they were

51

sufficiently organized in Parliament to deny the repeal of those laws. The introduction of private bills did not require an announcement and thus steam carriage supporters were caught by surprise such that the leader of the Radical Party introduced legislation requiring that Parliament be informed of the filing of private bills henceforth.

Gurney's request for fair treatment for himself was introduced into the Commons after the political turmoil over passage of the Reform Bill and the act for the abolition of slavery had died away. A Select Committee gathered evidence and recommended that:

1. The portions of acts with tolls prohibitive to steam carriages be repealed and the tolls made equal to tolls on horsedrawn carriages.
2. Gurney's patent be extended for fourteen years beyond its legal termination.
3. Not less than £5,000 be given to Gurney in lieu of such extension.

The Commons' refusal to allow the *Report* to be put to a vote was a clear illustration of the advent of railway power in what was soon to be called the "Railway Parliament." From support for the steam carriage in the Commons of 1831 under the Whig party, led by Earl Grey with the agriculture-loving Viscount Althorp as chancellor of the exchequer, to the Commons of 1835 under the Whig party, led by Viscount Melbourne with Spring-Rice as chancellor of the exchequer, there had been a shift in policy. Melbourne was creating the new industrial order, reforming Municipal Corporations to lay the foundation of popularly controlled local government and requiring every incorporated borough to establish a police force.

The railway's great carrying capacity initially attracted the English capitalists. The early rail lines were laid with the imperative that they pass near enough to the industrial estates to allow for branch lines from the estates to the main lines. These branch lines were mutually beneficial as they greatly reduced the transport cost to the coalfield owners. Like tributaries feeding a river, they reduced the costs of loading and unloading at the stations because of the increased flow of merchandise they brought to the lines.

The steam carriage, on the other hand, appealed to the producers of agricultural products because its smaller carrying capacity and its flexibility of making short runs and connecting inland markets met their needs. The accumulating surplus value and the political power accompanying it, however, lay with the industrialists in the north.

By 1841 the opportunity for introducing the steam carriage had been lost. The railway interests were in control of the country for three reasons: (1) the benefits of railways to landed interests, whose lands over which railways ran appreciated in value by one-third; (2) the attraction of easy money for railway proprietors through stock exchange transactions; and (3) their monopolistic advantages which made entry into the railway field too difficult owing to the large amounts of capital required.

Did the steam carriage fail vis-a-vis the railway because railways brought a better return on investment? In a cost and profit comparison of steam carriage to railway, however, railways were the poorer investment as the next chapter demonstrates.

7

Cost Comparison Between the Railroad and Steam Carriage

ON RELATIVE TERMS

The travel route that offers the best comparison of road to rail travel in the 1830s is the London to Birmingham, where the road ran for 108 miles and the railway for 112 1/4 miles. Richard Cort, the son of the inventor of the process for puddling iron, in his capacity as secretary for the London-Birmingham-Holyhead Steam Carriage Company in 1834, drew up a schedule of expenses and returns for the company based on the experience of steam carriage builders up to that time. Since the London-Birmingham railway was still under construction, he could not compare his projected accounts with its accounts, but we can use its accounts, after the railway began operating in 1838, for this purpose.

Cort's figures for the working costs for steam carriages on the London to Birmingham road are presented in Table 4.[54A] Cort commented: "These estimates show a profit exceeding 100£ per diem, in addition to the interest and profit on the sum expended in roadmaking, which is to be secured by an additional toll on steam carriages."

The London, Holyhead, Liverpool Steamcoach Company, capitalized at £350,000, offered shares at £20 ("a deposit of 2£ per Share to be paid, upon Subscribers being recorded as Shareholders, and no further sum to be called for, until an Act of Parliament has been obtained"). Therefore, with 17,500 shares and a daily surplus of £100, an annual surplus of £36,500, the annual gross return per share would be £2. 1. 10, over 40 percent. Cort estimated net profit to be 20 percent.

Table 4
Working Costs for Steam Carriages on the London-Birmingham Road

Daily Expenditures	L	s	d
Hire of 30 carriages to run 108 miles each at 1d. per mile	13	10	00
Thirty engines kept in repair at 6d. per mile each	81	0	0
Coke for 30 engines, 3/4 bu. per mile ea. at 7d. per bushel	70	17	6
Engineer, Asst. Engineer, fireman for 30 engines at 18s each	27	0	0
Establishment at London, Birmingham and depots	10	0	O
Reserved fund for the purchase of new engines, equal to			
10% per annum of the original cost	8	15	0
	211	2	6
Tolls payable to trustees at 40s each engine	60	0	6
Interest and profit equal to L 10% per annum on capital			
of L 350,000 and L 30 per mile per annum for the repair			
of the road, to be secured by an additional toll			
on steam carriages	104	15	0
Total Daily Charge	375	17	6

Daily Return

	L	s	d
150 passengers at 23s each	172	10	O
350 passengers at 13s each	227	10	O
(N.B. - The average number of passengers traveling daily			
between London and Birmingham, exclusive of the inter-			
mediate stages, is 550, and the present coach fares are			
40s. inside and 20s. outside)			
Parcels	80	0	0
Daily Return	480	00	O
Deduct Daily Charge	375	17	6
Daily surplus, after paying interest and all charges	104	2	6

The steam carriage was expected to carry baggage and parcels. Because the hauling of freight was a natural advantage to the railway, we cannot abstract that element for a better comparison. Dionysius Lardner, the prolific writer on railways, estimated that the goods traffic on railways accounted for 31 percent of gross revenue, passenger traffic for 60 percent, and the remainder arising from baggage, parcels, and so on.[54B]

We have the working costs for the London-Birmingham Railway in 1842 and the detailing of expenditures for the latter half of the year. (Table 5) The cost of constructing the railway was set at L5,953,000 and its value in 1842 at L11,430,000. These figures will serve for the purposes of comparison to the steam carriage estimates despite the eight years between them, during which the railways were being constructed and established.

Table 5
Working Costs for the London-Birmingham Railway, 1842

Working Costs	L	
Expenditures	272,300	
Receipts	809,200	
Net Profit	536,900	
Paid percent per annum	11.2s	
Pays at market price percent per annum	4.18s.	

Detail of Expenditures - for half-year ending 31 Dec. 1842

		L	
1.	Police charges	6,200	
	Coach traffic charges	16,281	
	Salaries, wages etc. in merchandise traffic	2,135	
	General charges for direction, superintendence		L
	secretary, clerks, advertising, stationery, offices, etc.	8,309	32,925
2.	Maintenance of way	22,711	
	Locomotive power	38,640	
	Coach repairs	8,633	
	New stock an d depreciation in Locomotive		L
	and carriage stock	14,212	84,196
3.	Parish Rates	7,771	
	Passengers' Duty	14,077	21,848
			138,969

Source: William Galt, *Railway Reform*, London: Richardson, 1844, p. 29.

Receipts for the half year were £420,958.

We have found passenger statistics for the half-year ending December 31, 1841, which would be comparable to the half-year ending December 31, 1842.

First Class Passengers	161,044
Second	212,987
Third	32,043
	413,272

Cattle 9,232, calves 811, sheep 65,097, pigs 2,353, horses 1,616, carriages 1,616, and 79,261 tons of goods.

Fare Rate		Cost of Conveying each passenger the distance (i.e. 112 1/4 mi.)
First Class	31/3	10/4
Second	22/6	7/5
Third	14/0	4/8

The fares were extraordinarily high in relation to cost per passenger because passenger fares were expected to cover the costs of original investment and to add to the low profit from carrying freight. Moreover, the fares reflected the bias against carrying the working class. Reformers pointed out that by reducing fares to one-sixth of the present amount, returns would be much greater. Since the railway company had destroyed competition from stagecoaches (which had charged 40 shillings inside and 20 shillings outside), it did not see the necessity of risking the lowering of the fares. By contrast, the steam carriage fares were much lower and would have attracted the passengers from the railway.

If all the passengers had traveled the full distance, which, of course, they did not, the receipts would have totaled approximately £514,342 (i.e., first class, 252,302; second, 239,610; third, 22,430). The London-Birmingham railway was in the class of the more profitable companies. Since its profit would be absorbed into the profits or losses of the other companies, and since an examination of the railway industry is our true purpose, we take Dionysius Lardner's figures for the industry over several years (Table 6). He assumed (after close study) that working expenses were not less than 40 percent of the receipts, by which he figured the major limits of the profits from year to year.

Table 6.
Railway Industry Profits

	Length of Railway open (miles)	Capital Expended	Total Receipts	Receipts	Percent on Capital	
					Minor limit of expenses	Major limit of profit
12 mos. ending						
6/30/43	1,857	74,280,000	4,535,189	6.1	2.4	3.7
1844	1,952	78,080,000	5,075,674	6.5	2.6	3.9
1845	2,148	85,920,000	6,209,714	7.2	2.9	4.3
1846	2,441	97,640,000	7,565,569	7.8	3.1	4.7
1847	3,036	121,440,000	8,510,886	7.0	2.8	4.2
1848	3,816	152,640,000	9.993.552	6.5	2.6	3.9
6 mos. ending						
12/31/48	5,079	205,160,000	5,744,956	5.6	2.2	3.4

Lardner commented:

These figures show, that, whatever may be the advantages of particular railways as investments, the aggregate of the whole presents no signal advantages over other enterprises; and that they have been, since 1846, not much more productive to the capitalist than the public funds. It is probable, however, that the depression shown in the results of the last two years may be only temporary; nevertheless it is evident that the railways, taken in the aggregate, have never yet produced a net profit of 5 per cent.

Both steam carriage estimates and railway accounts included the primary cost of constructing a road or railway. Cort's estimates for the building of a granite roadway and way stations follow:

	Original Outlay	in L
Parliamentary and other preliminary expenses		5,000
Road Making		300,000
Depots and water stations		2,400
Engines		31,500
Contingencies		11,100
		350,000

In calculating the cost of the engine, which could be made at the time for £700 each, Cort made allowance for contingencies and costed them at £1,050 each. Thus, thirty engines cost £31,500. The outlay is considerably less than that for the railway when a comparison is made after the deduction of parliamentary costs: Steam carriage (350,000-5,000) £345,000, as compared to the railway: (4,751,135-72,869) £4,678,266.

The *Report* of the Select Committee on Railways of 1839 summarizes (Table 7) the capital expenditures of the London-Birmingham railway (in pounds).[54C]

Table 7
Capital Expenditures for the London-Birmingham Railway
in L

	Parliamentary Estimate	Expenditures to 31-12-38	Excess
Land and compensation	250,000	537,596	287,596
Works, road and Stations	2,070,807	3,707,589	1,636,782
Locos. etc.	80,000	194,343	114,343
General (inc. cost of Act. L 72,869)	99,193	208,676	109,483
Interest	---	102,931	102,931
	2,500,000	4,751,135	2,251,135

H. Pollin, an English economist, made a survey of all railway company lines and found that the cost of land averaged about 12 percent of total expenditure, although it fluctuated from a low of about 9 percent to a high of 27 percent.[54D] The cost of the works, road, and stations was the greater expense, as we see in the case of the London-Birmingham line.

When asked by the Lords Select Committee on the Tolls on Steam Carriages Bill of 1836 to submit a comparative statement of first cost and annual maintenance per mile when the supposed traffic was 250,000 tons per annum, Alexander Gordon gave the figures shown in Table 8.[54E]

Table 8
Gordon's Estimate of Building Cost and Maintenance for the London-Birmingham Roadway

	Edge Railway	Old Road Laid w/Blocks of Granite for Wheels to run on	Cassell's Bituminous Surface Laid on an Old Road	Gravel or Broken Stone Road
First cost	20,000	2,500	1,000	2,000
Annual Maintenance per mile	400 (not providing for depreciation)	50 (not providing for depreciation)	75 (providing fully for keeping it up)	372 (providing for renewal every 10 years)

Since the road from London to Birmingham was 108 miles, Cort's estimate of £300,000 for the cost of laying the blocks of granite for that distance leaves room for contingencies. (Cost would be £270,000.) Gordon's table shows that the rail line would be eight times more expensive than the granite road to maintain.

The cost per mile for the London-Birmingham railway (112 1/4 miles long) was £53,150, which was considerably higher than that for the average rail line, which was closer to Gordon's figure.

We conclude that if steam carriage service ran alongside the rail service, steam carriage profit would have been higher by 15 percent (and twice the return from stagecoaches, which averaged a net profit of 10 percent throughout the country). Since steam carriage fares considerably undercut railway fares, passengers would have preferred the steam carriages, thus increasing their profits and reducing railways to losing propositions.

In analyzing railway finances, Cort predicted correctly that railways would not pay above 5 percent. (He illustrated that the Manchester-Liverpool line could not pay even 1 percent). That his arguments went unheeded by the general public is a testament to the hegemonic influence of the railway companies over the press and the society generally. As for the availability of investment capital, it was in short supply from the commercial crisis of 1826 to 1832, but in great supply from 1833 through 1836 when many steam carriage companies were floated. After 1840, however, it can be argued that the railways did deprive steam carriage companies of capital. The chancellor of the exchequer reported the amounts spent on railways:

In 1841, 1842, and 1843, the amount was about L4,500,000; in 1844, it was £6,500,000; in 1845, it was £14,000,000; in the first half of 1846, it was £9,800,000 and in the last half-year it was £26,000,000; in the first half of 1847 it was £25,720,000; and if the works had been proceeded with, the expenditure in the last half of 1847 would have been £38,000,000 on Railways. . . . Let it be recollected that a great amount of capital was taken away which deprived men of the means of carrying on their commercial pursuits, and that we cannot avoid looking to the obvious consequences of converting £50,000,000 of that which had been floating in to £50,000,000 of fixed capital, and thereby taking it out of those commercial channels in which it was hitherto employed.[54F]

The foregoing figures do not support the suggestion that railways enjoyed economic advantages over steam carriages. High road tolls, about which steam carriage entrepreneurs complained, may have played an important part in the victory of the railway over road traffic and suggest that steam carriage companies encountered legislative restrictions which hampered their growth.

8

The Decisive Importance of Restrictive Tolls

Gurney found tolls to be a nuisance from the beginning of his experiments when he exercised his steam carriage in the Regent's Park barrack yard. The toll gate outside his factory in Albany Street was on the south side of the doors at first, but was mysteriously moved just a few yards to the north, between the factory doors and the barracks. It was a portent of his troubles to come.

When Dance was forced to stop his steam carriage service on the Gloucester-Cheltenham road because the tolls were suddenly imposed, and, at the same time, Gurney learned from his parliamentary agents that high road tolls for Scotland were being passed in private bills, Gurney immediately called a meeting of the partners to discuss the actions they should take.

Hanning considered excessive tolls in a letter to Gurney as early as August 1829:

To suppose that the Minister would for a moment think of crippling the energies of the engine is most improbable; the advocates of such a measure might as well petition against steam power on land, because it lessens manual labour, and against its use on sea, because we are now most powerful there under the use of canvas.[55]

Now in 1831 Hanning refused to advance more money and assessed the situation grimly:

It is no use to attempt establishing the subject in the face of the Government, or to lay out a single shilling further, until we see that the Government do not really intend to oppose us. Therefore you must lose no time in petitioning the House, and having the case investigated and enquired into, so as to arrive at the determination on the part of the Legislature.[56]

Dance wrote later: "it was not the particular Road on which the Tolls were laid then that stopped us, but the Fact that wherever we attempted to run, or Contracts were made, we were met by an Act of Parliament."[57] The Cheltenham Bill dated July 30, 1831, may be regarded as the spearhead of the assault on the steam carriage.[58] It named over 180 trustees with the power "to put this Act and the Several Acts relating to Turnpike Roads in England, not exceeding Three in the whole, to be Trustees hereby nominated." The act stipulated that tolls be taken "at each and every Turnpike, Toll Gate and Side Gate, Bar and Chain, which is now or which shall hereafter be set up or continued upon, across, or by the Side of the Roads by this Act directed to be made, improved and kept in repair."

The Cheltenham road toll charged 8d per horse for stagecoaches, which for a four-horse stagecoach came to 2 shillings 8 pence each time of passing. At six times daily the stagecoach paid 16 shillings, and for one week it paid £6.12. Dance's steam carriage, on the other hand, was charged 3 shillings for the steam tug and 3 shillings for the carriage drawn on each passing of the gate. At six times daily (three round trips) this amounted to L1.16, or on a weekly basis, £13.12.

Over the course of twenty weeks, the period during which we have Dance's cost accounts on his commuter service, he would pay £272 in road tolls, whereas the stagecoach would pay £132, less than one-half Dance's expense. Dance's working expenses for the twenty weeks were £132. The addition of £272 would bring the cost to £404. His revenue of £202 would have made the steam carriage service unprofitable unless Dance doubled the fare from 1 shilling to 2 shillings sixpence. However, Dance stated that if a toll were collected at Gloucester (which happened shortly afterward) he would pay 12 shillings on each journey. Thus, he would pay £808 to the tolls over a twenty-week period. His working expenses for the period would be £132 plus £808, or £940. To make a profit he would have had to charge 5 shillings per passenger, at which rate he could not have kept his passengers.

Before the passage of the private bill, road traffic on the Cheltenham-Gloucester road did not pay tolls. Therefore, the act was prejudicial to the stagecoach interest, although not prohibitive as it was for the steam carriage. The stagecoach could raise its fare slightly to cover the additional cost because the steam carriage would no longer be running in competition. On the other hand, the Cheltenham-Gloucester railway which was planned at the time would be competitive when it opened in 1836. Indeed, Parliament favored railways over stagecoaches with discriminatory legislation such that the regular stagecoach service was terminated throughout England by 1839. It appears, then, that the higher tolls benefited only the railway interests.

On the road to Liverpool and Edinburgh the tolls were based on horsepower that would cost a steam carriage £3.3 each time of passing. The toll on the Bathgate turnpike amounted to £1.7 each time.

Ward planned to run twelve to twenty steam carriages over the Liverpool-Manchester-London road and extend the service to Edinburgh on the Bathgate road later in the year. He found, however, that the high tolls discouraged the parties contracting into the Scottish patent. On the Highgate-Whetstone road leading north from London, the steam carriage was charged 5 shillings (2/6 each for drag and omnibus). The same amounts were charged on the continuation from St. Albans to Coventry, on the Birmingham-Broomsgrove, and on five other roads on the route as well as on the Liverpool-Preston road, Darlington, and other roads leading north to Edinburgh. Ward figured that his steam carriage would pay, on the average, 1 shilling toll per mile.

Hanning, whose steam carriages were to run on the London-Exeter-Plymouth roads, confronted tolls on the Exeter roads of sixpence per wheel, plus sixpence per wheel for every ton of carriage weight over one ton. On the Totness-Ashburnham road to Plymouth the toll was 2 shillings each passing.

Captain Dobbyn, with a contract for the roads from London to Bristol in the west, had to pass his steam carriages over the Pucklechurch road near Bristol whose trustees were authorized to charge the preposterous toll of 8 guineas.

From the moment in June 1831 when certain interests throughout the United Kingdom became aware of the success of Dance's commuter service until the end of the third week in August, fifty-one private bills with tolls prohibitive to the commercial running of steam carriages passed through Parliament.[59]

Two weeks before his death in 1834 Hanning requested that the two parliamentary members from Somerset try to get rid of the tolls, for he believed, as he had written to Gurney, "equality of tolls should be levied, as compared with what is paid by carriages drawn by horses, for without such protection from Parliament the invention must stand prohibited in this country."[60]

According to Alexander Gordon, the "gentlemen of money in the City" who were "much interested" in launching steam carriage companies in the event the tolls were repealed recognized that repeal would not come. If they put carriages where tolls did not then exist, tolls would be legislated on those roads to ruin them. After watching many millions of pounds being sunk into railroads for years, they suddenly turned to railways en masse.

In September 1833 Dance, in the company of a number of important civil engineers, drove the fifty miles from London to Brighton and back within five hours actual running time. Public misgivings over his failure at Cheltenham were put to rest by the engineers' favorable testimonial on his steam carriage. But his plans to launch a regular passenger service over the route were foiled by two private laws which set prohibitory tolls on steam carriages on the Brighton road. "I know he gave it up," said Gordon, "immediately after (the closing of Gurney's factory) and attributed it at the time to the imposition of those tolls, and the impression they had created."[61]

Downey felt a similar discouragement. After the Scottish company disbanded, he ran two steam carriages in December 1834 on the London-Greenwich road in competition with the railway, until, unable to get capital backing, he sold the carriages to Macneill.

By securing the financial backing of the road trustees, Macneill, Parnell and the promoters of the Holyhead-Birmingham-London Steamcoach and Road Company thought they had a guarantee that the tolls would be kept low. Nevertheless, still dependent on Parliament, they proceeded with caution and sold £20 shares in the company for a deposit of £2, with the remainder to be paid when "an Act of Parliament has been maintained." Their caution proved well advised. In 1834 when the company tried to run two steam carriages built by the Heaton Brothers of Birmingham, the trustees on the Birmingham-Wolverhampton road stopped them with high tolls after the first run.

The same stipulation—forming a company only after obtaining an Act of Parliament—was placed in the proposals of Maceroni's several projected companies. Capitalists feared to proceed without parliamentary approval lest some draconian legislation be passed against them. Meanwhile, they hoped for a policy change: "The impression among them all is," said Gordon, "that there will be a general Act passed placing a certain toll upon all steam carriages at a very small rate."[62]

In response to Robert Torrens' appeal to the House of Commons in 1831 to repeal the high tolls on steam carriages, the members appointed a Select Committee to consider the question of tolls. It enlarged its task to a thorough examination of the steam carriage. The committee came to the conclusion

that the substitution of inanimate for animal power, in draught on common roads, is one of the most important improvements in the means of internal communication ever introduced. Its practicability they (the Committee) consider to have been fully established; its general adoption will take place more or less rapidly, in proportion as the attention of scientific men shall be drawn by public encouragement to further improvement.[63]

The committee's *Report* recommended a three-year suspension of high tolls on steam carriages in local acts and that the rate be the same as for horsedrawn carriages. In the event that the common arguments against steam carriages were again raised, the committee specifically singled out nine points (one of which was that steam carriages caused less wear and tear on roads than did horsedrawn carriages), and supported them with detailed testimony from a variety of knowledgeable witnesses. The Commons concurred in the committee's recommendations, formulated a bill called "An Act to regulate for Five Years Road Tolls on Steam Carriages," and sent it with the *Report* to the House of Lords in 1832.

The Lords did not immediately accept the *Report*. Rather, they appointed a Select Committee to examine witnesses. Possibly no hearings were held for lack of a quorum, which was set at five. Henceforth, a parliamentary struggle to undo the high tolls raged in Parliament, particularly from 1836 to 1840 and again from 1860 through 1880.

In 1836 Gurney's supporters in the Commons brought in a bill "to repeal such Portions of all Acts as impose prohibitory Tolls on Steam Carriages, and to substitute other Tolls on an equitable Footing with Horse Carriages." When it reached the House of Lords, the Earl of Radnor, a Radical Tory, asked that the Lords not detain the bill in committee as the Commons had made an extensive *Report*. As a result, the quorum of the Select Committee was reduced from five to three.

This committee called Goldsworthy Gurney, Walter Hancock, Alexander Gordon, Thomas Harris (who had worked for Gurney and Dance), Joshua Field (a Gurney engineer who later joined with Dance to operate a carriage service in London), and the Reverend Williams, a self-proclaimed expert on steam carriages and no friend to Goldsworthy. The remaining witnesses represented either stagecoach or railway interests. As will be shown later, their testimony was misleading and provided the basis for the Lords' *Report*.

The Committee entertain serious Objections to the Bill referred to them; and they are not of Opinion that these Objections are counter-balanced by the Prospect of any great Public Advantage.... It is probable, therefore, that any Encouragement on the Part of the Legislation would only give rise to wild Speculations, ruinous to those engaging in them, and to Experiments dangerous to the Public. The Committee therefore recommend that this Bill should not at present be proceeded with: at the same time they have no Doubt that the further Imposition of prohibitory Tolls in Local Acts is not a desirable mode of Legislating upon such a Subject.[64]

Parliamentary supporters of the steam carriage took a new tack: the abolition of turnpike trusts. The trusts exacted the high tolls on steam carriages and became a point of contention around which innkeepers, stagecoach operators, and landed gentry could be rallied. They made excellent legislative targets because they were in serious financial trouble. Turnpikes, being supplementary to the original system of parish road repair, could not raise capital legally by issuing shares. Rather, loans were raised, often at high interest rates, through mortgages or on bonds issued on tolls to be collected. By 1834 the trusts spent 67 percent of their income on repair, 20 percent on interest payments, and 8.5 percent on administration.

Some parliamentarians delayed discussion on the Bill for the Consolidation of Turnpike Trusts until passage of the Highways Bill, which consolidated the laws on highways to relieve the pressure of the county rate on landed interests. Then the Turnpike Consolidation Bill was dropped as if by agreement. Thus the landed interests obtained a reduction of their tax for the upkeep of the highways in return for allowing the turnpike roads to remain in the control of private trusts and a barrier to steam carriage travel. Nevertheless, an M.P., who was a member of the Central Agricultural Society, headed a Select Committee to investigate the indebtedness, mismanagement, corruption, and wastefulness of the turnpike trust system. He invited Parnell to sit on it, and he asked Gordon and Maceroni to testify on the feasibility of steam carriages for revitalizing the turnpike trusts.

The railway interests, however, found room for one of their own as a witness—a clerk to the trustees of Middlesex and Essex turnpike roads and solicitor of one of the districts of the Eastern Counties railway. Ironically, he testified that Hancock's carriages frightened the horses in his district so badly that he had "to intervene." Hancock, the stolid mechanic, would have looked on this familiar fabrication with some amusement as he had given up the "great experiment" and had turned to railways. However irrational, it was to become the major argument for keeping steam carriages off the roads of England. The arguments of danger from bursting boilers, or poor economy, or the possibility of accidents could be applied to railway locomotives with more meaning and consequently had to be dropped by railway interests. In contrast, the shying of horses was a subjective judgment beyond the realm of scientific proof and inapplicable as an argument against railways.

Action was not taken until after the *Report* made by a Commons' Select Committee on Turnpike Trusts in 1864. This delay caused Anna Gurney to comment bitterly: "It is remarkable that the Tolls on steam carriages first began to be taken off in the very next session after my father was suddenly seized with irrevocable paralysis (viz. in October 1863)."[65]

The Committee of 1864 fully concurred with the conclusion which the Committee of 1836 had arrived at: "that the abolition of tolls throughout the Kingdom would be beneficial to the community.... Tolls appear to Your Committee to be unequal in pressure, costly in collection, inconvenient to the public, and injurious, as causing a serious impediment to intercourse and traffic."

Meanwhile, two lords, the Marquis of Stafford and the Earl of Caithness, revived interest in the steam carriage in 1859 by driving touring cars made by the engineer Thomas Rickett. A bill was introduced to the Commons, but testimony was taken only with regard to traction engines. The ensuing Locomotive Bill of 1861 brought tolls on steam locomotives equal to those on horse carriages, but there were two drawbacks: the locomotive could go no faster than 10 mph on the highway and 5 mph through the city (whereas the horse omnibus went 7 mph), and one of the secretaries of state could prohibit the use of locomotives found "inconvenient to the Public" in certain districts.

As a consequence, a bill to amend the law relating to locomotives on public roads was introduced but was stalled until the session of 1865. The stated objective of its proposers in the Commons was to stop the unnecessary interference with traffic and the charging of operators with frivolous complaints. The bill achieved this objective by making control of the locomotive a matter for the police rather than of highway jurisdiction under the secretary of state.

Passage of the bill through the Commons depended on resolving the argument over more freedom of movement for agricultural locomotives as against concern for the safety of the public. Apparently, public safety was an obsession with Conservatives who insisted that a third man be attached to each locomotive and that he walk 100 yards in front to warn other traffic of its approach. When some Liberals and Radicals tried to keep the distance at "less than 60 yards," they were outvoted by 90 to 32. The Lords added that the third man "shall carry a Red Flag constantly displayed," thus giving the Locomotive Act of 1865 its infamous name of "The Red Flag Act." They raised the penalty for not stopping for horses and for speeding from £5 to £10. Prior to the act, a tractor owner saved £358 over 250 working days by not having to use horses. Now, the costs of having to pay a third man and of having to move at less than half the speed eradicated the saving.

Although by 1878 there were over 3,000 traction engines in Britain, Parliament maintained its legislative repression in its Highways and Locomotives (Amendment) Act of that year. The only significant change it made in the Locomotive Act of 1865 was to replace the requirement that a man carrying a red flag precede a locomotive by at least 60 yards by one omitting mention of a red flag (by 1878 a symbol for international communism) and reducing "60" to "20" yards. The main purpose of the 1878 Act, however, was to form highway boards that would be responsible for the maintenance of the roads in a new system of Highway Districts and to control traffic. This was a necessity as the turnpike trusts were rapidly dissolving and would disappear in 1895 with the closing down of the last one—on the Anglesey section of the Holyhead road.

9

The Interest Group Basis of Restrictive Legislation

Figures in authority cast false aspersions on the steam carriage in an effort to turn the public against it. For years some engineers stubbornly claimed that the steam carriage could not climb hills, and, after Dance abandoned the Cheltenham-Gloucester service, the *Mechanics' Magazine* wondered maliciously if the "newly Macadamized road" had stopped it.

Hancock persistently misrepresented Gurney's steam carriage and, as a consequence, discredited all steam carriages. Gurney's carriages were not as strong as his, he often testified, and made too much noise: "If I adopted that Plan I should frighten the Horses off a common road." Every other witness, when asked, testified to the quietness of Gurney's engine and to the fact that horses did not shy at his steam carriages.[66] As for complaints that steam carriages damaged the roads, John Macneill silenced such charges. He invented a machine for measuring the damage done to roads by vehicles and demonstrated that horsedrawn carriages did far more damage than steam carriages.

The ultimate decision on the steam carriage, however, came from the Select Committee of the House of Lords in 1836 whose opinion was respected by the public and was paramount in legislation. The testimony of George Stephenson, William Cubitt, and John Braithwaite impressed the Lords' Committee, which wrote: "it appears that some experienced Engineers, after a careful Examination of the Expenses attendant upon it (the steam carriage) have been induced to abandon all Hopes of its Success as a profitable Undertaking."

George Stephenson, the famous engineer and "father of the railway," gave testimony that was so questionable that one may readily believe the well-known charge that he did ruin William James to advance his career. The railway historian Hamilton Ellis suggested that Stephenson's testimony was motivated by spite, directed against the son, W. H. James, because of W. H. James's devotion to the steam carriage. This reason was unlikely, however, inasmuch as James had taken his steam carriage to America some years before. It is most likely that Stephenson simply said what certain members of the committee had invited him to say. "I think they (the steam carriages) will never be made to do any Good on a common Road, " he said. "I do not see the slightest possibility of it."

Moreover, he said, steam carriages were too dangerous; they could not be stopped before 50 to 100 yards. They were also too noisy and smoky, but like rail locomotives (and here, he may have been just ignorant) they could not do without a chimney: "the Draught, without the Blast-Pipe, would be so much diminished as to reduce a Fifty Horse Power Engine to not more than Two or Three Horse Power." As for Gurney's steam carriage: "I think there is more Danger in Mr. Gurney's than in others, for there is a greater quantity of steam held in the pipes than what is held in the Chambers of Mr. Hancock's."

Alexander Gordon scornfully considered Stephenson "ignorant of the essential difference" between the steam carriage and the railway locomotive.

William Cubitt, a civil engineer and one of the great names in railway history, wagered other engineers that the steam carriage was not mechanically practicable. As a result, he helped finance the Maudslay-Field steam carriage and later had to admit to its perfectibility. However, he insisted that it was a losing financial proposition. When pinned down to an explanation of how the steam carriage differed from the locomotive engine, he testified that a common workman could drive a locomotive, but only a superbly talented person could be trusted to guide a steam carriage. Moreover, only with the introduction of scores of carriages could steam coaches become profitable. Were not companies formed to amass capital for large undertakings, he was asked. The answer was yes. Could not the capital be applied to steam carriages? Again the answer was yes. Cubitt, wrote Gordon, was forced from his position of the poor capital risk of steam carriages.

John Braithwaite, the third to give testimony, built the *Novelty* locomotive which did 45 mph to everyone's amazement when he competed with Stephenson on the Liverpool-Manchester railway. Braithwaite believed that steam carriages could never become profitable: the workmanship required was too costly. Besides, he said, nine out of ten horses shied from them.

Gordon commented that Braithwaite jumbled the facts and did not know the first principles of steam carriages. For his part Braithwaite, despite his status as an enterprising capitalist, was unnaturally considerate. He frequently refused to build steam carriages, he said, to save people from losing money by operating them.

The committee found that: (1) Steam carriages "still have the Effect of terrifying Horses. and that Accidents have occurred in consequence." (The evidence showed the contrary.) (2) Owing to witnesses' disagreement over the limit in the size of the boiler to prevent explosion, the Lords were unable "to recommend the necessary Enactments, if it was found expedient to proceed further with the Bill." (Gordon and Gurney set a definite limit; only Hancock insisted on a larger boiler.) (3) No adequate means were found to prevent the emission of sparks from the chimneys of the engines which could be dangerous. (As the testimony showed, the danger was on railways, not on roads with steam carriages. Moreover, at that time Gurney testified extensively before the Lords' "Select Committee to inquire and report whether any danger by fire is likely to arise from Locomotive engines being used on railroads passing through narrow streets," on which some of the Lords of the present committee were sitting. Gurney explained how a tray with wire gauze prevented hot cinders from falling on the road and how the separator in the eduction pipe prevented bits of fuel or sparks from being blown out of the chimney but rather emitted exhaust smoothly in the same manner as the upper leaf in a bellows. In the mistaken belief that it slowed the speed, railways had not adopted this method. The Lords preferred that the testimony on sparks from engines come not from steam carriage engineers but from railway engineers). (4) Since greater skill was needed to drive steam carriages than locomotives, "to find Persons properly qualified might be a Matter of considerable difficulty." (This was Cubitt's argument; Gurney and others had testified to their easy handling.)

In questioning the railway engineers the Lords neglected to look into their current activities. Further inspection might have revealed certain biases. Stephenson's connection to Lord Wharncliffe was clear. In the previous year, Wharncliffe had tenaciously steered the Great Western Railway Bill (London to Liverpool) to approval in the Lords, and the Manchester-Leeds Railway Bill was being considered favorably at that moment. In addition, the Grand Junction (Liverpool-Birmingham line) was expected to open the following year, 1837. In all of these enterprises George Stephenson was entrusted with the lead in order to open up the mineral wealth of the Midlands.

Cubitt's motives with regard to steam carriages were not free from bias. He did not tell the Lords that he was the contractor for the London, Chatham and Dover railway (in the course of building it, he was distinguished by the dynamiting of the Round Down Cliff between Folkstone and Dover with 1,800 pounds of gunpowder) and that for the past two years he had been joint

71

contractor for the most important company in the South of England—the Nine-Elms to Southampton Railway Company. The Liverpool to London railway interests supported the enterprise that was to develop trade with Normandy and Paris. The company chairman was W. J. Chaplin who came from one of the largest firms of carriers and stagecoach proprietors; board members were the Liverpool banker John Moss and Matthew Uzielli of the great international banking house of Devaux of London and Paris. George Stephenson was the chief engineer.

Braithwaite's extensive manufactory in London built locomotives for Cuba and elsewhere. He did not tell the Lords that he was the chief engineer on the Eastern Counties railway project under construction. His interest in railways extended to his founding the *Railway Times* in 1837.

"To recapitulate," wrote Alexander Gordon, "three principal witnesses, on whose evidence the Committee founded their 'serious objections' are all of them attached to railways."[67] The *Mechanics' Magazine* printed the testimony of these three engineers on "the Steam Carriage Job of Messrs. Goldsworthy Gurney and Co. . . . by which Report that very dirty job . . . was most happily frustrated."[68]

The falsity of the *Report* by the Lords Select Committee of 1836 must be attributed in large measure to the bias of the Lords themselves, for they had before them the evidence from two hearings in the Commons which thoroughly examined and endorsed the steam carriage.

Just four members of the 1832 committee which had encouraged the steam engine sat on this committee: Wharncliffe and Lord Radnor, who were on opposite sides of the steam carriage question inasmuch as Wharncliffe represented the Lancashire interests and had extensive investments in railways and iron and coal fields; the Duke of Richmond who, as the leading landowner in Sussex, led the landed classes against the Lancashire capitalists; and Salisbury, the reactionary, whose large landholdings in London and Liverpool brought him immense profits as the railways increased the centralization of capital in the large cities and drove the unemployed from the country into the city.

An examination of the Committee, aside from offering political insights, gives us a picture of what was meant by "the ruling class."

Members for the Reform Bill

Baron Wharncliffe
His peerage was created only in 1826. He married the daughter of the Earl of Erne. He led a group of Tories in the Lords known as

the "Waverers" who voted for a second reading of the Reform Bill and secured its passage. He was the largest shareholder in and active promoter of the pioneer Dundee and Newtyle Railway which ran across his Perthshire lands.

Earl of Radnor
Lord Lieutenant of a county; Recorder of Salisbury; High Steward of Wallingford; he was patron of eight Church livings worth on the average L 500 a year each.

A brother was High Commissioner of Stamps (L1,000) and another brother was Naval Commissioner (L1,000). A Whig, he was a member of the Free Trade Club and sat in the Commons in 1828. He was a senior partner in the Bouvier Bank in London which helped finance steam carriages.

Duke of Richmond
Pension (L6,339). He was a lieutenant-general in the Army, aide-de-camp to the King, a vice-admiral of Sussex, Postmaster-General and a cabinet minister. His mother's father was the Duke of Gordon and his wife was the daughter of the Marquess of Anglesea.

Baron Hatherton
Promoted to the peerage from Mr. Littelton of the Commons in 1835 for supporting Melbourne; married daughter of Marquess of Wellesley; patron of five livings and Chief Secretary for Ireland; owner of Midland coal fields.

Baron Strafford
An army general and, like Hatherton, a member of the Reform Club and supporter of Melbourne, he was created a peer in 1835.

Earl of Ripon
From Robinson of the Commons in 1833; had been president of the Board of Control, of the Board of Trade, Lord Privy Seal, Secretary for the Colonies, Chancellor of the Exchequer and First Lord of the Treasury. He married the daughter of the 4th Earl of Buckinghamshire and opposed Melbourne.

Baron Ravensworth
Created a peer in 1821, he was a patron of one living; opposed Melbourne's government.

Earl of Tankerville
Pension L400; was Treasurer of the Household; had patronage of one living; opposed Melbourne.

Earl of Chichester

Patron of four livings, an army major, opposed Melbourne; married the daughter of the Earl of Cardigan. His uncle was the Bishop of Exeter (L6,500) having 100 Church livings as well as precentorships and prebends in his gift.

Baron Dacre

Title dated from 1307; married Mrs. Wilmot; for Melbourne.

Earl of Burlington

A Whig in the Commons of 1834, succeeded to title; Chancellor of the University of London, patron of 14 livings; for Melbourne.

Earl of Morley

Created peer in 1815; for Melbourne.

Members opposed to the Reform Bill

Marquess of Salisbury

Lord Lieutenant of county Hertford (Lord Lieutenancy meant great patronage power); Joint Postmaster General (L2,500); High Steward of Hartford; father-in-law of Sir Henry Wellesley, the brother of the Duke of Wellington. His son, Lord Cranbourne, was Commissioner for the Affairs of India (L1,500) and Colonel of Militia (L1,000). He was said to hate "the slightest resemblance to change or innovation" and to abhor railways "with an incredible vehemence."

Baron Ashburton

Created a peer in 1835 from Mr. Baring in the Commons; was President of the Board of Trade and Ambassador to America; patron of seven livings; married daughter of William Bingham of Philadelphia; partner in Barings, the world's foremost international banking house, which in bidding for railway concessions internationally lost out to the Rothschilds; opposed Melbourne.

Earl of Hillsborough

Created a peer in 1836 from Mr. Hill in the Commons.

Viscount St. Vincent

Divorced first wife, the daughter of Lord Say and Sele; married daughter of Thomas Parker.

Baron Kenyon

Sinecure L930; a Bencher of the Middle Temple, and Custos Brevum of the Court of the King's Bench; married the daughter of Sir Thomas Hanmer; against Melbourne.

Baron Lindhurst

Lord Chief Baron of the Exchequer Court in the Grey Administration and Lord Chancellor for the Wellington administration; High Steward for the University of Cambridge: opposed Melbourne.

Duke of Cumberland

Son of William III; Field Marshal; Chancellor of the University of Dublin; opposed Melbourne.

Marquess of Bute

Lord Lieutenant and Costos Rot of Glamorgan, Lord Lieutenant and Heritable Coroner of Bute, High Steward of Banbury, Keeper of Rothsay Castle, Colonel of Glamorgansh. militia; patron of lO livings; first wife was daughter of the Earl of Guilford (with customs sinecure of L2,391), his second was the daughter of the Marquess of Hastings; opposed Melbourne.

Earl of Orford

High Steward of Lynn, Colonel of West Norfolk militia; Lord of the Admiralty and Commissioner for Affairs of India; patron of seven livings; opposed Melbourne.

Viscount Gage

Opposed Melbourne.

Of the 22 members, 18 were among the great landowners of the United Kingdom. Of these 18, there were seven obviously favoring the railway (Wharncliffe, Hatherton, Ripon, Ravensworth, Tankerville, St. Vincent, Orford) because their lands covered the coal deposits of northern England. There was also one (Baron Kenyon) whose land was in the industrial north of Wales, one (Baron Strafford) whose land in Middlesex soared in value with the influx of population and wealth brought to London by the centralizing tendency of the railway, and one (Marquess Bute) who owned large mineral properties in Ayrshire.

One (Marquess Salisbury) who opposed all technological innovation would have opposed the steam carriage and thus inadvertently aided the railway interests.

The positions of four of the great landowners cannot be ascertained: the Earl of Chichester and Viscount Gage whose lands lay in Sussex, Baron Dacre in Hertfordshire and Essex, and the Earl of Morley in Devon, though it is interesting to note that they did not participate in the agricultural defensive societies led by Richmond and others of the landed aristocracy. Strong support for the steam carriage came from the "Red Tory" Radnor and Richmond among the landed interests. The four nobles who were not great landowners (Burlington, Hillsborough, Lyndhurst and Cumberland) would have supported the policy of the majority as they belonged to the industrial class (with the exception of the Duke of Cumberland, destined to become King of Hanover in the following year). The last, Baron Ashburton of the international banking house of Barings, may have favored the steam carriage, since his eldest son was a leading participant in the National Institution of Locomotion.

The cooperation of the great landed interests of England with the railway capitalists cannot be easily squared with early virulent opposition to railways exhibited by the landed aristocracy. The economic historian J. T. Ward, however, has commented: "Each famous case of opposition can be matched by examples of landowners' support."[69]

When the House of Lords threw out the first bill for the Birmingham-London railway in 1832, Lord Wharncliffe, who chaired the parliamentary committee for the bill, said: "There is no doubt that to landowners the failure of the bill must be attributed." By the end of the year, the bill was reintroduced and passed the Lords easily. The opposition had been bought off. "The land, which was overestimated at £250,000, cost three times the amount. "

Aside from attracting many of the large landed interests to their side by large payments for the use of their lands and royalty payments for the minerals extracted from their lands, the Quaker industrialists of Lancashire gave the landed aristocracy favored treatment as investors with the railway industry. With each new railway the "free-trade" industrialist, increasing his control over the market, weakened the opposition until only the smaller landed interests were left to defend the agricultural economy.

The movement of the social forces, seemingly autonomous, was discernible to the men in power through their dealings with its leaders. Thus, in 1838 the third Earl of Radnor wrote to the fifth Duke of Richmond in exasperation over their growing political weakness: "Confound those three W's—Wharncliffe, Winchilsea & Wynford—I wish they were in the Penitentiary or on the Tread Mill." These men characterized the alliance that promoted the railway over the steam carriage: the aggressive greed of the large industrialist linked to the defensive greed of the privileged professional class which, in turn, owed its power to the industrialist and the conservative majority which feared change.

The railway opposition to the steam carriage appeared to come from the House of Lords which revoked the House of Commons' early efforts to develop it. The Reform Bill brought little real reform. It even increased the influence of the great landowners in the Commons by the addition to the county electorate of leaseholders and tenants-at-will. The upper chamber allowed its gradual decline in political importance because it retained control of the Commons through the anomalies of the political system. From 1832 to 1846 a large proportion of the membership of the Commons consisted of sons and brothers of peers whom they expected to replace in the Lords. Between 1834 and 1841 when Liberals and Radicals, who were solidly behind the steam carriage, held the balance of power and could have pressured the Whig government for real change, they were hopelessly divided on issues. The alliance of the Whigs with Daniel O'Connell, the Irish politician, over his agitation for repeal of the Union provoked Tories through their majority in the Lords to obstruct all Whig legislation in the 1830s.

Within ten years of reform, the Tory-Conservative element controlled legislation in the Commons which it dominated for decades to come. That the majority of this element should have supported the railway in preference to the steam carriage indicates a concern somewhat more profound than that of protectionism versus free trade. After the mid-1840s, therefore, the railway, despite its disruption of rural life, was generally perceived as an innovation supportive of the status quo and the ruling class.

The interdependency of the various groups behind the railway not only gave them political stability in the long term, but it also exemplified the total commitment of British investment in railways. The industrial crises of 1837-1838 and 1846-1847 which brought to public scrutiny the corruption and mismanagement of English railways did not weaken that commitment. Indeed, in an effort to overcome public reluctance to pay installments on railway shares in the early period, railway companies depended on loans in excess of the one-third ratio to authorized share capital stipulated by law. The rate of growth of capital funding for railways was about 20 percent per annum in the United Kingdom in the mid-1840s and settled down to 5 percent per annum during the 1850s and 1860s before falling to 2 percent for the 1870s and 1880s.

The alliance of the great landowners with the industrialists left the landed aristocracy with the appearance of power and the industrialists with the real power. As late as 1890, according to the English historian F.M.L. Thompson,[70] landowners would forego the profits to be made by converting their wealth to industrial investment because of the prestige which the owning of land gave them. They overlooked the demise of English agriculture because of the benefits that their ties to the industrial class and its imperialist designs had brought to England. For instance, all but one of the lords on the Select Committee on the Locomotives Bill of 1865, which formulated the Red Flag Act, was a great landowner. Moreover, an economist, G. R. Hawke, demonstrated that railways as an innovation in the economy of England and Wales "could not have been sacrificed in 1865 without the need to compensate for a loss of the order of 10 per cent of the national income."[71]

Hawke came to this conclusion by studying the linkages from railways to other sectors such as the iron industry, the building industry, and "technical external economies induced through changes in the location of industry in adaptation to the railway economy." "Railways," he wrote, "could not have been replaced without some diversion of resources or alternative technical change which would provide replacement for 4.1 per cent of the national income of England and Wales for freight services, and 2.6 per cent or 7.1 per cent of Railways: national incomenational income for passenger travel depending on the degree of comfort which could be sacrificed."

England's rulers probably believed that it was very unlikely that an alternative to travel by rail could arise. The steam carriage, if it were to prove itself capable of limited passenger transport, would take decades to develop in order to support the returns to the social capital which railways had been developing since the 1840s. Hence, the traditional conservative bias, coupled with an inclination to protect the immense investment in railways and an intolerance for anyone who seemed to interfere with it, brought forth the wrath of the ruling lords.

The English landed classes, who were unable to develop the steam carriage in England, opposed their development in Scotland and Ireland because English agriculture would be undermined by the increase in the supply of produce from those countries through a mechanical and cheaper system of cultivation and the reduction in consumption as Scottish and Irish horses were replaced by the steam carriage and the steam plough. The Scot, Lord Caithness, drove his steam carriage in 1860 over the Ord of Caithness, which rises one thousand feet in five miles with sharp turns, in his vain effort to persuade the Lords to allow it to develop. The Irishman, Sir James Anderson, spent his life and fortune developing the steam carriage and suffered the defeat of one project after another. Without the support of English agriculturists, the Scottish and Irish agriculturists, who could have provided the large capital needed for the establishment of the steam carriage, dared not mechanize lest the English who controlled Parliament legislate against them. Whereas steam carriages would open up Irish towns, allowing for labor mobility and intertown trade, railways isolated some towns and fostered trade with England rather than within Ireland.[72] Their construction cost Ireland 20 million pounds which the impoverished country could not afford, and of this amount 15 million were going to England for iron and machinery.

This flow of money from Ireland to England benefitted the absentee landlord as well as the English manufacturer. Richard Cort, the steam carriage advocate, warned that by sending this wealth, which would have to be largely in raw produce, to England, Ireland would undermine the English farmer and increase the English manufacturer's profits by drawing back more luxury goods from England. The largest share of the produce from Ireland, which the railway would bring more quickly to market, would enable the absentee landlord to draw more quickly on bills on England to be met by the sale of such produce and therefore encourage absenteeism. And then, prophetically, when one considers the Great Hunger of the mid-forties, Cort warned in 1834, "Nor is this all; for precisely as the produce is thus sent more quickly away, less will be left in stock for home consumption; and all the evils of famine, with which Ireland has been afflicted so frequently during the last fifteen years, will be felt with double force, should a similar series of unfavorable seasons again occur."

English landowners owned large tracts of land in Ireland and, in order to control the Irish laboring class, favored an exploitative trade policy that forced Irishmen to find work in England. Thus the hard-pressed English laborer was set against them, distracting both from the real causes of their poverty.

IN AMERICA

In America, where the roads were poor and the use of canals had only recently been established in the East, the steam carriage was not outlawed, perhaps because, under the circumstances, such action was thought to be unnecessary. A Philadelphian visiting London in 1835 to evaluate steam carriages expressed the prevailing wisdom on the subject, which has been mistakenly accepted by historians of today as generally true of the period. Whereas in England steam carriages, he said, could compete with horses because horses were costly to buy and maintain and steam power was cheap owing to the low price of metals and fuel, the opposite was true in America where horses were maintained at one-half the cost in England, and where fuel and labor were expensive and the roads badly constructed. Since many wooden roads were laid in America and since the remaining restraints also

79

applied to railways, the discouragement of the steam carriage would seem to have other causes, chiefly financial.

The Quaker families in Lancashire and Norfolk, whose private country banks such as Gurneys had invested heavily in the railways of northern England, quickly seized the opportunities of investing with their Quaker brethren in the United States. They built the first railways, that is, the Baltimore and Ohio (1828-1833), the Philadelphia and Reading (1832-1843), and the Erie Railroad out of New York City (1832-1851).

At the close of the American Revolutionary War, a great concentration of trade flowed between the United States and Liverpool, and there was an increasing capital investment of Lancashire in America. In 1843 out of a total of $231.6 million in American federal and state securities, $150 million was in foreign ownership. When investment in these securities declined after 1848, investment in railway securities replaced them and the American railway boom began. The dependence of American rail development on English capital was so great that by 1853 the foreign holdings of U.S. railway debt amounted to $70 million (Ll4 million), of which one-half represented securities obtained in return for purchases of British rails which came to America via Liverpool from Staffordshire and Wales. The merchant banking houses of Lancashire assumed the major role in the export of these rails.

WHY THE STEAM CARRIAGE FAILED IN AMERICA

Unlike the outlying regions of the British Isles such as Scotland and Ireland, the United States was not governed by the English Houses of Parliament in the 1830s. Therefore, a stronger argument than the predominance of Lancashire capital in America is needed if we are to account for the failure of the steam carriage to develop in the United States. As a counter argument, one might claim that venture capital was more available in the United States where the saving rate was possibly 150 percent of the United Kingdom saving rate, and where the multiplicity of wealth and political entities might free locales from regulatory influence on behalf of railways. Certainly, the United States government imposed no restrictive tolls on steam carriages in the early years. Yet in 1832 the subject of steam carriages was hotly debated in the House of Representatives and in certain local areas eager to develop their commerce.

A large conservative voice in Congress opposed in vain that body's printing of the British House of Commons' *Report on Steam Carriages* of 1831 and the appointment of a standing Committee on Roads and Canals. Conservatives, largely from the South, feared the taxes which the federal government would impose on the states for internal improvements. But they were not the real enemies of the steam carriage, for they encouraged road travel for the sake of local development and emigration to the West. The real enemies of the steam carriage were the supporters of railways, such as Churchill Cambreleng of the merchant firm of Cambreleng and Pearson in New York City. In the House of Representatives he broke into an angry exchange with Charles Mercer, the chairman of the Committee on Internal Improvements (and later of the Committee on Roads and Canals) over the efficacy of steam carriages.

Cambreleng, a director of the proposed Utica to Schenectady Railroad, declared that "whoever proposed to employ on ordinary roads, locomotive engines, travelling at the rate of fifteen or twenty miles an hour, recommended that which in practice would prove speculative and fallacious." Cambreleng's railway was being threatened by competition from a proposed steam carriage passenger service between Troy and Schenectady. "Tens of thousands, who visit the Springs from the South and East,--and New York from the North and West,--would then have an opportunity without additional expense," the *Railroad Journal* commented in 1832, "of testing both; and, from that comparison, spread, as the information would be, to all parts of the country."

On the other hand, Mercer, president of the Chesapeake and Ohio Canal Company, "insisted on the practicability of introducing steam cars upon common roads, by which one-half the present cost of transportation would be saved."

The railway mania could not be stopped. A historian of Congress concluded:

As one turns over the indices of the journals of Congress, he is struck by the sharp decline in the frequency and importance of measures concerning roads, both post and military, which occurs about the year 1840; and, though it practically came nearly five years earlier, we may name that date as marking the time when railways clearly superseded roads as a national improvement.[73]

Therefore, it was the capital interests in Boston and New York which promoted railways as the best means of exploiting the West. The direction of all available capital to this great and expensive undertaking meant that none remained for the competing industry of the automobile which could not serve the need for transport over long distances as well as railways.

Hopes that railways would prevent gluts and scarcities because they were free from limitations of topographical conditions and would lead to social and political unity proved illusory. Railways led to the concentration of wealth.

81

THE RATIONALE FOR PREFERENCE FOR THE RAILROAD

If the steam carriage proponents in Parliament had forged a lasting alliance between radical Whigs and Conservatives, the railway would have been stopped in its tracks. The period 1833 to 1836, one of prosperity in England, provided plenty of investment capital for steam carriages. By 1833 the innkeepers, stagecoach owners, and their employees recognized that the railway was ruining them and that the steam carriage was their only hope to keep road traffic alive. Canal proprietors saw the steam carriage as their natural ally against the railway. Led by the dynamic Sir Henry Parnell in Parliament and the universally respected Thomas Telford in the preparation of routes, the steam carriage advocates were overcoming the opposition from turnpike trustees. William Hanning, the agriculturist who counseled the Whig leaders and who withdrew his financial support of Gurney when he learned that the steam carriage was to be stopped, represented an important link between the conservative landed classes and the ruling Whigs. His work on the committee to legislate for joint stock companies laid the groundwork for the concept of limited liability which would have made the promotion of steam carriage companies safe for investors had the principle been adopted in the 1830s rather than held in abeyance for twenty years. In this effort, he and Viscount Althorp reflected the desire of the landed classes to invest safely in industry where returns were much higher than in agriculture. Yet, at the same time, they would be able to free the control of capital from the growing power of the Lancashire group and, through the agency of the steam carriage and mechanization in agriculture, reverse the flow of capital so that it went from the city to the country.

The first victory marking the success of such an alliance would have been the defeat in the House of Lords of the Birmingham to London Railway scheme. This plan had been floundering in 1835 owing to immense difficulties of construction and lack of funds. Certainly, opposition to railways was intense and could have been turned to political advantage. Small titleholders ruthlessly thrown off their lands, great estate owners furious with the disruption caused to their scenic lands and sporting pleasures, and small entrepreneurs fearful of monopolies whom, as we have seen, joined in societies of agriculture and associations of artisans to oppose the government—all of them denounced railways as unprofitable, dangerous to the economic health of the society, and destructive to the countryside. If the House of Lords, using these reasons, had thrown out all railway bills and prohibited tolls on steam carriages, steam carriage companies would have sprung up under the control of small entrepreneurs throughout the country. Capital would have been localized because the steam carriage would have benefited agricultural trade and local communication. Investment, therefore, would have gone for internal improvement, and the consumer sector would have created the surplus value with which it could have purchased the machinery produced by the producers goods sector. Since agriculture was mechanizing, a balance between the sectors could have been maintained.

In time, competition among steam carriage capitalists would have led to improvements in the steam carriage and to its wide distribution. On the negative side, it would have brought about a concentration of capital in regional centers as steam carriage companies were forced into amalgamation.

Although the landed aristocracy would have invested in these companies, the middle-class entrepreneur in both the consumer and capital goods sectors would have gained the surplus value as raw products from the estates grew cheaper in exchange and machinery became increasingly necessary to agricultural production. Owing to the regional prosperity, the middle class would have grown in numbers, brought about the decentralization of political power, and usurped political leadership from the landed aristocracy and the Lancashire industrialists. Thus, although it could have earned profits, the conservative-industrial interests kept the steam carriage off the roads. Their preference was for railways which enhanced their industrial investments and helped them to keep economic and political control.

It may be supposed, in a moment of fanciful speculation, that the steam carriage would have generated great economic activity in the nineteenth century as the automobile did in the twentieth and would have brought prosperity through the inventions and innovations it spawned. As a result, economic development could not be centrally dominated, and the aristocracy might have faded from power decades sooner than it did. Advances in communication and education might have followed shortly afterward, and historians may not have had to record two world wars that effected the social and economic adjustments which an unhindered technology might have brought about on its own.

The England of the 1830s, however, could not have departed on this flight of fancy. The Lancashire capitalists had established firm control over the wealth-producing means of production (textiles and trade) on which the economic health of the nation depended. By their control of capital they influenced royalty and shaped government policy. In the years of the Napoleonic Wars, they built up international money contacts through their employment of merchant bankers such as the Rothschilds, and laid the groundwork to facilitate their foreign trade in peacetime. Just as they used the railway to draw wealth from the English and Welsh countryside and from Ireland and Scotland to the banking center of London and to undermine the English landed aristocracy whose power came from their great landholdings in all four countries, so they were about to use their merchant bankers and English foreign policy to develop railways abroad and draw the wealth of foreign countries into England.[74]

10

Financing the European Railways

Private bankers who supported steam carriages confronted a powerful alliance of the Bank of England, private banks tied to Lancashire interests,[75] and merchant bankers such as the Rothschild Bank whose business was largely with the Lancashire manufacturers. Merchant bankers had worked with Lancashire capitalists from the early years of the Napoleonic Wars when the government caused the Bank of England to suspend payment in gold. As a result, gold remained in the hands of Europeans for buying English manufactured goods, the surplus abundance of which threatened to sink the English economy. Since the science of selling for export required perfect knowledge of the needs of the buyer, shippers of these goods could obtain credit at Manchester and Liverpool only if the market was certain. It was at this point that Nathan Rothschild, with information provided by his family connections in Germany, became useful as a banker to Lancashire shippers. Along with this relationship, Rothschild formed a close relationship with the British government after helping to raise the money to pay the French indemnity to the allies after 1815, and he worked with John Charles Herries, financial secretary to the English Treasury, to keep English influence strong in Europe.

James, the French Rothschild, who took his cue from his older brother Nathan, quietly prepared for the advent of the railway through northern France. Unlike the English capitalists who had to buy concessions from the English Parliament, the Rothschilds waited for the French government to take the first step in order to work with it. James was an early participant in the Societe Generale de Belgique, which became the central banking authority in Belgium after its revolt from Netherlands rule in 1830 and led in the financing of the development of large industry in Belgium between 1834 and 1838. Through it he invested in the coal and iron fields of Belgium and northern France.

King Leopold's first action after England placed him on the throne of the new Belgian state was to initiate the building of railways and thus carry out the English foreign policy of developing a means of swift communication with Britain's rich and rebellious colony, India.[76] The Belgian government forwarded a scheme to build a railway from Anvers (which had been the first military port of Napoleon's empire) to Cologne, Germany, thus linking the Escaut and Rhine rivers. In August 1831 it sent two young Belgian engineers to the Stephensons in England to learn railway construction, and two more to the French government of Louis Philippe proposing a railway between Anvers and Marseille linking the North Sea to the Mediterranean. Failing to procure a loan of 18 million francs from the legislature for the railways in 1834, the Belgian government received a credit for 10 million francs from the Treasury which issued bonds. By a royal decree in 1836 it borrowed 30 million francs from the legislature (about 25 million was spent on railways, 2.5 million for a canal on the Sambre River, and less than 0.5 million for paving the roads) which was again raised by floating loans. The Rothschild banks placed all Belgian loans from 1831 to 1836 with investors in London and Paris.

Lancashire capital also invaded France quite easily after it overcame some difficulties. James de Rothschild was Louis-Philippe's banker through a series of government bond issues from 1831 to the Revolution of 1848.

In April 1836 an English deputation led by an English member of Parliament met in Paris with the French government to formulate a plan for uniting France, England, and Belgium by rail.[77] In November King Leopold journeyed to Paris for the same reason. The French, however, were not so easily persuaded, despite the enthusiasm of some of their leaders. Fear of the monopoly power of the railway companies was expressed by the left wing bourgeois poet-politician Lamartine: "And you partisans of liberty and of the enfranchisement of the masses, you who have overturned feudalism and its tolls and its rights of way, and its boundaries, and its stakes, you would allow them to be used by the feudalism of money to shackle the people and wall up their land."[78]

In 1838 the French government rejected a bill to construct seven major lines, but it approved the building of a line from Paris to Orleans in the south and a line from Paris through Rouen and Le Havre to Dieppe. The Orleans line was conceded to Casimir Leconte, sometime manager of the important stagecoach company, Messageries Royales, but the members of his board were dominated by Rothschild, who deposed him and turned the company over to Francois Bartholony who was allied with Paris banking interests neutral to Rothschild at the time. The latter

6. Poet-politician Lamartine depicted reclining on his automobile in France in the 1840s. He warned that railways would enchain the masses to capitalism just when they had broken the bonds of feudalism. (Courtesy of Henry Allemagne, *Prosper Enfantin et les grandes entreprises du XIXe siècle*, Paris, 1935).

line, Paris to Dieppe, was quickly abandoned by its original French concessionaires and seized on by Edward Blount, the most ubiquitous English capitalist in France among a great number. Blount's capital came from the Lancashire-London financial group and the London-Dover-Southampton railway which had an outstanding interest in a railway connecting Paris to the English Channel. "I practically financed the West of France Railway," Blount wrote. But the object of swift communication with the East was on his mind. He was a member of the projected Euphrates Valley Railway Company which "would have carried our troops to India in much less time than is now required."[79]

By the French railway law of June 11, 1842, the government paid for the infrastructure while the companies paid for the superstructure (rails, stations, etc.) for which the government gave them subsidies.

Concessions were seized eagerly. James de Rothschild and his English nephew, Nathaniel, led English and French capitalists in the construction of the Great Northern Railway of France (du Nord). Among these capitalists were the Hottinguers of the Haute Banque and the Lancashire banking group led by the firm Glyn, Mills, and also Robert Stephenson. The granting the concession of the railway to the north to James de Rothschild provides us with an illustration of the complicated involvement of the English government and capitalists in French affairs. James's tentative efforts to win the railway concessions to the north had been forestalled by the argument in the French legislature over government or private control of the railways and by an economic depression. But after the passage of the 1842 law, he negotiated for the concession by maneuvering English capitalists, Belgian capitalists, and the French government in both the interests of the British government and the Rothschild banks.

Nathaniel Rothschild, a son of Nathan in the English house, had moved to Paris to help administer the Paris house. He acted as the communicator of news to his brothers in England who had taken over the English house upon Nathan's death in 1836, and during these negotiations represented Lancashire-London interests in the proposed northern railway. In early January 1843 George Carr Glyn informed Nathaniel that he did not see the slightest chance of English capitalists taking up shares in the proposed railway. Nathaniel shared this view with his brothers of the London house, crossed over to London, and met with capitalists and political leaders. Four days later, he wrote: "Busy all day with Belgian railroad people and as yet have not come to terms with them or with the Government."

Prompted by the English Rothschilds, Sir Robert Peel, the prime minister, made a speech expressing confidence in France. His words engendered confidence in investors for the northern railway on the French stock exchange. English capitalists, however, were not as amenable as the English government. "Our railroad affair was going on in the best possible way," Nathaniel wrote from Paris, "when the English parties (i.e., of the Dover Railway Company led by David Salomons) told us they had made proposals to the French government (i.e., for a railway to Calais as well as to Lille). They were backed by nobody and being in Treaty with us it was blackguard behaviour, and our friend D. Salomons is perhaps more to blame than anyone else. They have however confessed their fault and now wish the affair to take the turn we propose. The misfortune is we shall not get such good terms from the government."[80] An agreement was soon reached, however. "This morning we paid visits to M. Teste and nearly all the members of the Cabinet and after having agreed upon the terms with the former, we communicated to the latter gentlemen that we are the fortunate candidates of the Belgian railroad. . . which did not surprise them. Tomorrow we shall have the *Cahier des Charges*. . . . Tell Mills that in the contract we only wish to introduce his name, ours and those of Mallet, Lefebre and Eichthal . . . not all the principals."[81]

Mills of Glyn, Mills represented Lancashire capitalists (including Thomas Weguelin, a director of the Bank of England, and member of an important firm in the Baltic trade, Thomson, Bonar and Company, William Gladstone of the same firm, and John Moss, the Liverpool banker). Like Robert Stephenson, Mills worked for the London-Dover group. The English Rothschilds communicated news to them both. "We are very satisfied," wrote Nathaniel to his brothers, "with the manner in which you have arranged the railroad affair with Mills. I have no doubt (the cabinet council) will agree to our suggestions and it will pass the Chamber without difficulty."[82] By signing a treaty with the French minister in advance, however, Nathaniel raised suspicions in the French legislature which attacked the treaty and encouraged a rival French company, Compagnie Durand, which was supported by the Barings, English banking rivals to the Rothschilds. Suddenly the project was dropped.

On October 31, 1843, James wrote in French to Nathaniel, who was then visiting the London house, that the French cabinet had decided to negotiate with the Rothschilds again over the railway to the north. He also observed that the prime minister Francois Guizot would use their former agreement as a basis to which modifications could be made over such points of dispute as a tariff and the number of passenger classes. (The elitist House of Pairs, that is, Nobles, sided with the Rothschilds for two classes, whereas the House of Deputies wanted three.) James suggested that his nephew find out what the English were thinking and come to an agreement with them:

89

I know that Mr. Mills intends to come to Paris; but I think that his presence alone will suffice to stir up all our competitors, and put them on guard, and cause them to start slandering us and begin their intrigues.... It would be therefore absolutely essential . . . to keep as secret as possible the resumption of negotiations for the railway du Nord in order to arrive at the Chamber with a final proposal before our adversaries would have had time to collect themselves. For this reason it would seem to me preferable to get a preliminary agreement in London over what needs to be done here and in this way ensure that we proceed both silently and directly towards our goal.[83]

While the English capitalists were being lined up, Baron James disingenuously informed his Belgian ally, the Societe Generale de Belgique:

With the guarantee of 150,000 francs per kilometer (600,00 francs per league) that the Government has adopted as the minimum for all undertakings, that business reduces itself to an enterprise of 40 to 50 millions. Since it is intended to link England with France, it is probable that it will find a certain support on the London Stock Exchange, and as happened on the Paris-Rouen line, English capital will join forces with French capital.[84]

As it turned out, the English Rothschilds and the Barings took 8,000 shares in the du Nord railway.

At the same time, James de Rothschild gave Paulin Talabot, engineer protégé of the Stephensons, the initial financial support to organize a company to build the Lyon-Avignon line. After purposeful yet inexplicable delay and the failure of a competing syndicate in the crisis of 1847, Rothschild continued his support. Another company, involving the politician Louis Mole, the St.-Simonist Michel Chevalier, James de Rothschild, P. Hottinguer, and the financier Achille Fould, provided 30 million francs on one side and involved 40 million francs of English capital on the other. This company competed for the line to Strasbourg which became the Chemin de Fer de l'Est. James de Rothschild won the concession by amalgamating seven companies and maintaining himself and his opponent, Fould, as the principal subscribers with a quarter of the capital representing English interests. The railway Amiens to Boulogne in the south undertaken by Charles Lafitte had a large representation of English directors from the board of the English South-Eastern railway. The Railway of the Center (du Centre), directed by Casimir Leconte, was strongly supported by London bankers. All of these railways employed English engineers such as Stephenson, Joseph Locke, and the Mackenzie brothers, English contractors such as Thomas Brassey with their tens of thousands of English navvies, and English agents. With their advanced technological knowledge, the English had established firms in several manufacturing industries in France with hundreds of English workmen. Now the manufacturers of railway equipment followed suit.

Although iron rails and railway implements were allowed into France free of duty, the English engineers required faster service than the shipments from England to France provided. As a result, Locke established the English firm of Allcard and Buddicom at Sotteville alongside the construction of the Paris-Rouen line. It became the principal supplier of locomotives to French railways. Allcard and Buddicom coming from the Grand Junction railway owed their business to the Lancashire interests.

French capitalists, somewhat resentful of the encroachment of English capitalists, began to develop factories to make machinery. Francois Cave constructed huge factories in the Paris suburbs in 1835, and a joint stock company built the Cail-Derosne factories in Chaillot in 1838. They were given easy credit by Paris joint stock banks and the old bank of Seilliere which took a large role in the development of railways and coal mines. Another old bank, Gouin, built factories in 1845 with the view of competing with England at the moment when the railway and steamship enterprises called for an immense joining of all industrial forces.

At the same time Lieutenant Thomas Waghorn, who devoted years to making an overland route to India for commercial interests in India and England, warned the English public that the French opposed the English in the East and had brought a stop to the railway he had been building for the past ten years across the Egyptian desert.

Although the rail route from Ostend to Cologne was completed in 1846, it took some international intrigue to have lines built through Austria. Waghorn wrote from Trieste to Baron Homalauer in September 1846 that he urged Prince Metternich and Baron Kubeck to take the lead in constructing a railway through the Tyrol Mountains from Durno to the Rhine "coupling Vienna with it afterwards, at any point Vienna pleases. To keep the French Railways in check, at once, is what I am at, for if it be not done at once they will beat you."[85]

Waghorn's suggestion took years to realize. Meanwhile, a line from Vienna to Breslau was completed in 1847 to link up with Dresden, Berlin, Magdebourg, Hanover, Cologne, and through Belgium to Ostend. By January 1851 the rail from Vienna to Trieste shortened the route from London to India considerably over the route via Marseilles. Letters arrived forty hours sooner in London than in Paris.

The very liberal terms by which the French government encouraged capitalists to build railways, as if paying them scandalous sums from the treasury for the purpose, revealed the government's eagerness to catch up with its neighbors in all-important advances in internal communication and international connection. (It was a sign that the finance bourgeoisie, as the ruling class, controlled the government.) Waghorn could not have known, however, that English capital controlled so many lines in France and Belgium. Although the recession of 1848 caused much construction to cease, the Belgian government bailed out the companies with generous loans throughout the 1850s. As for the French government, an historian wrote in 1860: "Since their origin the railways did not cease demanding sacrifices from the state; they ran only under conditions of perpetual crises; and it was only through state aid that they were able to run at all."[86]

The Second Republic almost succeeded in nationalizing the railways. It took two lines in the south over from Talabot; the other lines, particularly Rothschild's du Nord, were attacked by the unemployed and hungry workers. But with their resources in Germany and England the Rothschilds kept up French credit and confidence until the Socialists were outmaneuvered by the Saint-Simonians and conservatives in Parliament who refused to consider nationalization.

It has been conjectured that Britain was behind Napoleon III's seizure of the government in 1852. If one considers the amount of British investment in French railways alone, the fear of its loss would have prompted British political intervention. The Duc de Morny, Napoleon's half-brother, who is credited with planning the coup d'état, epitomized the French businessman deeply involved in railways, particularly in the Chemin de Fer du Centre. The Bank of France possibly provided Napoleon III with 25 million francs for the coup, and Napoleon, possibly in gratitude, employed the Bank to facilitate the building of railways. He paid back government debts to the Bank (50 million francs in two installments in 1852 and 75 million in annuities of 5 million over fifteen years), and extended its privilege of issuing notes. Because its capital was tied up, however, the bank of issue could not extend credit to business. The Second Republic ameliorated this situation by forming Comptoirs d'Escompte in Paris and sixty towns to create capital for loans to business. In his turn Napoleon III, a St.-Simonist at heart, with help from the Foulds, other Paris houses, and international bankers, created the Credit Mobilier under the Pereire brothers to pursue the St.-Simonian goal of revitalizing France.

The Pereires centralized the financial and administrative affairs of the railways through the Credit Foncier and the Credit Mobilier by lending them 1.5 milliard francs within five years. In 1853 the Duc de Morny and English capitalists (notably the president of the London stock exchange) took over a network of railways in

Central France under the name Grand-Central and reduced fifteen companies to four.

As deeply as the French worker hated the railway for inflicting the 1848 depression on him, and resented the hordes of English workmen who were supplanting him in his own country before 1848, he began to respect the prosperity which the railway enterprises engendered in the country. He welcomed his employment in the railway and its supplying industries under the Second Empire and in foreign countries to which the French, in competition with English and German capitalists, expanded their operations.

The capitalists, meanwhile, bought up iron works, coal fields, and supply industries in connection with their railways. James de Rothschild invested in Belgium and the north of France which was traversed by Rothschild's Chemin de Fer du Nord. The Talabots, still under the financial control of the Rothschilds, managed an industrial network: the Paris-Lyons-Marseilles railway (PLM) (which had absorbed the lines in the south), the shipping on the Rhone River connecting with the mineral fields and forges in South-central France, their newly acquired metallurgy of Anzin, and their mines and factories in Algeria. Owing to such widespread investment opportunities, the relationships among the international capitalists of Europe were as complicated as a spider's web. Yet with the venture of the Pereires' Credit Mobilier into insurance, real estate, railways, and maritime shipping, there developed a distinct national-minded banking interest in opposition to the private international bankers, most notably the Rothschilds.

Various writers have discussed the enmity between the Pereires and the Rothschilds, even suggesting that James de Rothschild resented the Pereires (who had been in his employ) for buying an estate, Arminvilliers, bordering the Rothschilds' Ferrieres near Melun. According to the economic historian Jean Bouvier, Baron James "got even with them blow for blow on all the markets and tracked them down throughout all of Europe."[87]

Bouvier thought that the Pereires broke with Rothschild because, faced with the anarchy of capitalism, they wished to form a planned organization of production where producer, state, and economic groups could function in concert. They wanted harmony in place of the struggle for capital. Faithful to their St.-Simonist principles, they sought a modern system of banking, and in the process they took over the stock exchange and modified the credit structure. They aimed to eliminate pauperism and thus stop progressive movements. When the Pereires tried to organize the circulation of state and industrial values as interchangeable credit obligations, that is, money, they confronted the Bank of France over its right of issue and restrictive policies on discounting. This confrontation became openly vicious when the Pereires allied themselves with the Bank of Savoy (when Savoy was annexed by France in 1861) in support of its right to continue issuing bills in competition with the Bank of France.

The Rothschilds defended the "political tradition" of the Bank of France's right to issue money. Fearing inflation, they supported the Bank's right to raise interest rates when menaced by financial crises.

When the Credit Mobilier expanded its operations into railways and banks in Austria, Germany, Spain, and Russia at the end of 1855, the private bankers became worried. When the Credit Mobilier's finances dried up from its refusal to issue preference shares, it sought funds from amalgamation and tried to make the Grand Central under Morny join with the Chemin de Fer du Midi to take over the Chemin de Fer Pyreneens. Morny, breaking with the Pereires, joined the Rothschild camp which had money. Rothschild formed the enemies of the Pereires into a banking syndicate, the Reunion Financiere. It limited the Credit Mobilier's actions abroad and blocked all of its new enterprises in Brussels, Naples, Rome, and Russia. English bankers who were behind the Rothschild group tried to replace the Credit Mobilier as a new credit establishment strictly within France and introduce the cheque and other English banking practices.

If the Pereires were to be effectively fought abroad, their enemies needed a powerful alliance of international capitalists. They formed the Societe Generale de Credit Industriel et Commercial in which William Gladstone represented the English, David Hansemann, the Germans, and Morny, the French from the Loire; Adrien Delahante and Talabot stood for the Rothschilds. Actually, half of the directors were linked to the PLM railway, with others linked to Swiss and Italian railways. Eugene Schneider represented the industrial and political groups, while Simons came from the Messageries Maritimes, a trading competitor of the Pereires Companie Transatlantique.

In defense, the Pereires joined forces with the Bank of Darmstadt and the International Bank of Luxembourg for more capital to pursue their investments in Austrian and Italian railways and Turkey. Other bankers, such as Salomon Heine of Hamburg, Salomon Oppenheim of Cologne, Simon Sina and Arnstein of Vienna, and the Baring brothers of England, joined with the Pereires. A great battle took place for the concessions to open up the Ottoman Empire between these capitalist camps, an affair which although involving railways, takes us beyond our theme. Once the Pereires struck out to conquer distant lands, they ceased to represent the development of national capital. Caught in a shrinking home market, they had been stubbornly hampered by the Rothschilds, the Haute Banque, and the Bank of

France, and they mistakenly decided to beat their opponents with capital from investments abroad. Instead, they weakened their home base and overextended themselves in investing in the docks and real estate of Marseilles, which they saw as an international port, and in financing Napoleon's intervention with the ill-fated Maximilian in Mexico. Finally, by the government's refusal of a loan, they lost their bid to build a railway in competition with Talabot's PLM from Marseilles to Central France. The Bank of France was behind the rejection.

In that year the Bank of Savoy's treaty with the Credit Mobilier, which established the Bank of Savoy's right to continue to issue notes despite opposition from the Bank of France, was ratified by the General Assembly. In 1865, however, in an about-face, the Assembly dissolved the Bank of Savoy, abrogated its issuing privilege, and transformed its two houses into branches of the Bank of France.

The failure of the Credit Mobilier in 1867 resulted in a loss of nearly 200 million francs and ruined millions of small shareholders. "Because there is not a village in France where that disgusting disaster did not claim victims."[88]

Napoleon III, the former Saint-Simonist, had supported the operations of the Pereires in opposition to his wife Eugenie who supported the Rothschilds. Perhaps owing to his commitment to the Bank of France and English investors in France, Napoleon turned away from the Pereires after their projects in foreign countries began to compete with English interests. On Morny's advice he refused permission for the Pereires, who like all bankers had been hurt by the financial crisis of 1857, to fuse the Credit Mobilier with the Comptoir d'Escompte. He also turned against the Pereires in the battle among capitalists for control of French railways through merger.

The Bank of France had tremendous influence in railway questions owing to its indispensable support in the construction of the lines. The Franqueville Conventions of 1859, however, formed six railways for all of France and virtually reduced railway shares to preference stock. The future of railways was no longer in the hands of the government or the Stock Exchange, but in those of the small saver. Great capitalists lost all interest in them.

Nevertheless, French bankers venturing into distant and greener fields administered the railways in France, particularly the Rothschilds who kept a close eye on their PLM and Nord lines. In addition, the English administered the French railways for decades to come as exemplified by Edward Blount. He kept his chairmanship of the Chemin de Fer de l'Ouest until 1894 when he was forced out by a government suspicious of foreign control of such a major line of communication.

95

11

The Repression of the Steam Carriage on the Continent and the Development of the Petroleum Automobile

Jean-Chretien Dietz of Belgium had inventive traits in common with the Gurney brothers of Cornwall. Like them he invented musical instruments, and like Goldsworthy Gurney he experimented with a steam carriage but met with technical success only after he corresponded with Goldsworthy. He built a drag with three wheels and a two-cylinder motor in 1832. He followed it in 1834 with a larger drag that pulled a train of carriages from Brussels to Anvers, and in 1836 with an eight-wheeled carriage that operated around a central wheel.

While Jean-Chretien built steam carriages in his Brussels workshop, his son, Charles, built them in Paris. Charles won acclaim for driving about Paris with distinguished members of the Academie de l'Industrie in 1834, for instituting a regular passenger service from Paris to Versailles in 1835, and for offering a service with a six-wheeled carriage between Bordeaux and Libourne in 1840.

As for the Bordeaux passenger service, Charles and his brother Christian, who directed their Societe de Remorqueurs, encountered public hostility, particularly from the stagecoach drivers who wanted to break up their steam carriage and throw it into the Garonne River. Once Charles had to be rescued by police on the Suresne Bridge as he was defending himself with an iron bar. But with the official support of a prestigious committee whose members were from the Academie Royale des Sciences, the Dietz steam carriage attracted spectacular enthusiasm within three trips to Libourne. This response occurred despite a false rumor that a passenger had been thrown off and killed, and despite the temporary inconvenience caused by the mysterious disappearance of the coke at one of their refueling stops. Unfortunately for the future of the automobile, the Dietzes abandoned the service after a few months because they began to suffer from competition with the rapidly developing railways. Charles Dietz, half-ruined, returned to his Paris workshop where he diversified production into engines for vessels and turbines.

A Dietz descendant claimed that the Rothschild Paris-St. Germain railway, conceded in 1835 and finished in 1837, took away the steam carriage business: "The struggle between the road and the rail was already taking place and was the principal reason why Charles Dietz, forsaken by the public authorities, abandoned this service after several weeks."[89]

There were other steam carriage promoters in France: Lotz who ran a small carriage between Nantes and Paris for a short time from 1865 to 1866,[90] and, at the same time, Servet's Compagnie d'Orleans whose five-ton carriage ran a special passenger service at night at 12 kilometers an hour between Grenoble and Lyons, a distance of 100 kilometers.

Obviously sensing a steam carriage revival, the minister of public works instituted an arrete or decree on April 20, 1866, which was not rescinded until March 10, 1899. Those persons establishing a steam carriage service for passengers or goods were required to submit a detailed itinerary, an assessment of the total weight of machinery and haulage and the average length of the drag and carriages to the regional prefect for approval. If the request was denied, an appeal could be made to the minister of public works. In addition, the steam carriage could not be driven over 20 kilometers an hour and had to be slowed when passing through towns and villages.

Meanwhile, in Germany the steam carriage encountered the restrictions that repressed it in England. In 1836 Colonel Dance was turned down when he proposed to the Ober-Regierungs president of Koblenz that he provide English steam carriages for transport of troops, arms and ammunition, and the wounded at £1500 for each carriage, ten of which must be bought from him. £500 was his fee for introducing the vehicle to Prussia. Berlin advised Koblenz that, despite praise in some journals, steam carriages were not in practical working order. When some workshops in Hanover and Koln built road locomotives after the English Boydell model in the 1860s, the minister of the interior appointed a commission which in an official report published the same opinion as the English House of Lords' Committee of 1836. A spirit of steam carriage-building in Koln in 1873 was cut short by police ordinances and swift arrests of the drivers, thus concluding a short-lived German flirtation with steam on the roads.[91]

Gottlieb Daimler, who developed the petroleum automobile, knew of experiments with the steam carriage, worked some of the heavy road locomotives such as Boydell's and Aveling's in the machine factories in Birmingham and Manchester, and studied the fourteen steam carriages at the World's Fair in London in 1862. Daimler, however, saw no future for them. Preferring to experiment with gas engines, he quit a job building steam locomotives and spent a year in Paris to study gas engines. Fortunately, he landed the position of technical director at the Otto and Langen Gas Engine Works in Deutz into which he brought his close friend, Wilhelm Maybach, a first-rate technical designer who shared his passion for developing an automobile.

Otto's stationary two-stroke gas engine at 1/2 horsepower stood 8 feet, weighed almost a ton, and was noisy and erratic. Between 1872 and 1876 Daimler and Maybach helped Otto design a four-stroke gas engine which Otto insisted on concentrating on for purposes of production. Daimler, however, realized that to increase the power and reduce the engine size, he needed to increase the speed of motor rotation. He persuaded Deutz and Company to purchase the rights to the American Brayton engine which he improved in a special department and for which the firm gave him shares in the company.

Since dynamos were being developed to run at 400 to 500 rpm, the gas engine of 150 rpm needed a belt and pulley arrangement to step up the speed to drive the dynamo, which Daimler saw as a waste of space. A jealous Otto argued that the inventive Daimler should be allowed no further experimentation. Daimler was sent to Russia to scout the market for Deutz engines and confirmed his conjecture that a small light engine run on petroleum would find many uses in remote areas where there was no gas supply. On his return Otto forced him out of the firm. With some bitterness Daimler and Maybach set up an experimental workshop in Cannstatt.

The terms of Daimler's separation from Deutz were: a credit of 106,094.50 marks and 112 shares added to his 75, making 187 shares worth 121,200 marks. In ten years with Deutz he earned 400,000 marks in dividends and royalties. Through both dividends and royalties over the next eight years he received 300,000 marks. Consequently, he and Maybach were not lacking for finances. In 1885 Daimler produced a vertical, high-speed, and compact gasoline engine which was the direct ancestor of practically all modern car engines—and furthermore of the engines that made mechanical flight possible.

Dissatisfied with both electric and gas ignition, which could not function efficiently for an engine with over 250 rpm, Daimler and Maybach invented the hot tube ignition by the end of 1883. A small platinum tube closed at one end and open at the other screwed into the cylinder head of an engine so that the open end communicated with the combustion chamber. The exposed part of the tube was kept at bright red heat by a suitable burner, and on the compression stroke of the engine (at the moment of maximum compression) a little of the explosive charge was forced into the narrow tube and was ignited by coming into contact with the red hot metal. This ignition arrangement was automatic and self-contained, easily understood, and with no moving parts to wear out or need adjustment. It was a great improvement on the gas jet and slide valve affair, and it was capable of working at speeds up to 1000 rpm. Its problem was that the engine speed could not be altered because the faster an engine ran, the earlier was it necessary for combustion to take place in relation to the position of the piston in the cylinder. This constant speed of the engine was fine for motor-boats and lathes but poor for automobiles in traffic.

Electric ignition was the answer. Lenoir developed it in 1860, Carl Benz used it for his slow-running automobile in 1885, and Robert Bosch of Stuttgart perfected it for the modern automobile in the late 1890s.

Benz, a rival to Daimler, used and improved the Deutz four-stroke gas engine on a light, tubular-framed, three-wheeled automobile with a simple belt-and-pulley transmission gear in 1885. This slow-running horizontal engine, similar to a stationary engine, was incapable of much development. Benz conceived the automobile from the point of view of the bicycle. Maybach, on the other hand, designed it along the lines of a carriage, and after experimenting with an early 1886 model, he came up with the prototype of the modern automobile. Benz, however, was more fortunate than Daimler in his financial backers because clearly they were supporting him to build an automobile. In Daimler's case, as we will see, the financiers, interested only in the petroleum engine, discouraged Daimler's automobile experiments.

No cars were sold in Germany. Benz was arrested for breaking a police ordinance of May 13, 1882, which forbade motor vehicles in the streets.

Maybach was almost arrested for driving a Daimler motor launch on the river, but the police quickly relented when they learned that Count Bismarck had purchased one. German discouragement of the automobile went to the extreme of the authorities committing Benz's first German buyer to an insane asylum.

France, and later Belgium and the United States, therefore, were the only open markets for the automobile. Benz motors were made at a French firm, the Societe de Forges d'Aubrives in the Ardennes. They were also exported by Emile Roger, Benz's French sales agent, who arranged to have the Paris machine manufacturers, Rene Panhard and Emile Levassor, construct the bodies. Panhard came from a long line of coachbuilders, which may have inclined him to the Maybach coach design when

Daimler's French agent, Sarazin, approached him in 1887. After constructing the Daimler petroleum engine, Panhard and Levassor needed little persuasion by Daimler of its potential.

7. Gottlieb Daimler being driven in his petrol carriage of 1886, five years before his improved engine and Maybach's carriage design produced the petroleum automobile in France. (Courtesy of *Historie de la locomotion terrestre*, Paris, 1935-36.)

Levassor, who became a zealot in promoting the automobile, accompanied Daimler to Valentigny in November 1888 where they met with Armand Peugot of the long-established family of tool and machine makers. Peugeot was producing bicycles after studying their manufacture in Coventry and was constructing steam carriages, yet almost immediately he converted to the petroleum automobile. Under Daimler's patent and Maybach's designs, Panhard and Levassor built the engines to fit into Peugeot's automobile frames. Peugeot made their first automobile too heavy to run, and Levassor took months to develop an engine that ran only 12 miles. But in September 1891 they produced an automobile that ran from Peugeot's Valentigny factory to Panhard and Levassor in Paris, a distance of 260 miles, in four days. The remarkable French automobile industry was underway.

100

A famous proponent was the sportsman-playboy Comte de Dion, who persuaded the steam carriage builder, Georges Bouton, to build a small, high-speed petrol engine. Bouton produced an electrical ignition using a dry battery.

De Dion's sudden interest in petrol engines came from another socialite, Baron Etienne van Zuylen de Nyeveldt. Van Zuylen represented the immense capital of the Societe Generale de Belgique, which his family founded. It helped control the Compagnie Financiere Belge des Petroles in which the Paris Rothschilds had a strong (perhaps the main) financial interest from 1889. Van Zuylen financed the de Dion-Bouton firm from 1894 and became a partner with a 400,000 franc investment in 1898. Moreover, a fact not without significance in this society, he was married to a Rothschild.

8. Messrs. Panhard and Levassor on the first Daimler voiturette brought to Paris in 1890. (Courtesy of *Le Technologiste*, 1900.)

One of the directors of the Paris Rothschilds, Arthur de Rothschild, a son of Nathaniel, was from the English family but was French in thought and action. He played an important, though shadowy, role in the development of the automobile in France. A leader of French society, Arthur stood behind Baron van Zuylen in his energetic promotion of French automobilism.[92] He was an early purchaser of Panhard-Levassor cars with their Daimler motors. He probably took shares in the de Dion-Bouton firm when its financier, van Zuylen, changed it in 1898 to a limited partnership with a capital of 800,000 francs, 400,000 of which came from van Zuylen. A subtle link in the automobile financing between van Zuylen and the Rothschilds appeared momentarily in 1901. A small automobile firm, Societe Francaise d'Automobiles, begun in 1897 by an engineer from de Dion-Bouton and financed by Baron van Zuylen, became part of the Bardon Company, a Rothschild automobile firm. Bardon, which had been operating in Paris since 1899, received a large infusion of Rothschild funds when it merged with van Zuylen's company.[93]

Arthur de Rothschild stirred an interest in automobiles in his nephew, Henri, pediatrician, obstetrician, book collector, and playwright. Henri entered the early auto races under the name of Dr. Pascal. His involvement in automobilism as a financier is intertwined with investments in the industry by the Rothschild Bank. Both reflected an ambition to produce a dependable cheap car to reach the widest possible market. Other French automobile firms of this early period, such as Panhard-Levassor, which had no connection with petroleum distribution as had de Dion-Bouton and the Rothschilds, produced expensive automobiles for the aristocratic and bourgeois rich. This is not to say that the Rothschilds abstained from producing luxury cars. In 1902 Henri established a short-lived factory to make the powerful and expensive Pascal racing car with the intention of devoting the profits to his children's hospital. But Henri's long-range goal may be seen by his financial support in 1904 of Georges Richard and Cie., which avoided races and luxury cars to concentrate on one low-cost model. Named "Unic," it brought the firm great success. Half of its production was used as taxis, especially in London where no English cab could stand up to the treatment or show such economic running figures.

Actually, the Rothschild Bank capital also was behind Unic, as Georges Richard and Cie. merged in 1906 with the Societe Anonyme d'Automobiles et Traction (Systeme Bardon), the Rothschild project. The new Societe Anonyme des Automobiles Unic had a capital of 2.5 million francs, the stockholders of each of the constituent firms receiving I million francs in shares. It sold the remaining shares for cash. The Bardon Company made chassis, motors, automobiles, and trucks. It appeared to have lost money by promising a delivery price on chassis and motors to other firms lower than the eventual production cost. The firm's accountant informed the Rothschild Bank in 1906 of a loss of 91,000 francs.[94]

9. The Bardon automobile came from the joint venture of van Zuylen and the Rothschilds in 1900. (Courtesy of *Le Technologiste*, 1900.)

Profit on orders, or in other words surplus on the price invoiced to the clients on the total cost of the material and workmanship exclusively employed in their construction. FR. 125,993.48.
Expenses in general of the factory (materials, labor, salaries, etc.... for which there is no possible basis of distribution according to the cost price of the orders). FR. 217,000.78
Deficiency of profit. FR. 91,015.30.

The accountant added, however, that the filling of orders received in December 1905 could bring the loss for the year down to 65,000 francs, as against 110,000 francs lost in 1904.

A look at these 1905 orders still to be filled gives an idea of the firm's role as a supplier to other firms and, consequently, of the central role played by the Rothschild Bank in the automobile business.

35 motors L.F. (Leeds-Forge, an English firm which made pressed steel chassis frames for cars)
150 motors G.R. 2 cyl. (Georges Richard & Cie.)
60 motors Bolide

10 motors Turgan, 4 cyl. (Etablissements Turgan, reorganized by an English Engineer in 1905)
103 motors Unic G.R. (Unic model. Georges Richard)
100 B.V. (boites de vitesse—gear boxes)
50 motors Herald 4 cyl. (Herald was one of the smaller French firms which hurt by the recession in 1905/6 converted to English limited companies hoping for strong recapitalization but without success)
50 B.V. Herald.
4 chassis C & Ste. B. (possibly Botiaux company of Paris which made automobile bodies)
2 motors
100 motors G.R. (Henri de Rothschild's company seemed to be giving the Bank's company plenty of business)
175 B.V. G.R.
2 motors for motorcyles
12 B.V. G.R.
40 chassis Herald.

The firm's customers were varied (there were 104 in 1904), including Edouard de Rothschild, Alphonse de Rothschild, Henri de Rothschild (Arthur died in 1903), Compagnie Routiere de France, Peugeot Freres, Michelin and Cie, Forges and Acieres, Cie. Voiture Electromobiles, Cie. du Nord, Grand Garage de l'Opera, Henri Deutsch (the oil refiner in the Rothschild group), and Holtzer and Co. (the long-established fabricator of special steel for armaments and cutting tools). Holtzer helped to introduce light chrome steel and nickel steel to the automobile industry which it entered at the turn of the century. Holtzer's manager, Paul Menard-Dorian, took a seat on the board of Panhard-Levassor when it became a public company in 1900 and rose to chairman in 1903.

The Rothschilds' Georges Richard Unic company eventually offered five different passenger car chassis in the medium-price range and low-powered cabs that made it the ninth largest automobile company in France before World War I. Henri de Rothschild with Jacques Bizet, a Unic dealer and founder of the Banque Automobile specializing in installment loans to automobile buyers, financed the *Zebre*, a small one-cylinder, 5 horsepower car. Nevertheless, most automobile promoters intended to keep prices high, a fact which the public resented. In July 1907 the Societe Protectrice Contre les Exces de l'Automobilisme pressed for stricter legislation on automobile usage and responsibility for accidents. The substitution in Paris of mechanical for animal traction with the coming of the large autobus and the taxi caused a contemporary to complain: "So— that which is healthy democratic progress is putting at the disposition of the poorest purses a type of locomotion which will remain always, apparently, one must admit, as a form of individual ownership, the prerogative of a privileged class."[95] But, at least, he added, if the automobile was not yet a force for democracy, it was already an instrument for decentralization. The people, therefore, did not fear the automobile; they feared the automobilists.

We must step back for a moment, however, to see how it was that the Rothschilds would want to develop the automobile in the first place.

12

The Breaking of English Capital

The rise of English capital to a position of dominance in industrial development around the world, through the agency of the Lancashire capitalists and the railways, subjugated national capital and its particular aims both in Britain and abroad, despite significant political and financial opposition in France. After 1870 the English domination was challenged by a newly united Germany. Buoyed by the French war indemnity for the Franco-German War, there arose a capitalist nationalism in Germany that resolved to wreck the control of English international high finance over Germany. Two banks spearheaded this attack: the new Deutsche Bank of Berlin, and the new Wurttembergisches Vereinsbank of Stuttgart in the south.

The Deutsche Bank, with strong links to long-established banks in Berlin and other cities, attracted provincial banks and the Frankfurter Stock Exchange, both of which wanted to break London's financial control of the German export trade. When the Bank set up a network of affiliates abroad, the London Rothschilds became alarmed and wrote to a Frankfurt journal friendly to them: "A necessity, to double the share capital is not, in any case, foreseen, save when it may come to pass that the Bank in the hands of reef pirates, Kaffirs, and Blackfoot Indians wishes to establish limited liability."[96] With the doubling of capital in 1871, the London financial grip was loosened and the banks of southern Germany, including Frankfurt, switched over to the Deutsche Bank with their stock exchanges and business life. One bank that joined the Deutsche Bank was the Wurttembergisches Vereinsbank. Under the leadership of Kilian Steiner, it financed a series of German industrial trusts and cartels to undermine foreign monopolies in Germany, in particular those of the Rothschild group.

Kilian Steiner has been called "the first, who generally and purposefully carried forward the concentration of the until-now united banking institutions into a powerful organization."[97]

Steiner came from a Jewish merchant family, studied law, joined the national-minded German party which planned his founding of the Wurttembergisches Vereinsbank in 1869, and formed a wide circle of friendship with politicians, bankers, artists, and businessmen throughout the country. Although he was not a director of the Deutsche Bank until 1886, his close friendships with the Bank's administrators gave him a guiding role from its beginning.

Steiner took an important step to obtain capital in 1870 when he founded the Rheinischen Kreditbank in Mannheim with the aid of the big merchants of Hamburg. This bank raised the capital for industry in that area; the Ladenburg bank in Mannheim could not be counted on to get the capital owing to its ties with the Rothschilds. Up to this point M. A. von Rothschild und Sohne ruled the finances of the south German states like a sovereign. This sovereignty encountered its first challenge in 1870 when it found itself in competition for handling a loan for the state of Wurttemberg, which, with the indiscreet help of official disclosure of the bids, it was enabled to win. Because of the outbreak of war, however, it failed to place the loan successfully. The Vereinsbank and other Stuttgart banks had to take over a quarter of the shares, thus creating a Vereinsbank group that took a second state loan in the following year away from the Rothschilds.

Faced with the weakness of their Frankfurt house, the Rothschilds formed an alliance with what became known as the Berlin group; the Diskontogesellschaft, the Darmstadter Bank, and S. Bleichroder (Count von Bismarck's faithful adviser). Soon, however, they felt the bite of the Deutsche Bank outside Germany when it competed on the international market for the first time, that is, for the Austrian-Hungarian loan of 1877. The Rothschild group had placed the first loan successfully and was expected to win the second, but the Diskontogesellschaft bid was rejected in preference to the Deutsche Bank. The Rothschild-Berlin group withdrew, leaving the field to a union of banks, including the Deutsche Bank and the Wurttembergisches Vereinsbank. From this time the Deutsche Bank enjoyed years of success in floating Austrian state loans. The Paris Rothschilds, on advising their English cousins to discount the advice of their Frankfurt house, wrote, "We have been thinking for some time that the Frankfurt house was a German house because she has the shape to incline her to have an affair in Germany."[98] This contributed to its rapid decline.

Meanwhile, the Wurttembergisches Vereinsbank under Kilian Steiner's leadership struck out into many fields of industrial development in Germany: south German railways and railway construction; gasworks in Stuttgart; machine-building factories in Alsace; the armaments factory of the Mauser brothers; the amalgamation of the Stuttgart chemical and dyeworks with the anilyne and soda factory in Ludwigshafen to create the largest chemical industry in the world; the uniting of metal and machine factories in Geislinger, Cannstatt, and Esslinger into a high-powered industry; and the takeover of the gunpowder factory in Rottweil, from which Steiner built the biggest dynamite and gunpowder cartel in Germany, known as the Koln-Rottweiler Pulverfabriken.

Two circumstances intervened to arouse Steiner's interest in the automobile: the involvement of the Deutsche Bank in 1883 in the German petroleum market; and the undeniable embrace of the world's largest producer of dynamite.

13

The Petroleum Connection

John D. Rockefeller's Standard Oil was a prime example of capitalist cunning: its union of oil refiners contracted with three American railroads for exclusive cartage of their oil in return for secret reduced freight rates and the doubling of rates for competitors; and Rockefeller arranged with Cornelius Vanderbilt of the New York Central for secret freight rebates which led to his monopolization of oil refining in the United States and his early pursuit of monopoly marketing of illuminating oil or kerosene in Europe and Russia. But then Standard Oil's kerosene monopoly in Europe met a challenger in the Nobel Company from the Baku oilfields of Russia. Nobel increased oil production from 40,000 barrels in 1863 to 3 million barrels in 1880 to 29 million in 1890 to 76 million in 1900.

Emmanuel Nobel, of Swedish origin, made a fortune manufacturing cannons in St. Petersburg for the Crimean War. One son, Alfred Nobel, invented dynamite and became rich through his patents and dynamite factories. Another son, Robert, bought oilfields in Baku in the 1870s, but it was his brother, Ludwig, who revolutionized the industry by constructing pipelines from the fields to the refinery and from the refinery to the harbor on the Caspian Sea. Transportation facilities were the avenue to the successful marketing of Russian oil because, although American kerosene was thought to be of better quality, its transportation costs were greater. An American consular report of 1886 warned: "Good refined petroleum at Baku commands at present 2 1/2 cents per gallon. If it could be readily transported to Batoum or Poti, on the Black Sea, and thus reach water transportation to Marseilles and other European ports, the days of American petroleum in these countries would soon be numbered."

At that time petroleum was increasingly being used. The world burned 1.5 million gallons a day, which could be supplied by Russia, but Baku's oil route from the Caspian Sea up the Volga

River, by rail across Russia or by rail from Baku over the Caucasus Mountains, at 4,000 feet at one point, to Batoum raised the price of a barrel of oil from 18 to 92 1/2 cents. A proposed pipeline from Baku to Poti on the Black Sea would cost $10 million, of which only $1 million worth of stock had been placed in London. The Russian government would not grant the pipeline until all the money was raised: "The fact is, that the present railway is owned by parties sufficiently powerful in the Russian government to prevent any pipeline or rival railway from being built, and the project is therefore, for the present, at least, definitely abandoned. The Caspian, Volga, Moscow route will make Russian petroleum at Berlin and Antwerp too expensive to seriously threaten American supremacy there."[99]

The Americans were concerned, however, over the Ilskin fields on the Black Sea where Standard Russe (backed by the Rothschilds) produced 100 barrels of light oil, and 400 barrels of heavy lubricating oil daily. Since Russian lubricating oil was cheaper and superior qualitatively to the American, its transport from the Black Sea to European ports was supplanting the use of American lubricating oil in Europe.

To understand the competition between oil producers, one must understand that it took place according to the differing types of oil produced. Crude oil is a mixture of hydrocarbons that have a variety of boiling points and that are separated through the refining process into hundreds of different products. They can be classified into six main types. *Kerosene* or *illuminating oil* was used worldwide by 1890. Standard Oil gave 500,000 lamps to Chinese peasants, followed by free kerosene to open the market in the Far East, and performed the same public relations gesture in Australia, Africa, and South America. *Gas oil*, piped from the refineries to storage depots, was rapidly adapted for illumination and for energy in manufacture after the Otto gas engine was developed in 1872. *Lubricating oil* had been in demand for years by industrializing societies. *Paraffin wax* found early use in, among other things, food preservation. *Fuel oil* (representing the heavier fractions after refining, or after lighter fractions called naphtha, were topped off in a distillation process) quickly found markets in the 1880s. Uses for *petroleum*, the sixth classification, which provided a motive force from a rapid series of explosions, were under experiment in the 1880s.

In 1873 Thomas Urquhart, manager of the Grazi-Tsaritsin railway in Russia, experimented with fuel oil in his locomotive engines and found the cost greatly reduced, the efficiency higher, and the conversion from coal very simple. Within a few years Russian fuel oil replaced coal-burning on all railways, in factories, and in inland water navigation throughout Russia. The Russian government set a high tariff on imported oil to favor its home industry. The Nobels built the first oil tanker in 1879 and soon had a fleet on order from Sweden and England. Having chased American oil out of Russia, the Nobels, together with the Deutsche Bank, founded the Deutsche-Russiche Naphtha-Import Gesellschaft in 1883 to market Russian petroleum in Germany. They transformed the Lingheim Company in Austria into the Oesterreichische Naphtha-Import Gesellschaft to distribute its oil in south Germany and Switzerland. At the same time the Nobels made overtures to the Paris Rothschilds whose access to and control of consumer markets in Europe would be invaluable to them.

Edmund and Alphonse de Rothschild were running a refinery at Fiume on the Adriatic Sea which refined Standard Oil and distributed kerosene into Hungary. In 1879 they financed Alexandre Deutsch de la Meurthe et Fils, a French oil explorer and refiner, in its explorations in Spain and after 1883 in Parma, Italy. The Rothschilds cleverly held the Nobels at arms length while they financed Nobel's Russian competitors, Bunge and Poliakowsky, in 1884 to form a new company, BNITO, and financed a railway from Baku to Batum on the Black Sea. Realizing the potential of Russian oil if it could be cheaply exported, they arranged credit to many small Russian refineries by paying for kerosene in advance and thus making these refineries dependent on them. They took over BNITO in 1886 as the Societe Commerciale et Industrielle de Naphte Caspienne et de la Mer Noire, and pressured the Russian government into favoring a pipeline over the Suram Pass from Mikhailova to Kviril. Thus oil could be sent cheaply to northern Russia and the markets of Northern Europe.

Since their refinery at Fiume now refined Russian oil, the Rothschilds prepared for competition with Standard Oil in 1885 by directing Deutsche de la Meurthe et Fils to form a French refiners' syndicate with Ferraille et Despaux and Desmarais Freres. The syndicate combatted Standard Oil, which by lowering oil supplies had at times forced French refiners to sell out to it. Now with Russian oil and Rothschild backing, the French syndicate attracted the seven remaining French refiners to it and brought Standard Oil to terms: Standard would supply crude oil at low prices and not interfere with French refining if the Syndicate agreed to regulate the import of Russian oil into France (through Nobel's agent, Andre and Company) to proportions set by Standard.

Meanwhile, in 1886 the Rothschilds finally advanced the Nobel brothers the capital needed in their fight with the Rockefellers and formed a Russian syndicate of the Nobel firm, Naphtha-Produktionsgesellschaft, the S. A. Tagjeff Company, the Caspian refinery Aracloff, and the Rothschild firm of Baku-Naphtha. Later, in 1893, the Rothschilds built a second syndicate of 135 Naphtha industrial firms at Rostow. In that same year, they merged it with the Nobel group, so that henceforth Russian oil was known as Nobel-Rothschild. The Nobels' agent in England, the Bessler-Waechter Company, was underselling American oil because of cheaper delivery by the Nobels' oil tankers. By 1888 Nobel as well as the Rothschilds, who had opened two English distributing companies, had 30 percent of the English market. The shipping firm, Lane and MacAndrew, who had helped Nobel in its shipping trade, brought one of the largest houses in the Eastern trade, Wallace Brothers, into the Rothschild orbit for shipping oil to the Far East to undersell Standard Oil there. In 1891 the same firm negotiated an oil-shipping contract between the Paris Rothschilds and Marcus-Samuel and Company, traders to the East in shells and lamps, soon to be known as Shell Oil.

Standard Oil fought back through its five German subsidiaries. The new sense of nationalism in Germany, however, brought fears of dependence on foreign oil in the event of war. The German government declined to nationalize the companies lest it could not guarantee oil supplies, but it encouraged the Deutsche Bank to finance exploration in the Galician and Romanian oilfields where the Bank founded the most important Romanian oil company, Steaunu Romana, in the mid-1890s. The Deutsche Bank's role from 1883 as founder of the Nobel's Naphtha-Import Gesellschaft allied it with Russian oil in fierce competition with Standard Oil. Until 1904 it also competed with the Rothschilds. By 1895 Standard Oil sued for peace with the Rothschild-Nobel group, agreed to divide the European market, and kept only 40 percent of the oil consumption markets of northeast Germany and England.

The Germans, who often had complained of the ups and downs of the oil price war between the Rockefellers and Rothschilds, must have been pleased by the agreement. Unfortunately, it did not end the war over petroleum. As the leading adviser in the Deutsche Bank, Kilian Steiner tried to benefit its alliance with Nobel against the dreaded monopolists of Rockefeller and Rothschild as early as 1886 when he made overtures to the fledgling Daimler Motoren-Gesellschaft in Unterturkheim, the only builder of petroleum engines.

Another circumstance that no doubt directed Steiner's attention to the possibilities of the petroleum engine was the merger in 1886 of the German general dynamite and gunpowder cartel with the British Nobel factories, in which Steiner played a major role. Negotiations had continued out of Hamburg for some years owing to Alfred Nobel's determination to combat the glycerine interests which kept raising the price of an indispensable material. Steiner's associate, Max Duttenhofer, whom he had set in charge of the Rottweiler gunpowder factory, was given a seat on the board of this worldwide Nobel trust. It was Duttenhofer, an old friend of Gottlieb Daimler, who made the personal overtures to Daimler for Steiner in 1886, and, no doubt, for Alfred Nobel, who had heavily financed the Nobel oil company and was anxious for it to expand its consumer markets.

Actually, Steiner's grouping of the Daimler Company within his industrial empire, when he finally took it over in 1890, reflects his conception of it as military. His successful melding of the Mauser weapons factory with the giant Berlin armaments firm of Ludwig Loewe and Company, thus magnifying its capitalization, his joining to it of the Deutsche Mettalpatronenfabrik in Karlsruhe in 1878, and finally his binding of the much enlarged Rottweiler gunpowder factory to this group, made a powerful syndicate or "Vertrustungspolitik," which took two-thirds of the shares of the Daimler Motoren-Gesellschaft. Since the syndicate was controlled by the Vereinsbank, Kilian Steiner made the decisions for the Daimler Company. In 1891 Steiner took control of the military gunpowder supply for the German nation.

Gottlieb Daimler had to surrender his firm and accept one-third of the shares because the success of his gasoline motors in the late 1880s required a capitalization far greater than he could manage. Moreover, Duttenhofer had been pestering him to form a stock company for years, promising him that he would keep control of the works. Daimler's wife had been pleading with him to let up on his long gruelling work-day, a habit from his early apprenticeships in metal and machine factories, so that he could spend time with his family and look after his failing health. When his wife died suddenly in 1889, Daimler gave in, though not without misgivings.

Daimler had the foresight to secure an American agent, William Steinway, for his automobile patents in the United States, and his motor launches were becoming widely popular even in Germany and England, which forbade the automobile. However, he soon encountered difficulties with his fellow shareholders.

Max Duttenhofer of the Rottweil gunpowder factory and Wilhelm Lorenz of the Karlsruhe metalmaking factory, despite promises to the contrary, ignored his suggestions, appointed managers and engineers, and interpreted the agreement of 1890 as a mandate for developing a stationary engine that could compete with the Deutz Company's gas engine sales to factories. Indeed, Duttenhofer almost merged the firm with Deutz.

Instead of my efforts being allowed full scope (Daimler complained in an open letter) so that the experience I have gained which as the originator of the petrol engine, places me in a preferential position to other members of the Company, may be turned to the best possible account without undue restrictions, I found myself, from the very beginning, held in check by the majority of the Directors and by the Chairman in a wholly unjustified manner and which increased in severity as time went on; I was deprived of all initiative and even my honour was attacked, all of which operated to the detriment of the Company.... I was, moreover, specially anxious to ensure . . . that my authority should be recognized and respected in accordance with the provisions come to previously on July 1886 between Herr Duttenhofer and myself. It seemed to me that the act of joining issues with these gentlemen would secure this because they had previously given me this assurance both personally and in writing....

After careful study of the law about joint-stock holdings I have come to the conclusion that the form in which my position as Director of the Company was assured is inadmissable according to Section 249 of the Book of Commercial Law, and it would bring me into conflict with the law if I were to make use of the concessions granted to me.

In addition, I find that my position, as a Director, is limited to a comparatively short period, and when this has expired, my authority in the management of the business will cease.[100]

Responding to Daimler's efforts to invalidate the contract or to buy out the other two-thirds of the shares, Kilian Steiner's brother, Herman, who acted as solicitor for the firm, wrote:

His [Daimler's] latest demand about the first agreement with Lorenz and Duttenhofer is simply ridiculous; this agreement became absolutely null and void by the establishment of the company and the syndicate agreement. The claim on the joint use of the patents is just absurd and does not warrant a serious reply....

To this Daimler replied, dispelling their belief in his political naiveté:

When he [Steiner] described my wish, for joint use of patents, as "just absurd," he has used an expression which can justly be applied to the method you adopted when you made a present of the Daimler master-patent to the Gas Engine Manufacturing Company of Deutz....

My demand for maintaining my direct relations with the owner of my patents in France and in the United States, was obviously in the interests of all parties; if your solicitor, Herr Steiner, suspects that in acting thus, there is something underhand in progress, he just shows that he lacks the necessary experience and insight into matters affecting patents.[101]

What was "underhand," of course, was the French development of the petroleum automobile.

Daimler's secret meeting with Levassor and Peugeot at Valentigny in November 1888 reveals that petroleum producers were not directly involved in the initial stage. The German industrialists' wish to restrict the petroleum engine to a stationary engine and the relative freedom to drive mechanical vehicles in

France (since the 1866 arrete was not enforced in the 1890s) made France the logical choice for the development of the automobile. The van Zuylen-cum-Rothschild petroleum interest in the automobile became evident with its investment in de Dion-Bouton in 1894, the year in which the petroleum automobile proved its viability in the Paris-Rouen road endurance test.

This was one year after the Rothschilds and the Nobels merged their Russian oil firms to gain monopoly control of Russian oil. This merger, however, did not affect the Nobel-Deutsche Bank petroleum alliance and the continuing battle between the Rothschilds and the Deutsche Bank over European petroleum markets, an antagonism that was exacerbated by the general conviction that war between Germany and France was imminent. Van Zuylen's encouragement of Bouton to invent a light petroleum engine to compete with Daimler's engine appears to be an extension of the battle for markets.

Impressed with the potential demonstrated by the Daimler automobile in the run between Paris and Rouen, the Rothschilds would have understood that the German entrepreneur, despite his pig-headed antagonism to the automobile, was now bound to recognize the value of the Daimler patents which he owned. On the other hand, long before they invested in the petroleum automobile, the Rothschilds were involved in industries other than petroleum which could benefit from the development of the automobile.

After 1870 the application of electricity required increased production of copper which had been exploited by small firms dependent on loans from English smelting companies and large merchant bankers such as the Rothschilds who thereby controlled the industry. Gradually there was overproduction and a fall in price prompting the Comptoir d'Escompte (now directed by E. Denfert-Rochereau), PARIBAS, and the Paris Rothschilds to form the Societe Industrielle des Metaux in 1887 in order to fix the price. The syndicate overspeculated, sought English capital, and when the Comptoir d'Escompte failed, Denfert-Rochereau committed suicide, sparking a panic as people tried to recover their money. The ensuing copper crash and the demise of the Comptoir d'Escompte were said to be engineered by the Paris Rothschilds (who, it is said, could have found the capital to save the situation) because the Comptoir had been taking away from the Rothschilds the business of floating Russian loans. Both the American and English capitalists who had dominated the industry were suspected of aiding the Rothschilds in order to clear the field of this new French competition.[102]

Just as copper was being used in boat-making and land transport machinery, so other metals were being discovered and exploited for use in light machinery. This is a significant point when considering the development of the automobile. Because of its lightness and flexibility, aluminum (discovered in 1845) contributed to the development of light and fast automobiles. A heating method to bring it to a purified state brought the price down from 3,000 francs a kilogram in 1854 to 140 francs in 1863. By passing an electric current through it, the purification process was cheapened to 102 francs per kilogram in 1884, 15 francs in 1892, and 9 francs in 1893, which allowed it to come into general use as automobile construction began on a large scale. The Paris Rothschilds invested in aluminum, through Bernard Freres, in the early 1890s.

Of the three sources of energy--steam, electricity, and petroleum--which competed in the early automobile industry, electricity and petroleum represented industrial domains in which there was savage competition and from which great sums of capital could be commanded should their capitalists decide to exploit the automobile for the sake of providing a profitable consumer market for their investments in those fields. The involvement of these capitalists with the armaments industry later brought many of them to look on the automobile primarily as an instrument of war. But in the main it was the competition for markets between petroleum monopolists that provided the impetus for the development of the automobile industry, and this required the foundation of a resurgent national capital, such as the French were experiencing.

The petroleum automobile attracted not only large financial backing but also the continuous interest of investment banks as the industry developed. This financial support, however, did not appear until petroleum capitalists needed to expand consumer outlets owing to two developments: first, electricity began to replace kerosene and petroleum as a source for illumination in the 1880s; and, second, the competition among the big oil producers, Rockefeller's Standard, Rothschild's BNITO, and the Nobel brothers brought immense pressure to find ways of using oil profitably to relieve them of the glut of supply and the need for price wars, rebates to local refiners, and expensive government intrigue. As Alphonse de Rothschild confessed: "The rivalry of Russian oil producers with the Russian trade and moreover, on the other hand, from the American Co. was disastrous indeed for the whole world."[103]

The involvement of the Paris Rothschilds' bank in automobile production and automobile popularization brought their banking rivals into the industry. Aside from the interest of the Societe Generale de Belgique in the de Dion-Bouton Company, Swiss banks invested in the Richard and Peugeot motor car companies. The Banque de Paris et des Pays-Bas and two other French banks financed the separation of the French plant of Lorraine-Dietrich

116

motor cars from its Alsatian firm in 1905. The Zafiropulo brothers, bankers from Marseilles and owners of European oilfields, took over the Rochet-Schneider bicycle firm in Lyons in 1898 and devoted it to petroleum automobile production for the luxury market.

10. The Count de Dion in his factory, after a drawing by Frederic Regamey

117

14

Profitability of the Automobile Relative to the Railway and Canals in France

The losses suffered by the Rothschild Bardon Company were expected. This company was set up as a supplier to the industry, as a financial intermediary, because it was the automobile industry which the Rothschilds were interested in promoting, not a particular automobile company (other than the de Dion-Bouton and Richard-Unic companies). They would have continued to run the Bardon Company at a loss if the industrial recession of 1907 had not snuffed out many of the small automobile companies and obviated its usefulness.

If we look closely at the finances of the earliest petroleum automobile manufacturer, Panhard-Levassor, we find that revenue from its automobiles quickly outdistanced its income from wood-working machines. See Table 9.

Table 9
Panhard Levassor's Revenue, 1895-1910

Capital Turnover

	Automobiles	Woodworking Machines	Total	Industrial Profit
1895-99	-------	------	6,887,000	3,426,000
1903-04	15,771,000	1,375,000	17,146,000	7,904,000
1904-05	-------	-------	21,625,000	10,671,000
1905-06	19,724,000	1,576,000	21,300,000	--------
1906-08	--------	-------	14,000,000	5,554,000
1908-09	---------	-------	17,589,000	7,980,000
1909-10	--------	-------	23,471,000	9,595,000

Percentage of Profit to Capital Turnover

1898-99	49%	1906-07	32%
1903-04	45%	1907-08	39%
1904-05	49%	1908-09	45%
1905-06	--	1909-10	41%

Michele Flageolet-Lardenois, who researched these figures, commented:

We can draw some succinct conclusions. The wood-working machines represented a minute fraction of the capital turnover. They served as a life buoy in case of difficulty. The crisis of 1907 left a deep imprint on the results. The proportion of industrial profit to capital turnover is remarkable for a French industry (even exceptional): "It maintained its profitability despite the generally low price of vehicles. That was owing to the improvement in the tool-making and work methods," which led to a reduction in the cost price.[104]

Despite these signs of great profitability for the automobile industry, the opportunity to make these profits was open to very few large capitalists. The general opinion of the time was that automobiles could take away local or short-distance transport from railways, which caused passengers to wait at transfer stations and other inconveniences. For long distances, however, the automobile would never compete with railways. On the other hand, the railways had encountered financial trouble beginning with a serious falling away of investment in railway construction after 1884. A marked regression in passenger traffic, which became catastrophic between 1883 and 1887, did not reverse to an increase in traffic until after 1905. By the Freycinet Plan and Railway Conventions of 1883, the state guaranteed not only the interest on the bonds issued by the railway companies but also, within agreed-on limits, the dividends on the stocks. A critic of the railways, Edgard Milhaud, wrote:

The companies offer in effect a magnificent target for the opponents of capitalism. The capital invested in the railways represented, in 1895, about 20 thousand million francs (4 thousand million in shares and 16 thousand million in loans) about half of the fixed capital of France, figured by P. Leroy-Beaulieu at 38-40 thousand million, and one tenth to one twelfth of the total wealth of the country which has been estimated between 200 and 250 thousand million.[105]

It was predicted that the state's guarantee on the interest of the bonds would amount to 60 million francs in 1888 and as much as 176 million in 1895. But the railway companies made reforms that brought in greater revenues, so that within six years receipts increased by 195 million francs, more than 15 percent. Thus, the amount of the state guarantee on the interest fell by 80 percent in six years. The companies achieved these savings by reducing their expenses. For instance, the PLM reduced its expenses by 8 million francs, paid off its loans from the state, and became profitable. Despite opposition to the freight rates by the small producers in the countryside, the railways developed with sufficient capital between 1883 and 1914 to bring about "beneficial exploitation."

Nevertheless, as we have seen, railways were not interesting investments for the great capitalists of France after 1860. In addition, the iron and steel industry had good reason to be disappointed in the railways because of the decline in the construction of new rail lines. According to F. Caron, this decline was connected with the companies' efforts to decrease expenses. Aside from the burst of new construction of local lines after the Freycinet Conventions of 1883, the railway construction picture presented a bleak future to industrialists. New construction averages for 1854-1906 were as follows:

1854 to 1867, 833 kilometers
1868 to 1879, 587   "
1880 to 1885, 1128 "
1886 to 1892, 666   "
1893 to 1906, 322   "

The annual sale of rails to the companies paralleled this drastic decline. The judgment was, therefore, that the railway industry, though viable, was not healthy.

Meanwhile, the railways were threatened by canal and river transport in the competition over long-distance traffic. Beginning in 1880 all tolls on the canals and riverways were suppressed, thus creating an extraordinary development in commercial transport by water in France. The canals were not as easily victimized by the railways in France as in England because they were owned by the state and were open to the public at a small cost.

The figures shown in Table 10, expressed as percentages, illustrate that canal traffic over the whole of France maintained a steady share of business and that rail traffic accelerated after 1855.[106] The table also illustrates the rapid decline in road traffic in France. The railways eliminated stage-coaching in France just as in England. The automobile seems to have made no impression as a competitor for traffic between 1895 and 1913. Its main role was as a private means of transport.

120

Table 10
Interior Transport in France

	Passengers Carried		Traffic in Merchandise			
	Roads	Rail	Roads	Canals	Rail	Sea
1830	100	--	53	18	--	29
1841-44	85	15	49	23	3	25
1845-54	65	35	43	28	7	22
1855-64	36	64	31	23	35	11
1865-74	25	75	24	16	53	7
1875-84	19	81	17	14	63	5
1885-94	15	85	15	18	60	8
1895-1904	7	93	12	19	62	8
1905-13	6	94	9	18	67	6

The introduction of the automobile industry may have helped to stimulate the French economy, but its limitation to a few major producers and its smallness relative to other industries belie the supposition that it was introduced solely to stimulate the economy. Moreover, the automobile industry was not introduced as a cost-saving technology because it did not replace the railways which independently reduced their own costs under threat of being nationalized. On the other hand, perhaps entrepreneurs saw the automobile industry as a successor to other industrial technologies, such as the profitable bicycle industry. We will examine the industries preceding and subsidiary to the automobile industry to determine whether this may be the reason for the development of the automobile.

15

Technological Determinism as a Mode of Development

James Laux, the historian of the French automobile, argues that the automobile industry developed from the bicycle industry.[107] His first point, that mechanical devices were adapted for the automobile from the bicycle, should be stated in reverse. The steam carriage inventors developed devices that were used for bicycles. Robert Thomson's 1873 steam carriage, for example, had pneumatic tires. We have seen free-wheeling, speed gears, and so on in Gurney's steam cars. Laux's second point, that the automobile inherited bicycle assembling techniques, overlooks the fact that other industries used the techniques, which were attributable to the general level of technology. That the practice of making standardized interchangeable parts for bicycles was carried into automobile production is true, but this did not happen until after 1900 in America. Europeans did not pick it up until some years after automobile production was an established industry. The practice had been used in arms manufacture for decades. His third point, that the bicycle psychologically prepared a market for automobiles, is a romantic notion belied by the enthusiasm for private steam carriages which was in evidence as early as 1832.

The carriage industry, on the other hand, did not give birth to the motor car. Automobile engineers simply installed their engines in carriages, the only known form of passenger vehicle. As early as 1881 English carriage-makers formed a protective association in imitation of French and American coachmakers, but the constriction of their trade and the economic hardships they endured did not produce the automobile. Panhard and Levassor made saws and machinery, not coaches, though Panhard came from a coachmaking family which bore an influence on the firm's design of automobiles. Indeed, until 1898 in Paris the principal automobile manufacturers used only three carriage-making firms:

Bellavette, Labourdette, and Muhlbacher. New carriage builders entering the business that year were Felber, Rothschild, Bail-Pozzi, Hannoyer, Boulogne, and Kellner. In England after the passage of the Locomotives on Highways Bill in 1896, the carriagemakers watched the flotation of automobile companies with wonder and native caution.

As in bicycle-making, carriage-making offered techniques that were useful to automobile manufacturers—techniques of the following workers gathered together to make carriages: woodworkers, bodymakers, undercarriage makers, wheelmakers, blacksmiths, trimmers or workers in leather and cloth, painters, draughtsmen, and designers. It offered the services of subsidiary industries as well: special steel and iron work; fittings in ivory, silver, and varnished wood; and fabrics in silk and cloth. English coachmakers, on hearing that an antagonism had arisen between carriage builders and mechanics in France, called on engineers to help them develop structural changes in the automobile to give it the grace and lightness it lacked. The best way to keep motor-carriage building in the coachmakers' hands, they advised, was to look out for the best motor. Then the coachmaker, "owing to his special knowledge of carriage construction and suspension," could keep the industry as a distinct branch of his operations. Yet, here we emphasize, coachmakers gravitated to the automobile industry after it began.

Tool- and machinemakers contributed to the automobile industry more than the bicycle and carriage industries. Gurney was fortunate that men such as Joseph Bramah and his apprentice, Henry Maudslay, had developed metal-cutting and drilling tools. Maudslay improved the lathe in 1800 by combining the slide rest with change gears and a power-driven lead screw. By 1820 machine tools used steam power. Drilling machines using flat drills were available. The screw-cutting compound slide rest lathe was the most important tool perfected in the 1830s. Machine tools were designed according to the low cutting speeds of the tempered carbon steel, averaging 15 feet per minute. With wrought iron the cutting speed increased to 25 feet per minute, and with brass, to 40 feet per minute. For boring, the speeds were approximately 50 percent higher. Maudslay introduced the standardized screwing tackle which laid the basis for the nationwide standardization of screw threads by one of his mechanics, Joseph Whitworth, whose screw-cutting lathe pioneered precision work in large-scale engineering and in whose machine factory Daimler worked for a time. Both Peugeot and Panhard and Levassor made tools and machinery. They, therefore, were best prepared to begin manufacuring automobiles in France. Daimler and Maybach had spent their lives in tool and machinemaking factories. Nevertheless, the automobile industry did not rise out of the improved tool and machine industries, as technological determinists might claim.

Gurney, in 1823, and Amedee Bollee, in 1870, complained about the paucity of tools for making automobiles, but they made them, as did many other engineers throughout the century. In Coventry, England, where bicycles were first built as an addition to an ailing sewing machine industry, automobiles were built as an addition to an ailing bicycle industry. The later industry benefited from the tools and skills fashioned by the previous industry. But automobile firms grew from varied backgrounds such as marine engineers such as Vauxhall, gas-and-oil-engine makers such as Crossley, riflemakers such as Birmingham Small Arms, and toolmakers such as the Maudslay Motor Company.

Indeed, there is an internal dynamic to the industrial production process whereby solutions to technical limitations are developed in machinery through the interaction of capitalists to reduce production cost or improve the end product. But when we use the case of the automobile as an example, we find that a new production process can be hindered from developing despite the overcoming of the technical limitations. In this case, competition among capitalists led to an invention but fettered its diffusion. The growth of the automobile industry in France in the 1890s, therefore, was not induced from the influence of profitable industries preceding it.

As regards subsidiary industries, only after the automobile industry began did French industrialists view it as providing a market for the iron and steel industry which had been suffering from the decline in railway construction.

The interest of certain industrialists in the petroleum automobile, such as the Marquis de Chasseloup-Laubat, the foremost railway industrial magnate in France and a director of Schneider-Creusot, does indicate a certain impetus to automobile development arising from the iron and steel industries of France. Is it possible that this rising class of French industrialists in the Third Republic developed the automobile industry as a mode of production to meet the marketing needs of the nation?

The composition of the judging committee for the 1894 Paris-Rouen road endurance test is informative for the shades of interest in the automobile which it reflected. Aside from van Zuylen, de Dion, Henri Menier (the chocolate tycoon who became the second vice-president of the Auto Club), and Andre Lehidieux (the Parisian investment banker who became Club treasurer), we find an Englishman, Sir David Salomons, who belonged to the family that helped introduce English capital in the establishment of railways in France and who had decades of close relations with the Rothschild family. There was also an American, James Gordon Bennett, owner of the Paris *Herald*, whose name became immortalized in automobile history for the international race he promoted. With him was a Vanderbilt who represented the Rockefeller interest. We also find the Marquis and the Comte de Chasseloup-Laubat, father and son, both of whom led in organizing the Paris-Bordeaux and later races.

The railway and metallurgical interests in automobiles represented by the Chasseloup-Laubats reflected the desire for investment in promising new fields by capitalists disillusioned with the poor returns from railways during the long depression.

16

The Promotion of Petrol over Steam

Baron van Zuylen and the Comte de Dion became president and vice-president, respectively, of the Automobile Club de France which was formed under the committee that organized the Paris-Bordeaux automobile race in 1895. This club became a powerful force for the promotion of the automobile in Europe, and among its founders were proponents of petroleum and electric automobiles. It did not include steam carriage proponents such as Leon Serpollet, gas-engine promoters such as Emile Roger (who having redesigned Benz cars to four wheels and a four-stroke engine was successfully marketing them outside Germany), and Peugeot, whose petroleum automobiles had done well in the race to Bordeaux and back. The makeup of the members is the more interesting since Serpollet, Roger, and Peugeot were present at the meeting in 1894 which planned the 723-mile Paris-Bordeaux race. Marquis de Chasseloup-Laubat remarked later: "The characteristic feature of the race of 1895 is the triumph of petroleum over steam."[108] Perhaps the steam carriage promoters lost some prestige when eight petrol cars and just one Bollee steam omnibus returned to Paris. These results echoed those of the 78-mile Paris-Rouen road test the previous year in which only one steam carriage finished.

The titled distinction and great wealth of the members of the Auto Club, including railway financiers, bankers, industrialists, and distinguished automobilists, implied a restriction in the use of the automobile: that is, it should be allowed to go no lower than the upper middle class. Possibly Armand Peugeot excluded himself from the group inasmuch as he was a member of the reserved Protestant clan of the Montbeliard region on the Swiss border. Moreover, he formed an automobile company in 1896, separate from the great Peugeot industrial works, the shares of which were taken up by family and friends. If he ever needed more capital than his family could provide, he could call on his cousins, the Koechlins, industrialists in Alsace, or on the Swiss banking capital that had been at the Peugeots' service for decades. Peugeot, therefore, was in a class apart from the Parisian high society.

The electrical car promoters in the club were represented by men such as Charles Jeantaud, owner of a fashionable carriage factory in Paris who produced electric cabs that achieved some popularity in the 1890s. The problem with electric cars, however, was that they could not be taken far from the recharging centers, and, unlike petroleum cars, which had petrol depots throughout the countryside (Peugeot published an annual listing of petrol and repair stations), electric cars could not risk traveling far from the cities. Moreover, in France one drove with a chauffeur who was expected to look after any problems that might arise with a petrol engine. In the United States, on the other hand, electric cars were more popular in the beginning years because ladies liked to drive themselves in the cities and found them less complicated to handle.

The big electrical companies which might have promoted electric cars found that they could not compete with steam carriage companies because the primary battery that produced electrical power cost twenty times more than steam power. Steam carriage companies were sweeping Europe and the United States with steam street railways, but after 1888 electric street cars with overhead feeder lines replaced steam in the United States. This was ten years before they appeared in Europe because the Europeans objected on aesthetic grounds to overhead lines and instead placed them underground at twice the operating cost.

At the Autocar Congress in Paris in 1900 Amedee Bollee claimed that steam carriages, owing to the large boiler required, could only be considered for tramways and heavy industry. Many others whose interests were in the electric and petroleum automobiles voiced this opinion. And to drive his point home, Bollee stated that twenty years' experience with steam cars had taught him that a vehicle costing 14,000 francs would last only five years during which it would need 15,000 francs for repairs. It was at this point that the Comte de Chasseloup-Laubat moved that manufacturers give preference to watertube boilers for heavy steam cars and to internal combustion engines for light cars. Many automobile promoters resented this obvious political pressure on the market to adopt petrol cars, and they began to suspect the Automobile Club of France and the road races it sponsored as a method to discredit steam cars. For instance, in the race of 1,061 miles from Paris to Marseilles and back in September 1896, twenty-nine of the thirty-two cars returned to Paris; the three that broke down were the only steam cars in the race. Yet, unexpectedly, and perhaps embarrassingly, in the Marseilles-Nice-Turbie race of 145 miles in January 1897, which was meant to test the practical value of the cars over heavy downgrading, Chasseloup-Laubat's steam car came in first.

Opponents of the Automobile Club published the *Velo* newspaper, demanded that the authorities stop issuing permits for road races, formed the Union Automobile de France, and elected Leon Serpollet, the steam car promoter, as its president. The Automobile Club, sensing a threat to its authority, replied through its official organ, the *Auto-Velo*, by disqualifying all contests or trials organized by the Union Automobile de France. The New York *Horseless Age* commented: "That an organization of the strength of the Union Automobile, whose members to a large extent are in the automobile business in order to gain a livelihood and who do not look upon the movement as a fad, could be forced out of existence by a resolution of a rival club, which follows, however, quite different lines, is highly improbable to say the least."[109] But the Auto Club de France had a "treaty" with five French clubs, eight European clubs, and the Automobile Club of America in New York that they would follow its lead; consequently, the Union Automobile had to disband in August 1901.

In May 1902, the Automobile Club formed the Association Generale Automobile "to aid the progress of the extension of industries related to automobilism and to bring together for the defense of their common interests, all those who design, build, sell or own motor vehicles, as well as those taking an interest in mechanical locomotion." The association offered technical, administrative, legislative, legal, and financial help "to establish or to aid in the establishment of stations for gasoline and alcohol and stations with electric charging facilities."[110] The battle line between petrol and electric cars on one side and steam cars on the other was becoming clear. The quarrel over sports car elitism versus practical middle-class vehicles simply concealed this real issue, although it was well known that petroleum automobile manufacturers needed the hoopla of races to attract buyers from the sporting and monied classes, whereas steam carriage promoters sold to an established market of tradesmen and professional people.

Leon Serpollet, however, determined to beat the petrol automobile with his steam car in racing competition. As early as 1833, Richard Trevithick had invented a boiler which obviated any need to add water because the original water could be constantly reused. Serpollet now developed the flash boiler by which water was injected through a metallic tube and instantly transformed into vapor, thus creating "le generateur inexplosible" and replacing the boiler. The tube's wide surface passed over the fire grate. Should Serpollet wish to accelerate, he would inject a little water from his reserve into the tube or tubes where it became instantly hot and arrived at the motor under great tension. This superheating gave steam its power and allowed the driver to manipulate the vehicle, speeding up, slowing down, on the instant. Serpollet also did away with coke for fuel by substituting an oil burner, thus reducing the bulk. By running the oil burner by a pump in tandem with the water pump, Serpollet could feed the engine proportionately. With simple valves that opened and closed quickly, the steam car's motor was uncomplicated, completely sealed against dust, strong, and indestructible.

Using the capital of a rich American, Frank Gardner, Serpollet built steam speedsters that found markets in France and England. He entered his Gardner-Serpollet steam car in the Paris-Nice race of 1902 and 1903, came first, and set a speed record of 130 km per hour in 1903. Despite the publicity from his victories, the sale of small steam cars for personal use declined. The Gardner-Serpollet company went bankrupt the following year, and steam cars were put irrevocably out of competition.

The rivalry between steam and petrol car promoters continued in the United States but was cut short in Europe owing to the superior sources of capital open to the petroleum automobile manufacturers. Aiding the progress of the petroleum automobile were the interlocking relationships among the Rothschilds with petroleum and national railway interests, other bankers financing the national economy, and the metallurgists who through amalgamations became a small and powerful leadership for the national purpose. This group consolidated its political strength through the Comite des Forges from 1890 to 1898 and organized all branches of French industries, including the mechanic and electric, between 1898 and 1903 under its seigneurity.

The automobile companies consolidated their business by expanding horizontally. For instance, in 1901 van Zuylen and de Dion established, for thirty years' duration, the Compagnie des Messageries Automobiles (Puteaux) which bought and sold automobiles, equipment, garages, and so on, and granted concessions for tramways and all routes of communication. In 1899 Armand Peugeot and French and French-Swiss colleagues set up a similar company, the Societe des Voitures Automobiles de Franche-Comte (Quingy).

The petroleum automobile manufacturers consolidated their position vertically after World War I when the Comite des Forges created as one of its subgroups "La Federation nationale de l'automobile, du cycle, de l'aeronautique et des industries des transports," of which de Dion was president. The organization contained twelve separate syndicates dealing with all aspects of the automobile industry and its suppliers.

11. Automobile race on the road from Triel to Meulan, from a drawing by Louis Blombed in 1896 (John Grand-Carteret, *Voiture de demain*, Paris, 1898).

The decisive factor in the victory of the petroleum over the steam automobile, however, was the international influence of the Automobile Club de France, which, owing to its promotion by the Rothschilds, benefited from the international connections of the Rothschilds. Thus, the French exported the petroleum automobile, influenced automobile makers and dealers in countries following the French lead to develop petroleum automobiles, and gained for French petroleum auto manufacturers an insuperable advantage over the steam car industry by winning the revenue from the international market. The activities of automobile manufacturers in England, Germany, and America confirm the decisive influence of French petroleum producers

17

The Diffusion of the Petroleum Automobile

ENGLAND

The Political-Economic Formation in the 1890s

The railway interests in England, as in France, were on the defensive. "How far ought savings to be embarked in railway ordinary stocks?" asked the *Investor's Review* in 1892. "Looking at the high market premiums on many of these stocks, and at the smallness of the return they give at current dividends, it seems obvious that the small investor ought to avoid the bulk of these stocks altogether."[111]

The English railways were scrutinized for their gross earnings per mile as against their capital expenses (Table 11).

Table 11
Increases in Gross Earnings and Capital Expenses of English Railways, 1869-1899

Years	Total Receipts	Working Expenses	Ratio to Receipts	Net Revenue	Ratio to Capital Paid-up
	L	L	%	L	%
INCREASES ONLY					
1869-99	55,971,138	39,310,609	10	19,660,529	0.61
1879-99	39,890,362	28,045,414	7	11,844,948	0.54
1889-99	24,642,048	19,966,571	7	4,645,477	0.60
1894-99	17,356,234	12,882,374	3	4,473,800	0.16

From 1871 throughout 1880 the paid-up capital of the railways increased 13 2/3 percent, whereas the gross earnings per mile open rose 14 1/2 percent. From 1880 through 1890, however, the capital spent rose 23 percent, and the earnings per train mile 8

132

1/2 percent. ". . . nothing short of a substitution of capital for revenue, in meeting working charges and repairs . . . can keep up the dividends upon the ordinary stocks." The figures looked ominous.[112] The fall in profits was blamed on the increase in working expenses, over £39 million or 200 percent within the past thirty years, more than one-half of which was chargeable to the past ten years.

Two other points worried the investors: (1) the increase in capitalization from £34,100 per mile in 1870 to £53,100 per mile in 1899, and (2) the decrease in the proportion of passenger receipts to total earnings by 5.68 percent. On the first count, railway management had to take the blame for poor planning; on the second count, the increasing demand for more, easier, and cheaper transportation must have accounted for the very low average receipt of 9 3/4 pence per passenger journey in 1899 as against 1 s. 8 1/2 d. in 1859.

Railway companies defended the fact that rates in some counties were higher than those in others because richer counties helped to subsidize the poorer counties, but they had difficulty explaining why imported produce was charged a lower freight rate than home-grown produce. The Railway Association's parliamentary committee found itself confronted by a series of new opponents, such as the Farmers' Alliance formed as early as 1879, joined by the Central Chamber of Agriculture and followed by the Railway and Canal Traders Association.

Meanwhile, the number of railway directors in the House of Commons was declining and, by preference of the companies, was shifting from largely a Liberal to a Conservative representation. As the Liberals became state interventionist, they lost their free-trade reputation and were seen as dangerous to property rights. But the parliamentary Conservatives, traditionally defenders of protection for home produce, had difficulty forwarding the railway interest while bodies among them such as the Fair Trade League were rising to do battle with the freight rates. In 1889 all of the bodies antagonistic to railways (including chambers of commerce and agriculture) formed the Mansion House Association, which after 1891 became the premier negotiating body on behalf of the fair traders in Parliament.

An M.P., George John Shaw-Lefevre, presented a draft report of the issue in 1893: "The railway companies cannot be considered as exempt from the ordinary fluctuations in the trade of the country, or as being justified in raising their rates at any time in order to maintain their dividends at the expense of the other traders." This sentiment was echoed in the Railway and Canal Traffic Act of 1894.

The railways in symbolizing the greedy rise of the monied class had to bear a social guilt for the catastrophic situation of English agriculture after 1880.

Before [1875] for many years the price of wheat had never fallen below fifty shillings a quarter. Thereafter, it dropped steadily, reaching a figure of 23 s 1 d in 1895.... The causes were clear enough. The development of railways opened up the virgin wheat lands, first of the North American prairies, and a little later of the Argentine.... The collapse of prices meant an equal collapse of rent. Farmers went bankrupt, and landlords were ruined.... The greatest of the nation's industries was simply and completely ruined; perhaps the worst and biggest instance of crass ignorant stupidity produced by the dreadful thirst for money and power.[113]

In response to a strong protectionist resolution arising from a Conference on the Depression of Agriculture organized by Conservatives, who also formed a National Agricultural Union to abolish preferential railway rates for foreign produce, the Liberal government set up a Royal Commission on Agriculture to take volumes of evidence from 1894 through 1896. The concern of the class responsible for running the country was shifting dramatically to side with agriculture.

A greater danger to the railway companies arose in the shape of the Railway Nationalization League which was supported by the Amalgamated Society of Railway Servants. Company attacks on the Railway Servants coupled with the indiscriminate raising of freight rates to the maximum allowed by law caused the public to see the railway interest as politically on the extreme right.

Stockholders organized "rebellions" against the railway directorships which were disproportionately influenced by landed interests and biased toward the self-interest of coalowners, brewers, shipowners, and steelmasters of whom they were comprised. Many English industries opposed them as well: iron and steel in Birmingham, cutlery in Sheffield, sugar refining, gun and watchmaking, ribbon, bicycle, boot and shoe, shipbuilding, tinplate and silk, demanded an end to Britain's free-trade policy of which the railways were the backbone. These contradictory forces within the Conservative Party forced the railway companies into accommodation with the Conservative government on "reform issues" as Great Britain's economic position rapidly deteriorated vis-a-vis the growing strength of Germany and France.

Between 1892 and 1895 first the Liberals and then the Conservatives abandoned free trade. The government shifted emphasis to developing agricultural production and intercolonial reciprocity, which provided an economic climate for the automobile.

The French-German Automobile Rivalry in England

English automobilists were confronted by the restrictive law of 1878 by which, as late as February 1896, an Englishman was fined sixpence plus nineteen shillings sixpence in costs for neglecting to have a man precede his Panhard and Levassor motor carriage. Two groups, led respectively by Frederick Simms and Harry J. Lawson, on one side, and David Salomons on the other, lobbied to repeal the law.

Frederick Simms, who grew up in Germany and was friendly with Daimler, began the Daimler Motor Syndicate in England as a company with limited liability in 1893. In 1895 he sold the syndicate for £35,000 and his rights to Daimler patents for £18,750 to bicycle capitalists, namely, E. T. Hooley, Martin D. Rucker, and Harry J. Lawson.

All of the parts and motors were supplied by the Daimler factory in Germany at 25 percent discount. Following the lead of Hooley who made 10 million pounds recapitalizing the Dunlop tire company and recklessly refinancing and repromoting bicycle and accessory companies on the English market, Harry J. Lawson, renaming the firm the British Motor Syndicate, began his career as England's notorious promoter of the petroleum automobile and floated an array of automobile firms under its sponsorship.

Monopolizing all automobile patents, the British Motor Syndicate frightened new firms from entering the field until after the turn of the century. Bringing Henry Sturmey, Britain's foremost journalist of cycling and photography, into his company, Lawson financed Sturmey in a new journal, the *Autocar*, from 1895 and set him to work gathering names on petitions demanding the repeal of the 1878 law. When David Salomons organized a motor car exhibit at the Crystal Palace in May 1896, Lawson promoted a more successful show one week later and with Simms formed the Motor Car Club.

Sir David Salomons, a member of the Automobile Club de France, represented the French group that promoted the petroleum automobile in England. He organized a motor show at Tunbridge Wells to which van Zuylen, de Dion, and Bouton came from Paris, and from which the Self-Propelled Traffic Association was formed. To invite the few motorcar owners in Britain to a much-publicized dinner at Hurlingham, Salomons skirted the law with the help of the chief commissioner of police who ordered his men to overlook the automobiles running in the streets for that occasion.

In drafting a Commons Bill which took into account many differing interests, Salomons won two important points: that the car be considered national, not local (as were the road locomotives), and that it be viewed no differently from a horsedrawn carriage.

The two factions competed to attract English buyers—on one side to the German Daimler and, on the other, to French cars—until 1897 when Simms, tiring of the business promotion of the Motor Car Club, formed the Automobile Association. David Salomons and his Self-Propelled Traffic Association merged with the Automobile Association in the following year. At its Richmond Automobile Show in the summer of 1899 Baron Arthur de Rothschild joined the club.

Overcoming the Law

A Commons Bill "to amend the law with respect to the use of Locomotives on Highways" was introduced in 1895 by the Right Honorable George John Shaw-Lefevre. A Liberal who held the cabinet post of minister of the Local Government Board, Shaw-Lefevre was a grandson of Charles Shaw-Lefevre, an early supporter of Gurney's carriage, and an ardent agriculturist. He had driven in a petroleum car in Paris and saw that the French had a remarkable head start in a promising new industry, but he used a visit by a deputation of the Traction Engine Owners Association as an excuse to bring in the bill. The association complained that, by the 1878 act, County Councils imposed different regulations on traction engines, making it impossible to drive through two or more counties. Shaw-Lefevre's bill intended to liberate traction engines from this restriction and gain the support of the agricultural interest. Its second section nullified for light locomotives all the previous acts on locomotives and sections of Highway Acts concerning locomotives, thus rallying the support of commercial interests. But within five days the Liberals had to resign, and Shaw-Lefevre, losing his seat in the ensuing election, joined the deputation from Salomon's Self-Propelling Vehicle Association to Henry Chaplin, now Conservative minister at the Board of Trade.

Although Chaplin led support in the Commons for the bill to repeal restrictions against locomotives on roads, the bill actually was drawn up by Lord Harris and was introduced into the House of Lords. It thereby became a Lords Bill and had the meaningful support of that Conservative House when it arrived in the now Conservative Commons. The Commons referred it to a Standing Committee whose members disagreed over restrictions to the automobile's operation to the point of a division only once, that being 20 ayes to 13 noes over the inclusion of the words "or visible vapour" in the clause, "and is so constructed that no smoke or visible vapour is emitted therefrom." The division obviously reflected the fact that the "ayes" were interested in petroleum cars, whereas the "noes" were steam car advocates. This distinction became particularly obvious when one of the "noes," Mr. Hopkinson, immediately proposed that "of offensive gas" be added after "vapour," but, seeing himself outnumbered, he withdrew his amendment."[114]

The Locomotives on Highways Act, becoming law in August 1896, liberated the English automobile but limited it to 14 miles an hour.

In 1900 there were seventy-five railway directors in the Commons and fifty-eight in the Lords, sufficient to take advantage of the public perception of automobiles as the prerogative of the rich and to raise a storm of opposition to a bill proposing a 25 mile per hour speed limit in built up areas and no speed limit elsewhere. A bill finally emerged in 1904 with a speed limit of 20 miles per hour throughout the country.

Financing the Industry

In November 1895 Lawson registered the British Motor Syndicate at a capitalization of £150,000, in shares of 1 pound. He issued seven shares to seven subscribers and 135,000 shares to H. J. Lawson and others "considered as paid" in return for £72,500 which he had spent for patents. Lawson increased the syndicate's capitalization to one million pounds in May 1896 and in July arranged for the syndicate to acquire the license for two patents from him for £250,000 (paid in 12,993 shares).

Meanwhile, Lawson floated the Daimler Motor Company in February with a capital of £100,000 in £10 shares, of which £40,000 was paid to the British Motor Syndicate for the license to use the Daimler patents. When he acquired an abandoned textile factory at Coventry for the Daimler Company, he leased a second building on the estate through the British Motor Syndicate to the Great Horseless Carriage Company which he formed in May 1896 at a capitalization of £750,000 to manufacture automobile bodies. The motors were purchased for these bodies from Daimler Motors at 10 percent under the cost to others. Lawson continued to set up syndicates with phantom financing and to purchase patents from American and French automobile companies with share capital.

Lawson's entrepreneurial optimism was encouraged by the boom in the bicycle industry about which it was reported that from January 1896 through November, eleven million pounds had been invested in new cycle companies. English cities such as Coventry, which had lost its ribbon and horologerie industries through foreign competition, owed their revival to the bicycle, which, likewise, brought their collapse when the industry crashed in 1897. The *Investors' Review* totaled the loss to the public in Hooley's English bicycle enterprises in 1898 in this manner: "Sixteen cycle issues with a nominal capital of £8,875,000; value at prices obtainable . . . £3,885,000; Loss to the public if it held the issues . . . £4,990,000."[115]

Because of the close connection of Lawson's automobile industry with the cycle industry, the Daimler Motor Company's £10 shares were offered at £4 in October 1897, and the Great Horseless Carriage Company's £10 shares were down to 22 1/2 shillings. The Daimler Motor Company, after bankruptcy in 1901, was recapitalized at £100,000, received the Royal Warrant from Edward VII in January 1902, and built up confidence through the sale of debenture and preference shares which allowed it in time to place its ordinary shares. In 1910 when its profit reached one million pounds, it was taken over by the Birmingham Small Arms Company Ltd., through which, like the German Daimler, it had a strong connection with the military.

The indomitable Lawson carried on his financial activities by floating the London Steam Omnibus Company Ltd. in July 1898, with a capitalization of £420,000 in £10 shares (2,000 being the founders' shares), the patents for which were licensed from the British Motor Syndicates. Warned the *Investors' Review* starkly: "Those who take shares will lose their money." Only after Lawson's claim to a monopoly on patents was overturned by a court suit did he bow out of the English automobile industry. Automobile historians called him "visionary" and "bold," but contemporaries regarded him as they did Hooley: "He simply went on buying and selling and mortgaging and transmogrifying with the heated fury of an ignorant 'bounder' blown out with his own conceit."[116]

GERMANY

Overcoming the Law

Carl Benz took over the task of forcing a change in the German law against automobiles; he had the necessary perseverance. When his first employers refused to let him experiment with designing an automobile until their gas engine firm made a profit, he found a capitalist, admittedly a retailer of benzine, who did encourage him. In the same manner, after the police arrested him in 1885 for driving in the streets, Benz managed "mit allen Waffen Ciceros" (with all of Cicero's oratorical power) to get permission to experiment in the streets of Mannheim if he gave written notice. By 1893 he won the permission of the Baden minister of interior

138

to drive about within the state at slow speed, and in 1895 the Benz Company succeeded in repealing the speed limitations of 6 kilometers an hour in the city and 12 in the country.

Promoting the Company

Meanwhile, Daimler went into litigation with his firm and was found not guilty of depriving it of his services when he left the firm in 1891. He was upheld in his rejection of the Deutz Company's claim on his petroleum motor patent. The firm produced only eleven automobiles in 1892 and 1893 before stopping production altogether. Frederick Simms' payment of 350,000 marks in cash for the license to manufacture the Daimler car in Britain revived the moribund German firm. But what brought Daimler and Maybach back into the business in 1895, as president and technical director respectively, was a change of heart of the board of directors. This change had been brought about by unsentimental alarm at the great advances the French were making in automobilism, coupled with the fact that seven Daimler-engined cars raced in June 1895 the 732 miles from Paris to Bordeaux and returned without engine trouble of any note. Frederick Simms (who spoke German) took a seat on the board of the German Daimler Company, and helped Max Duttenhofer and Wilhelm Lorenz, whose duties were now solely on the business side, to reform the company and regain its foreign business.

German automobile production was low and for several reasons. Firms were few, cars expensive, the German aristocracy ignored the automobile, and the German government owned the railways and disapproved of competition from the automobile, particularly as it threatened to disrupt the well-ordered German society.

THE UNITED STATES

Overcoming the Law

Some states, such as Vermont, had adopted Red Flag Laws in imitation of the British 1865 law against steam carriages. The New York State legislature passed a law in 1886 requiring a person to walk ahead of a steam carriage by one-eighth of a mile to warn traffic, but it left a speed limit to city councils which usually set it at 6 miles an hour within the city.

These laws came under fire from hundreds of automobile clubs which sprang up throughout the nation. By 1902 the New York law was amended to apply only to tractors, which left automobiles free of restrictions. As for speed limits, an Indiana judge gave a landmark decision by ruling against the speed ordinance of Kokomo: the right to set speed limits was not granted to cities in their charters. State legislatures, however, in cooperation with the Automobile Clubs began to fix speed limits in order to curb the excesses of speeding playboys.

Actual American opposition to the car came only from horse-breeders, livery stable owners, and horsedrawn vehicle associations which saw it as a threat to their established economic interests. Carriage manufacturers and blacksmiths, on the other hand, adapted to it and profited. This was true in France as well. In fact, the Paris carriage trade, stagnant since 1850, leaped to life with the advent of the auto. Moreover, the tradesman opposition in France was easily and quickly overrun by the fast-driving aristocratic entrepreneurs, whereas in America it succumbed to the undeniable opportunities for profit that the early automobile industry appeared to offer.

Unlike the envious French farmer who could not fulfill his wish to own a car until after World War I, the American farmer was indifferent to the petrol car when it appeared in the States in 1900. In 1904 he hated it for penetrating the countryside, spreading dust over the crops and farmhouses, and exuding the unpleasant sulphur (which refiners were just beginning to eliminate). But his dislike lasted only until the urban market was saturated in 1906 when he welcomed the cars that manufacturers began to design for him.

Financing the Industry

In America, the financing of the early automobile industry demanded only small amounts of capital, owing in large measure to the development of standardized interchangeble parts.

In exchange for granting territorial rights to dealers, automakers demanded from them an advance deposit of 20 percent in cash on all orders, full payment on delivery, and acceptance of the vehicles according to the prearranged price schedule immediately upon production. Added to the capital formed by dealers' deposits, the automakers received from thirty to ninety days credit from makers of automobile parts during which time they assembled and sold the automobiles. In effect this arrangement acted as a gift of fixed capital from the parts-makers. Moreover, although imitating the French models, American manufacturers were saved from the need for large capital funds had they been obliged to compete with them. The Payne-Aldrich protective tariff added an ad valorem duty of 45 percent to the price of foreign cars entering the American market.

The Rockefellers did not apparently invest in the automobile industry, possibly because their attention was focused on the antitrust court action against Standard Oil during that period. The Rockefellers' partners, the Vanderbilts, took an active role in racing petroleum cars and developing the market. But it was the Ford Company with the Model T in 1906, and General Motors under the leadership of William Durant which won the market— the first through a cheap, dependable car, and the second through amalgamating smaller firms.

Steam Versus Petrol in America

The Stanley Steamer, which sold steadily for twenty years without advertising, was recognized by aficionados as the best car of the day. The problem with the steam car industry was its lack of capitalization. The Stanley brothers sold 650 steamers a year whereas Ford sold 650 petrol cars a day. And when Abner Doble devised a method in the 1920s to raise steam in 45 to 90 seconds which "represented the final word in automotive performance and economy of operation," he landed in jail "almost immediately among accusations of 'skulduggery' from all sides."[117] Automobile historians concluded that the steam car could not survive in an automobile industry monopolized by giant manufacturers of the petroleum automobile.

18

Rationale

With reference to the Introduction of this book, the reader will recall that to be adopted by entrepreneurs an invention must have quantitative efficiency, that is, it must provide more output with the same amount of input than does the current machinery. In addition, it must have qualitative efficiency, that is, it has to reinforce the controlling power of the dominant economic groups in a given social formation; in other words, only when an invention does not undermine the control of the ruling group over the primary mode of production will it be accepted. The quantitative efficiency of the automobile over the railway we have demonstrated. The question remaining is, at what point did the railway lose qualitative efficiency and the automobile gain it? Profound changes in the class structure in France and the emergence of a strong national capital formation are the talismans which produced this seemingly magical turn-around.

In England the finance bourgeoisie, that is, the big bankers, merchant traders and stockbrokers, developed from and were subservient to the industrial bourgeoisie. But on the continent, the finance bourgeoisie, owing to its links with English capital, nurtured and controlled the industrial bourgeoisie.

Prior to 1830, the Belgian bourgeois class was formed out of the industrialization encouraged by William I. It comprised nobles, churchmen, merchants and a few industrialists. The enclosure of forest and commons began under French rule and continued under Dutch rule which caused the revolution of 1830 to be undertaken by a new large proletariat. As compensation for the shift in power, the largest landholders demanded concessions from the Dutch government. It took about 25 years of interior accumulation (with the aid of English capital, workers, and stolen machinery) for Belgium to develop capitalism. Owing to its need to raise capital abroad, particularly in building railways, as we have seen, the Belgian finance bourgeoisie had the upper hand and worked closely with royalty.

In France the probing fingers of English capital had to find a less direct route. The House of Rothschild provided it. The governing French middle class under the bourgeois King Louis Philippe grasped the English hand that would make a fortune for French capitalists. But here railways had not developed in tandem with the developing economy as in England. They were superimposed on an economic base of bad harvests, failing textile industry and spreading unemployment. The rising cost of English imported iron rails brought a decline in profit to the railways and sparked the revolution against the corrupt ruling bourgeoisie and their English allies. Narrowly avoiding nationalization of the railways, French capitalists welcomed the coup d'état of Napoleon III. He centralized capital and political control in Paris by promoting a web of railways radiating from it under the guise of strengthening the national economy. Here again the superior qualitative efficiency of the railway worked through its productive force to stabilize the relations of production throughout the period of the Second Empire. As in England, the surplus value in agricultural France was drained from the provinces to the industrial centers such as Paris and Lyons. Great machine-making factories such as Gouin and Cail in Paris were set up and engaged in the unequal trade of machinery for raw products from the land.

Through their growing independence on the banks of Paris (the Bank of France established branches in the various regions of France), the French farmers became tied to the interests of the Haute Bourgeoisie in the cities. The farm laborers, becoming unemployed through the gradual mechanization of agriculture, swelled the proletarian ranks in the cities and were kept occupied in vast public works programs, building railways, ports and re-building Paris.

The subtle involvement of government in promoting communications internationally for the purpose of exploitation became noticeable by the exploits of Lieutenant Waghorn. With the overt backing of Lancashire capitalists, who petitioned Parliament for changes in the tax law on the transport of mail to help Waghorn in Egypt, Waghorn indicated by his memorials to England's rulers that his unofficial activities were understood mutually always to be in their service. Waghorn then, like the railways he charted, was a product of England's policy of free trade. England forged an alliance among the ruling classes of the industrializing countries and created an international banking class nurtured, like the railways, from London and Lancashire.

The industrial substructure in France was weak; for instance, French soldiers built the Paris-Versailles railway. The importation of English industrial firms such as Buddicom's, English surveyors, engineers, and workers was essential to France's capital development. A combination of English capitalists and the French Haute Banque controlled the development. Karl Marx analyzed the situation:

In England--and, the largest French manufacturers are petty bourgeois as against their English rivals--we really find the manufacturers, a Cobden, a Bright, at the head of the crusade against the bank and the stock exchange aristocracy. Why not in France? In England, industry requires free trade; in France, protection, national monopoly besides other monopolies. French industry does not dominate French production; the French industrialists, therefore, do not dominate the French bourgeoisie. In order to put through their interest against the remaining fractions of the bourgeoisie, they cannot, like the English, take the lead of the movement and simultaneously push their class interest to the fore; they must follow in the train of the revolution, and serve the interests which are opposed to the collective interests of their class.... And who is more directly threatened by the workers than the employer, the industrial capitalists? The manufacturer, therefore, of necessity became in France the most fanatical member of the party of order. The reduction of his profit by finance, what is that compared with the abolition of profit by the proletariat?[118]

During the Second Republic when the government had been retaken from the revolutionists by the finance bourgeoisie, the party of order prepared for the reinforcement of its hegemony over the countryside. It set prefects, sub-prefects and mayors under the gendarme. It promulgated the school-teacher law under which schoolteachers could be arbitrarily dismissed by the prefects and subjected to disciplinary investigation. "They, the men of talent, the spokesmen, the educators and interpreters of the peasant class were subjected to the arbitrary power of the prefect, they, the proletarians of the learned class, were chased like hunted beasts from one commune to another...." Finally, the education law of 1850 "put education entirely into the hands of the clergy and Jesuits."

Accompanied by the reintroduction of the hated wine tax, the repressive measures of the finance bourgeoisie drove the peasants into an alliance with the middle classes in general and the proletariat. Here lay the seeds of the undoing of the finance bourgeoisie. "This is the socialism of industry, of trade and of agriculture, whose rulers in the party of order deny these interests, so far as they no longer coincide with their private monopolies."

The main monopoly of the Haute Bourgeoisie was the railway. Although Napoleon III allowed national capital to develop French industry through systems of credit led by the Pereires, it was the Foulds and Rothschilds who directed policy in the interests of the finance bourgeoisie. The railway, however, presented a contradiction. At the same time that it subjugated the provinces of the center under the rule of the bankers, it linked the petty producers of the town to the agricultural producers in trade. Thus, it forged a common interest in economic and social progress between the industrial and agrarian capitalists.

Although the peasantry was gradually being ruined by the division of farm holdings, increased taxation and rising mortgages, France as a whole prospered under the Second Empire because of its industrialization. "The enrichment of the country had not been limited to a few families of merchant princes;" wrote Andre Maurois, "a great body of small industrialists, of small traders, conscious of their success, was demanding consideration. In every provincial city, the professors, doctors, lawyers, notaries, chemists, and veterinary surgeons constituted a liberal group thirsting for equality, richly endowed with talent, which some day might well challenge the pre-eminence of the Notables."[119]

The challenge was provoked by a serious industrial crisis in the early 1870s, which was followed by an agricultural crisis. Republicans counteracted the haute finance hegemony with a campaign of virulent anti-clericalism and cries for universal education to teach *solidarite*, class reconciliation. The rising of the Communards and worker resistance prompted the legalizing of trade unions in the eighties and the promotion of social democracy blessed by the papal edict of capitalist-worker cooperation, *Rerum Novarum*.

French farmers objected to a public works policy that excluded industrialists from sending them consumer goods and machinery while it favored railway monopolies and the export business. Joining with industrialists also victimized by the railway cartel, they formed the Republican Party and sought a finance policy to break the domination of financiers who controlled the lending of capital. They struck a political compromise called the Freycinet Plan and Railway Convention of 1883 under which 23,000 kilometers of railway line were to be built or taken over by private companies with the benefit of a partial state subsidy in order to make the final links in a comprehensive national market.

Supporters of the railway monopolists became isolated in the debates, but the plan came to terms with them. Three men—Charles Freycinet, Leon Say, and Leon Gambetta—met privately on January 8, 1878, to draw up its principles, which eventually proved beneficial to the railway companies. They reflected the political factions prepared to satisfy the complaints of the small producers for more rail lines at lower rates but to retain the administrative power in the hands of the bankers.

Freycinet, who held the public works portfolio from 1877 to 1879 and kept a close watch over it under his administration in the following year, pushed the Republican message of order, peace, and industry by tying the poor regions of France into the national system of transportation. At the same time he encouraged the economic concentration which favored the capitalists. Leon Say, a high official in the Rothschild Bank and an administrator of the Nord Railway Company, epitomized the aristocracy of high finance. Gambetta was Say's antithesis, the "people's politician," who led the petty producers, petit bourgeoisie, and small farmers onto the national stage—not to challenge the ruling class but rather "to support their claims to power."

The powers of high finance thwarted the proposals for an egalitarian marketplace because the state subsidies to the specific companies intended to operate the sections of the third rail network had to be paid through the large railway companies which thereby maintained control over them and began consolidating the lines. The state also guaranteed the interest on capital invested by the large railways in return for a stronger voice in fixing rates, especially on freight from private to state rails. This, in turn, led to the disappearance of competition as the lines gradually fell victim to the cartel.

The Freycinet Plan, therefore, reduced none of the pressures on the internal market. The bankers altered their strategy for gaining control of that market. Until the 1880s the predominant flow of capital was from the provinces to Paris and through Paris to foreign borrowers. But in the 1890s and 1900s this pattern worked in reverse. A study of the Credit Lyonnais demonstrates that after the liquidity crisis of 1882, the great bulk of the bank's deposits was invested domestically in the short-term money market. This caused funds collected in Paris to be dispersed to capitalists in the provinces. By this time, however, technological advancement had made the industrialist powerful. He, in turn, gave the power of demand to the agrarian petty producer, now flooded with commodities via railway, canal, and road. But these commodities competed with the agrarian producer's own production. Tariffs had to be imposed on imported foodstuffs, and Republicans adopted protectionism to offset the worldwide fall in prices.

The Republican coalition held together despite an inherent contradiction: the guaranteeing of the possessions of all property owners in furtherance of an egalitarian society while maximizing the gains of productive capital in cooperation with the finance bourgeoisie. The interrelationship of banking and industry in France provided the foundation for the contradiction. The concentration of capital and the increasing competitive pressure on small industries to resist the falling profit rate intensified it. A new technique to resolve the contradiction was at hand.

If consumer need was the primary motivating force behind the automobile industry, the industrialists would have financed the steam carriages of Bollee and his competitors in the 1880s in order to satisfy that need. If they feared boiler explosions from the steam

146

car, there was available an internal combustion engine of 100 CV made by Edouard Delamare-Deboutteville and Leon Maladin at Rouen. From Rouen it was sold to factories throughout France and adopted by Schneider-Creusot and the Cockerill Company in Belgium. In 1884 Delamare-Deboutteville completed a four-wheeled, two-cylinder-engined petroleum automobile. Since his automobile patents fell into the public domain in the same year and he could find no supporting capital, he abandoned the project. In the light of Schneider-Creusot's leading interest in the Daimler petrol automobile in the 1890s, its disinterest in the petrol automobile in the 1880s implies either that the industrialists decided to give the railways more time to respond to the nation's needs, or that the industrialists had become politically more powerful in the intervening decade.

By 1890 the attempt by the Republican right to stem both the tide of liberalism and the political growth of the middle class was weakened. The Rothschilds, as finance bourgeoisie who became deeply involved in the manufacture of the early petroleum automobile, were not political allies of the industrialists. Yet the great public response to the marketing of the de Dion-Bouton petrol motor tricycles may have encouraged industrialists and those among the finance bourgeoisie involved in marketing petroleum to form an alliance to develop a new mode of production. Moreover, the Rothschilds as administrators of the Nord and PLM railways knew that the railways made their profits in servicing the central markets along the main lines and that the automobile could remove the pressure on them to service the unprofitable areas along the local lines.

The competitive forces in the petroleum industry gave birth to the petroleum engine, at which point the real automobile industry began. France's metallurgy responded to its needs. Regardless of the superior speed and solidness exhibited by the steam automobile, the petroleum automobile was anointed for mass production. The anointers were the finance bourgeoisie.

In France the automobile was rapidly diffused on the same principle that the steam locomotive had been diffused in Britain: it consumed a product that the capitalist had to market. The locomotive not only carried coal from the collieries to market, but it also consumed it in large amounts along the way. Thus, it doubled its value to the Lancashire capitalist by saving on constant capital in transport as it produced surplus capital in its operation. Similarly, the petroleum automobile consumed petroleum for the refiner, giving him surplus value. But, of course, since it could not be monopolized as was the railway, the automobile reduced the costs in constant value to the entrepreneurial world at large rather than to the petroleum monopolist especially.

147

Thus, the petroleum automobile was perceived to have quantitative efficiency superior not only to other forms of transport but in a special way to the steam and electric automobiles. In 1898 it was calculated that, although the automobile cost 6,000 francs while a horse carriage cost 5,000, the automobile could be run for 2,150 francs a year whereas the horse carriage had an annual running cost of 6,360 francs.[120] However, aside from its quantitative efficiency from the viewpoint of the individual consumer, it had superior efficiency for the petroleum entrepreneur who regarded its potential for consuming petroleum greater than even the oil-burning furnaces, which were then widespread in Russia. By contrast, the steam automobile related back to the coalfield owners whose profits were being amply made in metallurgy and whose supplies in France had always been insufficient for the demands of big industry. Nor did the entrepreneurs of electricity find that the electric automobile was as promising a consumer as machinery in factories and the vast market for electric lighting. Therefore, quite aside from its quantitative efficiency, the petroleum automobile offered a "relative" quantitative efficiency that brought increasingly greater financial returns to the petroleum entrepreneur through the machine's diffusion, superior to the financial returns offered by the development of the steam and electric automobiles.

The petroleum automobile's quantitative efficiency may, therefore, be seen to be greater than that of the railway at this time. With all rail networks constructed, the French railways had fallen into a stationary state, in which investment had fallen pitifully low, as we have shown. The colliers and metallurgists could expect only decreasing returns from the railway companies whose demands for their products steadily decreased. On the other hand, the petroleum automobile in the view of the petroleum capitalist would multiply and consume petroleum over the highways and byways of the world for decades, nay, centuries to come. Its development would also provide a market for the consumption of the iron and steel products of the metallurgist.

Quantitative efficiency is linked to qualitative efficiency. By relating a technical innovation back to an established technology, in this case the petroleum automobile through the petroleum engine to the petroleum refiner, quantitative efficiency gives to the capitalist in control of the production of the established technology a certain measure of control over the mode of production of the innovation. The capitalists in control of petroleum production would perceive a qualitative efficiency in the petroleum automobile superior to that of innovations in competition with it.

The egalitarian democracy preached by the Republican bourgeoisie made it impossible for it to employ ideological grounds to deny the introduction of the "egalitarian" automobile. In addition, the competitive pressure on the home market ensured the automobile's adoption as a means of reducing the cost of constant capital. But could the Republican bourgeoisie use automobile production to give it control over the mode of production? It had neutralized the power of the financial aristocracy, yet it required a means of production to combat that class's control of railways and its subsidiary industries. Just as the large English industrialists had used railway construction to bring the workers under their command, so now did the French industrialists use automobile production to command large numbers of workers in factories that were run along the severe and rigid lines of scientific management introduced into France at this time. Although the industrial bourgeoisie ostensibly had taken over control of the economic policy in Republican France, it shared control for all practical purposes with the finance bourgeoisie which, as we have seen, monopolized the petroleum industry under the guidance of the Brothers Rothschild. Consequently, the "invisible hand" guiding the promotion of the automobile in France in response to the petroleum capitalists' pressing need to develop a consumer market was seen to belong to the Rothschilds.

The question as to who was to control the internal market must be answered from the evidence which points to a combination of the industrial and finance bourgeoisie. The finance bourgeoisie played a self-effacing role in France as befitted the social and political temper of the times. It played an exhibitionist role in England where international capital was king. As the strains on the marketplace increased, the automobile as a mode of production stimulated not only petroleum production but also a myriad of subsidiary industries through which the industrial bourgeois could extend his control over the nation and promote the hegemonic message of egalitarianism.

One can safely draw the conclusion that the development of the petroleum automobile, as with the earlier suppression of the steam carriage, was not merely guided by quantitative concerns for cost and profit maximization. Its development was dramatically affected by the vested interests of some particular fractions of capital and by the political forces that affected their ability to realize those interests. Costs are not everything, it appears, in shaping the diffusion of new techniques. Political economic power is also a contributing force.

Yet a third element required for the launching of a new industry is sufficient capital to sustain it. In 1895, the long depression which had begun in the 1870s, having reached its lowest point, began to experience an upturn in the long range business cycle. The economist Joseph Schumpeter pointed to a period just before this low moment in the cycle when the entrepreneur introduces an invention to bring about the upturn. From the case of the automobile, it seems that the economic upturn is created by the circumstance of competitive and political factors in combination, which give the entrepreneurs the confidence to invest in a new technology.

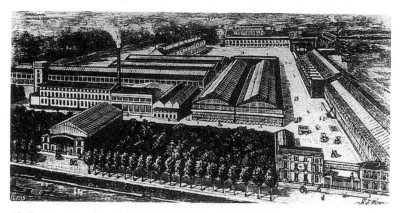

12 Exterior view of the de Dion-Bouton factory. (*Le Technologiste*, 1900.)

Notes

1. Jacob Schmookler, *Invention and Economic Growth* (Cambridge, Mass.: Harvard, 1966), p. 130.

2. There is relatively little synthetic work on technological change within the Marxian perspective. Insights into the role of technology in the economy were gleaned in Karl Marx, *Capital* (New York: International Publishers, 1967), Vols. 1-3. For reflections on the Marxian approach to technology, see, for example, the special issue on "Technology, the Labor Process, and the Working Class," *Monthly Review* (July-August 1976), particularly David M. Gordon, "Capitalist Efficiency and Socialist Efficiency"; Nathan Rosenberg, "Marx as a Student of Technology"; and Donald D. Weiss, "Marx Versus Smith on the Division of Labor." See also Michael Reich and James Devine, "The Micro-Economics of Conflict and Hierarchy in Capitalist Production," *Review of Radical Political Economics* (Winter 1981).

Terminology: a mode of production constitutes a determinate system organizing economic production and distribution within a social formation, the sum of the structured relationships shaping daily life. The mode of production shapes a class structure; within the ruling class shaped by that mode of production, there may be several class fractions or economic interest groups. When an invention or technical innovation has resulted in a substantial change in the methods of production or the character of output, I refer to the adoption of a new technique.

3. H. C. Report, 1834, ca. p. 10.

4. Anna Gurney, "Letter to the Editor," *Times* (London), December 27, 1875, P. 6.

5. H. C. Report, 1834, Gurney's evidence, July 7.

6. Memorandum, July 14, 1829, Hanning papers. Taunton, Somerset.

7. Herbert Taylor, *The Taylor Papers; being a record of certain reminiscences, letters and journals, in the life of Lieut.-Gen. Sir Herbert Taylor* (London; Longmans Green, 1913), pp.262-5

8. "Report from the Select Committee on Mr. Goldsworthy Gurney's Case with Minutes of Evidence." No. 483, pp. 80-81. Great Britain, Parliament, *Sessional Papers* 11 (1834), cited henceforth as H. C. Report, 1834.

9. Goldsworthy Gurney, *Mr. Goldsworthy Gurney's Account of the Invention of the Steam Jet or Blast* . . . (London: G. Barclay, 1859), passim. Letters were exchanged on this subject between Anna Gurney and Samuel Smiles in the Times (London) December 27, 1875, p. 6; January 1, 1876, p. 6; January 24, 1876, p. 11. A note from the son of Goldsworthy's friend, William Keene, supported Goldsworthy's claim to the invention (*Times*, December 29, 1875). As for Stephenson's

151

connection with Gurney's steam jet, J.C.H. Warren writes in *A Century of Locomotive Building by Robert Stephenson & Co., 1823-1923* (Newcastle-on-Tyne: Reed, 1923), p. 261: "Immediately after (Robert Stephenson's) return from South America in 1827 he had written a letter to the Liverpool and Manchester Railway Company explanatory of Mr. Gurney's locomotive engine for coaches and passengers." According to Warren, Stephenson wanted to put the engine on the side of the boiler or beneath it in imitation of Gurney, which indicated he was close to discovering Gurney's steam blast. The power of Gurney's boiler was widely recognized; his was the only engine on steamboats powerful enough to overcome the currents in the Euphrates River where it was used extensively in the 1830s.

10. Francis Maceroni, *A Few Facts Concerning Elementary Locomotion* (London: E. Wilson, 1834), p. 34. Other forms of fuel were considered at this early date. Alexander Gordon and his father, David, briefly experimented with the gas vacuum engine invented by Mr. Brown of Brompton, but it was too expensive, as coal-gas, the cheapest type, cost 3 shillings per 1,000 cubic feet and, to be used in a piston engine, it had to be compressed into portable shape at an additional cost of 3 s. 6 d. per 1,000 cubic feet. Richard Broun hinted at "a new motive power not yet made public . . . which will prove cheaper, simpler, and more effective . . . and affect society generally in a more important degree than did the discovery of Columbus (*Appeal to our Rulers and Ruled....* [London: Mortimer, 1834], p. 6n). Maceroni suggested liquid fuel as a motive force in 1826: ". . . whether oil, fat, or coal-tar, might not under particular circumstances, be injected into the fire-place, so as to keep up an abundant flame . . . more economical and compact . . . . Even at sea a whale ship might supply oil enough for a long voyage" ("On increasing the flame of fuel as applied to steam boilers." Letter from F. M., *Mechanics' Magazine* No. 170 (November 25, 1826): 480). "Until Maceroni republished his letter of November 25, 1826 I was wholly unacquainted with his views respecting the use of liquid fuel," *Railroad Journal* (New York), May 1834, referring to *Mechanics' Magazine*, No. 529 (1834): 453. Concerning the use of liquid fuel, Gurney responded to the House Committee of 1831 that he anticipated the replacing of steam by other elementary power, "but I do not think that will take place in our day." He referred to a compound "known to produce power by chemical change; some peculiarly explosive and aeriform bodies for instance." (See H. L. Gurney, "The Case of Sir Goldsworthy Gurney," Ms., pp. 18-19.)

11. Agreement, Goldsworthy Gurney and William Hanning, August 21, 1828, Hanning papers.

12. ALS, Gurney to Hanning, Regent's Park, November 23, 1829, Hanning Papers.

13. In comparing the power of Gurney's locomotive to other locomotives of the day, we have the report of Messrs. Rastrick and Walker that the conveyance of 48 tons at 5 mph was the greatest performance the directors of the Liverpool Railway could expect from their engines. Whereas Gurney's engine with water and coke weighed 30 cwt, the Manchester-Liverpool engines were far heavier, that is, Stephenson's *Rocket* with water and coke weighed about 7 1/2 tons;

Hackworth's *Sans Pareil* with water and coke weighed about 8 tons; and Braithwaite's *Novelty* weighed about 4 tons. Therefore, by pulling thirty times its own weight, Gurney's engine was much stronger than the larger locomotives which pulled about six times their own weight. The *Samson* weighing 8 1/2 tons plus 4 tons of fuel and water in the tender, making 12 1/2 tons, drew about 44 1/2 tons gross of goods and wagons at 8 mph at Rainhill in April 1831. To equate it with Crawshay's experiment with Gurney's engine (drawing at 4 mph from 30 to 35 times its weight), the *Samson* at 4 mph would have drawn 89 tons, which, when divided by its 12 1/2 ton weight, gives it pulling power at 7 1/2 times its weight. The most powerful of the rail line locomotives was five times weaker than Gurney's engine. This illustrates the superiority of Gurney's boiler.

14. H. C. Report, 1835, p. 12.

15. *Glasgow Courier*, July 4, 1834.

16. "Report from the Select Committee on Locomotives on Roads," Great Britain, Parliament, *Sessional Papers* 16 (1873): 142-143.

17. ALS, Woolcombe to Gurney, Devonport, April 7, 1836.

18. Great Britain, Public Record Office, Rail 10008/111 (August 28, 1838).

19. ALS, Woolcombe to Gurney, Devonport, March 29, 1836.

20. H. L. Report 1836, p. 333.

21. J. Lawrence Pritchards, *Sir George Cayley: The Inventor of the Aeroplane* (London: M. Parrish, 1961), pp. 153-154.

22. ALS, Downey to Deans, July 6, 1834, Downey papers. Soc. of Civil Engineers, London.

23. Henry Parnell, "Notebook, May 10, 1829 (i.e., 1829-41)" November 12, 1835, p. 32, and April 29, 1837, p. 36.

24. Telford Pocket Note Book for 1833. National Library of Scotland.

25. ALS, Robertson to Telford, January 24, 1834, Telford papers. Telford, Salop.

26. ALS, Macneill to Telford, February 4, 1834, Telford papers; see *Aris's Birmingham Gazette* (January 6, 1834), p. 2, for support from Trustees of Stratford, Dunchurch and Daventry roads.

27. Brougham Col. 33,190; Post Office Directory for London, 1847; List of Brokers, 1845; London City Corporations Record Office (Ms 17,959/45): Broker's Ledger. The involvement of "Wolff" in a steam carriage company is interesting for its connections. Ernst Wolff is not listed as a member of the English stock exchange at the time, but the address on Maceroni's letter, "26 Change Alley, Cornhill, London," is next door to the stockbroker, Lewis Wolfe, at 23 Change Alley. (Wolfe is the anglicized version of the German Wolff.) Lewis Wolfe went bankrupt during the railway financial crash of 1846 and reappeared in the *London Post Office Directory* in 1852 as a dealer in Chinaware. His banker was Glyn and Company whose chief officers had invested heavily in the London-Birmingham railway, of which George Carr Glyn was made chairman in 1837. Glyn's was also banker to the National Association of Locomotion which promoted the steam carriage. This leads to speculation that a compromise between the groups was being effected. Since the railways had taken over the Pickford Carriers and the Chaplin Coaching Company which they employed exclusively as

feeders, that is, as carriers of passengers and parcels to the train stations, thus shutting out other coaching companies, they now contemplated using steam carriages as feeders for passengers over longer distances. ". . . my steam carriages will take up and put down the passengers at their own doors," wrote Maceroni (Brougham Col. 33,198). See *Prospectus*, The Maceroni Common Road and Steam Conveyance Company, May 1839, Yale University Library.

28. Brougham Col. 33,223 (ALS, Maceroni to Brougham, June 6, 1841).

29. Gurney, *Mr. Gurney's Observations on Steam Carriages on Turnpike Roads* (London: Baldwin and Cradock, 1832), p. 40ff.

30. Walter Hancock, *Narrative of Twelve Years Experience (1824-1836).* . . . (London: Weale, 1838), p. 86.

31. "A steam carriage will be exhibited on Saturday and Monday the 3rd and 5th of July inst . . . constructed by Wm T. (i.e., H.) James, New York, 1833" Broadside 1 1/4 by 11 1/4 Streeter Collection; for comments on James and Anderson's steam carriages in England, see *Dingler's Polytechnisches Journal*, Bd.32,S.169; Bd.35,S.6. Gurney's engineer, Stone, and his backer, Captain Dobbyn, opened a steam carriage business in New York City in 1832, but Stone soon abandoned it for the plumbing business. In 1851 Stone helped promote J. K. Fisher's steam carriage in New York City.

32. *Mechanics' Magazine* 22 (1835): 348.

33. H. C. Report, 1834, p. 62ff.

34. ALS, Robertson to Telford (February 1, 1834), Telford papers.

35. H. C. Report, 1835, Gurney's testimony, May 26, 1835.

36. H. C. Report, 1834, McNeil's (i.e., Macneill's) testimony, July 11, 1834.

37. "Distress of Agriculture," Great Britain, Parliament, *Sessional Papers* 26 (1835). Lefevre published an unofficial report with a commercial publisher. Torrens thought that the economy provided by the steam carriage would make England prosperous both at home and abroad; see H. C. Report 1831, pp. 104-106. The Country Party broke from the Conservative government over the Tory Party's refusal to help resolve the distress of the agricultural population, brought defeat to Wellington's government, and gave the Whigs the parliamentary majority in 1830.

38. ALS, Richard Broun to Brougham, November 26, 1833. Brougham Col. 46,228; also see attachment: "National Institution of Locomotion for ameliorating the condition of the country by means of Steam Transport and Agriculture. " (*Prospectus*, November 1, 1833).

39. Edward S. Cayley, *Reasons for the Formation of the Agricultural Protection Society*, addressed to the industrious classes of the United Kingdom (London: Ollivier, 1844). If the Corn Laws were repealed, Cayley wrote, at least one-quarter of the L250 million invested in the soil by the tenant farmers (larger than that invested in cotton, woolens, linens, and hardwares) would be lost to the financial market. For Broun's attempts to keep the steam carriage an important issue and to save the Central Agricultural Society, see Committee of Superintendance Minutes HA 93/63/3, 2/4, February 1837-July

1840, Central Agricultural Society Papers, Ipswich Record Office, Ipswich, England.

40. See ALS, Registrar of Records to Charles Klapper, February 27, 1933, February 27, 1933, Gt. Br. P.R.O. Rail 1005-7, wherein it is denied that the Great Western Railway subsidized Hancock "because (his steam carriages) ran from Stingo Public House in Marylebone Road to the Bank of England." The Great Western Rail Company arranged for Sherman's, Chaplin's, Gilbert's, and Horne's stagecoaches to go between Great Western's offices in Princess Street, the Bank to Paddington Station. But J. L. Beaumont James writes in a letter to the London *Times* (June 22, 1936) that Hancock ran a steam omnibus passenger service between the city and Paddington from August 18, 1834. Hancock claimed before the Lords (H.L. Report, 1836, p. 318) that unlike Gurney he had no financial backing and paid £10,000 to 12,000 out of his own pocket; his round-trip passenger service between the City and Paddington took 1 to 1 1/2 hours. Francis James, (*Walter Hancock and His Common Road Steam Carriages, Alresford, Hamps.*: Oxley, 1975) in a 131-page biography of Hancock, preceding a reprint of Hancock's *Narrative*, states that his steam carriages were "financed out of profits from the almost unbroken monopoly of supplying manufacturing machinery (made in the family factory at Stratford) to the expanding rubber industry." Francis James continues (in 1975!) the discrediting of Gurney—"totally ignorant of engineering techniques, he had pursued a theoretical approach"—"Dr. Gurney considered himself Hancock's social superior" (p. 16) and looked down on this son of a cabinetmaker—". . . there is the strong possibility that Gurney preferred not to run the risk of subjecting Dance to a probing examination" (by parliamentary committee) (p. 41). (Dance was ill in Germany at the time.)

Is James continuing a "cover up" or is he simply being malicious? Hancock's steam omnibus failed, he said, because the public did not like being jolted. But consider this: when Gurney petitioned the Commons in 1834 for reparations for costs because high tolls prevented the development of his steam carriages, Hancock petitioned for "equal reward with Gurney" and discredited Gurney's grounds for recompense—". . . but Your Petitioner not having found any impediment on the common roads generally either in the shape of extensive tolls, or otherwise, during the many thousands of miles he has travelled over the common roads by Steam, intends during the present month to bring several of his carriages before the public for hire, on such roads." (Apps. to 16th *Report* of the Select Committee of the House of Commons on Public Petitions, App. 2,293 1834). In an off-moment Hancock allowed himself just one veiled comment on the opposition: "parties who do not desire that this branch of improvement should prosper against the interests of themselves." (*Mechanics' Magazine* 25 [1836]: 435, "Letter to the Editor").

41. Charles Dance, *A Letter. . . the Duke of Wellington* (London: 1837), "When Mr. Gurney and myself wished to introduce our boilers on railways, we found the monopoly was so exclusive that there was not the slightest chance of getting a *fair trial*."

42. ALS, G. C. Glyn to C. A. Saunders, June 1835, Gr. Br. P.R.O. Rail 1914-3. Glyn was a director of the railway from 1830 and became chairman in 1837. Glyn's banking concern was the financial motor behind the establishment of many railways worldwide, but its archives (I was told) were largely destroyed by bombing in World War 11.

43. *Correspondence* between the Board of Trade and T. Grahame, Esq., late chairman of the Grand Junction Canal Combination (London: Ridgway, 1853), p. 12.

44. ALS, R. Creed to J. B. Duboulay, 3.1.1834, Gt. Bt. P.R.O. Rail 1008.105.

45. ALS, Creed to Capt. Watts, Gr. Br. P.R.O. Rail 1008/105.

46. L.T.C. Rolt, *Thomas Telford* (London: Longmans, 1958), p. 160.

47. *Bankers' Circular*, No. 281 (December 3, 1833), pp. 164-165.

48. Bishop Carleton Hunt, *The Development of the British Corporation in England, 1800-1867* (New York: Russell and Russell, 1969, c. 1936), pp. 74-75.

49. H. C. Report, 1834 (July 10), p. 57.

50. "Minutes of Trustees under the 1798 Act. 1798-1851" (Gloucester Records Office D2041/2). Gloucester City Records: Walters, D6/a36/10; Baker, D726/1; Wood, D 63711/8/F2; D 690/IV/1-4, etc. *Directory of Gloucester*, 1820. Wood's Account Books in P.R.O. make no mention of a steam carriage. Wood was the model for a miser in Charles Dickens' *Bleak House*.

51. See, Wood, William Page in *DNB*.

52. "Report from the Select Committee on Turnpike Trusts," Great Britain, Parliament, *Sessional Papers* 9 (1839): 45.

53. Richard Cort, *Railway Reform* (London: E. Wilson, 1849), p. 100.

54. ALS, W. Downey to T. Deans, Edinburgh, July 2, 1834. Downey papers. For tolls on roads leading to Glasgow, see 4 Gulielmi IV, Cap. lxi (June 16, 1834), (stagecoach 1 s. and steam carriage "such Toll duties as shall be fixed by the Trustees at any general meeting assembled, or 1 d. per hundredweight") Gt. Br. Statutes. *Laws*, 1834.

55. H. C. Report, 1835, Gurney evidence, May 26.

54A. Richard Cort, *Rail-road Impositions Detected*, 2nd ed. (London: Lake, 1834), Appendices.

54B. Dionysius Lardner, *Railway Economy* (New York: Harper, 1855), p. 241

54C. Great Britain, Parliament, *Sessional Papers* 10 (1839): App. 17, p. 381.

54D. H. Pollin, "A Note on Railway Construction Costs, 1825-1850," *Economica* (November 1952), passim.

54E. H. L. Report, 1836, p. 336.

54F. James Morrison, *The Influence of English Railway Legislation on Trade and Industry* (London: 1848), p. 111 n. Speech to House of Commons, November 30, 1847

56. H. C. Report, 1834, p. 47.

57. H. L. Report, 1836, p. 332.

58. Gt. Br. Statutes, *Laws*, 1831 (I & 2 Gulielmi IV, Cap. xvi).

59. H. C. Report, 1834.

60. H. C. Report, 1835, p. 26.

61. H. C. Report, 1834, Ans: 812. For tolls on Brighton Road, see 4 Gulielmi IV, Cap. lxl, Gt. Br. Statutes, *Laws* (6 d. for stage coach, 2 s. for steam carriage).

62. H. C. Report 1834, passim. On the other hand, no toll was placed on the London-Stratford road where Hancock ran his carriage from his factory in Stratford to his commuting service within the City of London. Lest the group behind Maceroni's several companies be thought politically inconsequential, the leading role played in the formation of each of the Maceroni companies by the renowned Radical politician and economist Colonel Thomas Perronet Thompson, proprietor of the *Westminster Review*, stamps it as dynamic and influential. Thompson's promotion of the steam carriage has escaped his biographers.

63. H. C. Report, 1831, pp. 104-106.

64. H. L. Report, 1836. 65. Anna Gurney, "Letter to the Editor," *Cornish Gazette* (September 5,1879).

66. H. L. Report, 1836, p. 318. For example, Gordon's testimony to the same Lords' Committee on the noise from Gurney's carriage gave one a good idea of the sound as well as effectively contradicting Hancock immediately after whom Gordon testified. The noise could be heard at 5 yards distance but was not noticeable. It was "a sort of whistling or rather switching noise" (p. 319).

67. Alexander Gordon, *Observations on Railway Monopolies and Remedial Measures* (London: Weale, 1841), p. 51.

68. *Mechanics' Magazine* 26 (1836): 69.

69. J. T. Ward, "West Riding Landowners and the Railways," *Journal of Transport History* (Leicester, University Press, November 1960), pp. 242-243.

70. F.M.L. Thompson, *English Landed Society in the Nineteenth Century* (London: Routledge & Kegan Paul, 1963), p. 290.

71. G. R. Hawke, *Railways and Economic Growth in England and Wales 1840-1870* (Oxford: Clarendon, 1970), pp. 404-405. He estimated the social internal rate of return from railway investment, 1830-1870, to be about 15 percent.

72. Jasper W. Rogers, *Plan proposed* by James C. Anderson, Bart., and Jasper W. Rogers, Esq., C.E. for establishing steam carriages for the conveyance of goods and passengers on the mail coach roads of Ireland; also a proposed system for repair of roads by means of a road police and for telegraphing (Dublin: N. Walsh, 1841). Anderson's Irish Company cooperated with Parnell's Holyhead-Birmingham Steam Car Company in 1839 when they planned to shorten the voyage to America by weeks by carrying passengers from the London-Birmingham rail by steam carriage across Ireland to Galway and by steamer to New York City.

73. L. H. Haney, "A Congressional History of Railways in the United States to 1850," *Bulletin of University of Wisconsin* No. 211 (Madison, Wis.: 1908), p. 234. See also Robert Mills, *Substitute for Railroads and Canals: embracing a new plan of roadway; combining with the operation of steam carriages, great economy, in carrying into effect a system of internal improvement* (Washington, D.C.: Dunn, 1834).

74. John Francis, *A History of the English Railway: Its Social Relations and Revelations, 1820-1845*, vol. 2 (London: 1851), p. 18. "It will be seen that the state recognized the railways as a power to minister to its necessities, and was as eager to claim its service, as it was willing to influence its destinies."

75. The steam carriage promoters depended on their personal bankers: Hanning on Messrs. Cockburn and Company; Bouviers which acted for the Maceroni Steam Carriage Companies from 1837 to 1841 was the personal banker to Lord Brougham and, more significantly, had Lord Radnor as its senior partner. Praeds acted as banker for Maceroni's National Steam Carriage Company of 1835. Coutts Bank acted for the National Institution of Locomotion and for Parnell's London-Birmingham-Holyhead Steam Carriage Company.

The Bank of England, owing to its role as a bank of supply of notes to the London trade, was supported by London private bankers who existed to finance commerce such as Glyn, Mills which, on the other hand, owed its preeminence to its role as London agent for the country banks of Lancashire and Yorkshire.

76. Demetrius Boulger, *The History of Belgium*, Pt. II(London: 1909), p. 276. In 1830-1831 a British Army officer surveying the Euphrates Valley recommended it over Egypt as a railway route to India, and a House of Commons committee recommended his findings in an 1832 *Report*. See also Halford L. Hoskins, *British Routes to India* (New York: Longmans Green. 1928).

77. *Railway Magazine and Annals of Science* 1 (April 1836): 117. The leader of the delegation, Dr. Sir John Bowering (whose family was connected with the woolen trade of Devonshire), was a Radical reformer, an editor of the *Westminster Review*, and a member of Parliament for Bolton, Lancashire in which capacity he argued for more frequent communication with India, which railways would provide by shortening travel time to the national advantage. (Gt. Br., Parl., *Debates in H. of C.* (April 25, 1843), 68, 883; for Leopold see, *Railway Magazine. . .*, I (November 1836): 477. Radical reformers threw their lot in with the Lancashire free-traders when they supported the Opium Wars dispute beginning in Parliament in 1834 to open China to British trade.

78. Pierre Dauzet, *Le Siècle des Chemins de Fer en France (1821-1938)* (Fontenay-aux-Roses: Bellenand, 1948), p. 46.

79. Edward Blount, *Memoires* (London: Longmans Green, 902), p. 61. Although Disraeli as prime minister ordered the taking of Cyprus because the island lay opposite the approach to the Euphrates Valley from the Mediterranean, the English government did give guarantees to capitalists for building the line, fearing, according to Blount, that the Arabs would destroy it. Ironically, it was the old steam carriage promoter, Macneill (then knighted for his work with railways in Ireland), who just after midcentury was entrusted with building the rail line through Syria and the Euphrates to India.

80. ALS, Nathaniel to brothers, X1/109/55 (13), Rothschild papers (London). 81 ALS Nathaniel to brothers, X1/109/55 (44). Although Edward Wheler Mills was the partner of the Bank, the Mills referred to was his brother, Francis, who was not a partner but, according to Roger Fulford, *Glyn's 1753-1953: Six Generations on Lombard Street*

(London: Macmillan, 1953), (p. 80), brought "considerable business to Lombard Street through his promotion of railways in France and Italy." Francis Mills was vice-president of the Dover railway.

82. ALS, Nathaniel to brothers (Paris, March 10, 1843), X1/109/55 (46.).

83. ALS, James de R. to Nathaniel (October 31,1843), X1/109/54 (15).

84. Rothschild freres, *Lettres adressees a la maison Rothschild de Paris par son representant a Bruxelles*, T. II (Centre Univ. d'Histoire Contemporaine, Cahiers Bijdragen, 33), p. xi.

Arthur Dunham, *The Industrial Revolution in France, 1815-1848* (New York: Exposition, 1955), p. 447, App. B. The role of James de Rothschild provides the reader with interesting information on English investment in French railways. On August 29, 1845, the *Bankers' Circular* reported the composition of the board of directors for the du Nord line: Baron J. de Rothschild, president; Admiral de Rosamel, peer of France; P. Hottinguer; C. Lafitte; Pepin-Lehalleur; A. d'Eicthal [sic] regent of the Bank of France; E. Pereire, director of the St. Germain railway; A. Thurneyssen, banker; the Duke de Galliera; Caillard, senator; A. Gouin, deputy; Dellebecque, deputy; Jameson, banker; Blount, banker; Baron N. de Rothschild, banker; the Duke de Mouchy; F. Baring, banker; T. Baring, banker; J. Moss, president of the Grand Junction Railroad; Baron L. de Rothschild, banker; J. Masterman, M.P.; W. Chaplin, president of the Southampton Railway Company; and F. Mills, vice-president of the Dover Railway Company. We have encountered some of these names and can distinguish the unfamiliar ones as members of the Haute Banque in Paris. Caillard was the stagecoach entrepreneur. The English Rothschilds—Nathan and Lionel—are represented. Masterman, London banker, is given his member of Parliament status to indicate the interest of the English government. Capital for the line fixed at 150 million pounds was to be raised to 170 million in case of the junction of the Fampoux line and to 200 million in the case of the ulterior junction of St. Quentin.

85. ALS, Waghorn to Baron Homalauer, September 8,1846. Haddo House mss. (1/2) Bundle 1. For Waghorn's connection with the Lancashire capitalists, see ALS, Thomas Waghorn to Richmond (January 1833), Richmond papers 1463 f404,405. They petitioned Parliament for changes in the tax law on the transport of mail to help Waghorn in Egypt and petitioned the Treasury to overlook Act 59 Geo.3 Cap. III compelling steam vessels to carry letters for 2 d. to and from India. Waghorn indicated by his memorials to England's rulers that his unofficial activities were mutually understood always to be in their service. ALS, Waghorn to Sir Robert Peel, January 4, 1842: "In effecting this great object I have toiled gratuitously and unceasingly for fifteen years sacrificing my health, my prospects and my private property. I have nothing in return for this, on the other hand, am involved in debt to private Relations and Friends who assisted me with means years ago when I urged them to do so hoping that in all due course of time my Country would not fail to reward me and thus enable me to repay them." B.M. Add. MS. 40 499 f67; Parliament granted him money but not enough to cover his last trials with the overland route to Trieste, and he

died shortly afterward. See Marjorie Sankey, *"Care of Mr. Waghorn"* (Bath: Postal History Society, 1964).

86. M. Capefigue, *Histoire des grandes operations financiers, Banques, Bourses, Emprunts, Compagnies industrielles etc.*, vol. 4 (Paris: D'Amyot, 1855-1860), p. 216.

87. Jean Bouvier, *Les Rothschild* (Paris: Fayard, 1967), p. 170.

88. *Le Credit Mobilier et ses actionnaires* (Paris: le Chevalier, 1867), p. 24. Of course, the private fortunes of the bank's directors remained untouched: Pereires, 120 million francs; Duc de Galliera, 80 million; Cibiel, 10 million; Edouard Rodrigues, 10 million; Biesta, 10 million; C. Salvador, Dollfus, A. Thurneysson, Heeckerer, Renouard de Bussiere, and others, 20 million; totaling 360 million francs.

89. J. C. Dietz, *Histoire de l'Automobile: Charles Dietz, precurseur oublie* (Paris: Conserv. National des Arts et Metiers, 1955), p. 19.

90. "Arrete du 20 Avril 1866," Ministere de l'Agriculture, du Commerce et des Travaux Publics, F 14 10.007 (1866), Archives Nationales de France. My special thanks to Mme. Noel, archiviste.

91. Irmgard Lange-Kothe, "Zur Geschichte des Dampfwagens in Deutschland," *Automobil-Technische Zeitschrift*, Jahrg. 63, Heft 6 (June 1961): 196. A book appeared in Prussia in 1835 claiming that steam carriages were useless: Josef Ritter, *Die Unmoglichkeit, Dampfwagen auf gewoehnlichen Strassen als allgemeine Transportmittel einzufuhren.* A book dealer, Hoffmann, purchasing Gurney carriages, began a company in 1830 to carry passengers between Berlin and Potsdam. The Prussian postmaster-general, Nagler, was interested in Maceroni's carriage in 1834.

92. "It is doubtless true, in a way even general, that the taste for luxury and ostentation, the search for alliances among the old families, seen in the sovereign families, are particularly characteristic of the class of merchants and bankers, without becoming a rule of conduct, and distinguishes the heads of new families as well as the old families. In about 1880 the salons of Parisian high society could welcome . . . the young Baron Arthur de Rothschild, who passed his rich bachelor life between voyaging and participation in the reunions of the Yacht Club of France." Louis Bergeron, *Les Capitalistes en France (1780-1914)* (Paris: Gallimard, 1978), p. 53; Henri de R. spoke of Arthur's "valuable service to the French automobile industry" in a speech to the English Automobile Club in 1903, as published in *Allgemeine Automobil Zeitung* (January 25, 1903).

93. The discretion with which this relationship has been guarded caused James Laux, otherwise a meticulous historian, to report the firm as being under the guidance of Pierre de la Ville le Roulx, whose name does not appear in the Rothschild accounts. N. Salvago, however, was the largest shareholder after the Rothschild Bank and seemed to run the daily operations. See James M. Laux, *In First Gear* (Liverpool: University Press, 1976).

94. "Societe automobiles et de traction," 3K20 Rothschild papers (Paris.)

95. J. Aubin, *L'Automobile devant les chambres et devant l'opinion* (Paris: Jnl. "La Loi," 1908), p. 8. 96. Arthur Loewenstein, *Geschichte des Wuerttembergischen Kreditbankwesens und seiner Beziehungen zu*

Handel und Industrie (Tuebingen: Mohr, 1912: Archive fuer Sozialwissenschaft und Sozialpolitik. Ergaenzungsheft V), p. 94; quoted from the *Frankfurter Aktionaer*, 1871.

97. *Schmoller's Jahrbuch fuer Gesetzgebung*, 29 (1905), Heft 3, S.9; also see Gustav Schmoller, *Charakterbilder* (Muenchen: Duncker und Hublot, 1913), p. 233ff. which claims Steiner to be a "humane idealist."

98. ALS, Alphonse de Rothschild to English cousins, February 2, 1886. 101/8 Rothschild papers (London).

99. U.S. Manufacturers Bureau, *Monthly Consular and Trade Reports* 18, no. 61 (1886): 174.

100. "An den Aufsichtrath der Daimler-Motoren-Gesellschaft hier. Canstatt, 30 Maerz 1892," Simms papers 14/-.

101. "An den Aufsichtrath der Daimler-Motoren-Gesellschaft in Cannstatt. Cannstatt, 10 Oktober 1894," Simms papers 14/-.

102. Bertrand Gille, "Le Krach de Cuivres," *Revue d'histoire de la Siderurgie*, no. I (1968): 25ff.

103. ALS, Alphonse de R. to his English cousins, November 29, 1893. T 16, Rothschild papers (London).

104. Michele Flageolet-Lardenois, "Une ferme pionniere: Panhard et Levassor jusqu'en 1918." *Le Movement social*, No. 81 (October-December 1972): 44.

105. Henry Peyret, *Histoire des chemins de fer en France et dans le monde* (Paris: Soc. d'Ed. Franc. et Internat., 1949), p. 260ff.

106. J-C Toutain, *Les Transports en France de 1830 a 1965*, Cahiers de l'ISEA, No. 8 (Paris: Presses Univ., September-October 1967), pp. 244, 248.

107. Laux, *In First Gear*, p. 7.

108. Marquis de Chasseloup-Laubat, "A Short History of the Motor Car," p. 14, in Alfred C. Harmsworth, *Motors and Motor-Driving* (Boston: Little, Brown, 1902).

109. *The Horseless Age* (New York: January 16, 1901), p. 23.

110. *The Horseless Age* (New York: May 14, 1902), p. 587.

111. *Investors' Review* I (1892): 222.

112. "Railway Progress and Poverty," *Investors' Review* (October 20, 1900): 487.

113. R. J. Evans, *The Victorian Age, 1815-1914* (London: Arnold, 1968), pp. 263-265.

114. "Report from the Standing Committee on Law and Courts of Justice and Legal procedure on the Locomotives on Highways Bill, House of Commons," Gt. Br., Parl., *Sessional Papers* 10 (1896).

115. "Some Hooley Companies and Their Results," *Investors' Review* (June 10, 1898): 831.

116. *Investors' Review* (July 29, 1898), pp. 109-110.

117. George Woodbury, *The Story of the Stanley Steamer* (New York: W. W. Norton, 1950), p. 211.

118. Karl Marx, *The Class Struggles in France (1848-50)* (Moscow; Coop. pub. soc., 1934), p. 113, also pp. 121, 158, n. 58, 125.

119. Andre Maurois, *A History of France* (New York; Minerva, 1968 [c.1948]), p. 450

120. Daniel Bellet, "L'Automobilisme et son Avenir," *L'Economiste francais* (July 16, 1898): 72.

Comparative costs of steam to petrol cars: In the steam car, theoretically, one kilo of coke created 3,400,000 kilogrammetres of energy (a kilogrammetre equals the force expended in raising one kilogram one metre vertically, being about 7.2 foot-pounds). In Serpollet's steamer which used a petrol or oil burner rather than coke, one kilogram of petrol produced 4,250,000 kilogrammetres of power. In the petrol car, however, a kilo of gasoline produced 4,800,000 kilogrammetres. This was considerably more energy from a very small source and, although Serpollet's car was easily provisioned, the petrol car could be supplied with greater facility. For these two reasons, the petrol car had the advantage in the early years. What technical progress could have been made in the steam car had it maintained sufficient capitalization is an intriguing speculation. (L. Baudrey de Saunier, *Elements d'Automobile*. . . . (Paris: 1908), pp. 35-6).

On the other hand, the steam car could be started immediately whereas the starting of the petrol car required a manual of instructions in the early years.

Selected Bibliography

This bibliography comprises those materials considered the most helpful to an understanding of the subject.

ECONOMIC DEVELOPMENT

Clapham, J. H. *The Economic Development of France and Germany, 1815-1914.* Cambridge: Cambridge University Press, 1963 (c. 1921).

Dunham, Arthur. *The Industrial Revolution in France, 1815-1848.* New York: Exposition, 1955.

Evans, R. J. *The Victorian Age, 1815-1914.* 2nd ed. London: Arnold, 1968.

Landes, David. *The Unbound Prometheus: Technological Change and Industrial Development in Western Europe from 1750 to the Present.* Cambridge: Cambridge University Press, 1972.

Mantoux, Paul. *The Industrial Revolution in the Eighteenth Century: An Outline of the Beginnings of the Modern Factory System in England.* Rev. ed. New York: Harper and Row, 1961 (c. 1928).

ECONOMIC THEORY

Marxist

Coontz, Sydney H. *Productive Labour and Effective Demand.* New York: Kelley, 1966.

Gordon, David M. "Capitalist Efficiency and Socialist Efficiency." *Monthly Review* 28, no. 3 (July-August 1976): 19-39.

Neo-classical and Other

David, Paul A. *Technical Choice Innovation and Economic Growth. Essays on American and British experience in the nineteenth century.* Cambridge: Cambridge University Press, 1975.

Leon, Paolo. *Structural Change and Growth in Capitalism.* Baltimore: Johns Hopkins University Press, 1967 (c. 1965).

Nelson, R. R. "The Economics of Intervention: A Survey of the Literature." *Journal of Business* (April 1959).

Rosenberg, Nathan. *Perspectives on Technology.* Cambridge: Cambridge University Press, 1976.

Ruttan, Vernon W. "Usher and Schumpeter on Invention, Innovation and Technological Change." *Quarterly Journal of Economics* (November 1959).

Schmookler, Jacob. *Invention and Economic Growth.* Cambridge,
    Mass.: Harvard University, 1966.
Usher, A. P. *A History of Mechanical Invention.* Cambridge, Mass.:
    Harvard University, 1954.

THE AUTOMOBILE

For a bibliography of literature on the steam carriage, see Rhys
Jenkins, *Power Locomotion on the Highway.* A guide to the literature
relating to traction engines and steam road rollers and to propulsion of
common road carriages and velocipedes by stearn and other
mechanical power, with a brief historical sketch. London: W. Cate,
1896.
Bird Anthony. *Gottlieb Daimler, Inventor of the Motor Engine.*
    London: Weidenfield and Nicolson, 1962.
Bishop Charles. *La France et l'Automobile.* Contribution francaise
    au developpement economique et technique de l'automobilisme
    des origines a la deuxieme guerre mondiale. Paris: Genin, 1971.
Broun, Richard. *Appeal to Our Rulers and Ruled* in behalf of a
    consolidation of the post office, roads and mechanical conveyance
    for the service of the state. London: Mortimer, 1834.
Dietz, J. C. *Histoire de l'Automobile: Charles Dietz, pre'curseur
    oublie.* Paris: Conservatoire National des Arts et Metiers, 1955.
Gordon, Alexander. *A Treatise upon Elemental Locomotion* and
    interior communication wherein are explained and illustrated
    the history, practice and prospects of steam carriages and the
    comparative value of turnpike roads, railways and canals. 3rd
    ed. London: T. Tegg, 1836.
Gurney, Goldsworthy. *A Course of Lectures on Chemical Science* as
    delivered at the Surrey Institution. London: G. and W. B.
    Whittaker, July 2, 1823.
_____. *Mr. Goldsworthy Gurney's Account of the Invention of the
    Steam Jet or Blast,* and its application to steamboats and
    locomotive engines in reference to a mistaken claim put forth
    by Mr. Smiles in his "Life of the Late Mr. George Stephenson."
    London: G. Barclay, 1859.
_____. *Mr. Gurney's Observations on steam carriages on turnpike
    roads* with returns of the daily practical results of working; the
    cause of the stoppage of the carriage at Gloucester; and the
    consequent official report of the House of Commons. London:
    Baldwin and Cradock, 1832.
Hancock, Walter. *Narrative of Twelve Years' Experience* (1824-1836)
    demonstrative of the practicability and advantage of employing
    steam-carriages on common roads with engravings and
    descriptions of the different steam carriages constructed by the
    author, his patent boiler, wedge-wheels, and other inventions.
    London: Weale, 1838.
Harris, T. R. *Sir Goldsworthy Gurney, 1793-1875.* Penzance: 1975.
Herapath, John. *A Letter to His Grace the Duke of Wellington* on the
    utility, advantages, and national importance of Mr. Gurney's steam

carriage. London: Baldwin and Cradock, 1829.

Lange-Kothe, Irmgard. "Zur Geschichte des Dampfwagens in Deutschland." *Motorwagen*, Jahrg. 63, pp. 194-198.

Laux, James. *In First Gear, the French Automobile Industry in 1914*. Liverpool: University Press, 1976.

Nitske, W. Robert. *The Complete Mercedes Story: The Thrilling Seventy-Year History of Daimler and Benz*. New York: Macmillan Co., 1955.

Nixon, St. John C. *The Invention of the Automobile*. London: Country Life, 1936.

Seltzer, Lawrence. *A Financial History of the American Automobile Industry;* a study of the ways in which the leading American producers of automobiles have met their capital requirements. Boston: Mifflin, 1928.

Siebertz, Paul. *Gottlieb Daimler. Ein Revolutionaer der Technik*. Meunchen: Lehmanns, 1940.

Young, Charles Frederick T. *The Economy of Steam Power on Common Roads* in relation to agriculturists, railway companies, mine and coal owners, quarry proprietors, contractors, etc., with its history and practices in Great Britain . . . and its progess in the United States by Alex L. Holley and J. K. Fisher. London: Atchley, 1861.

RAILWAYS

For a bibliography dealing with railways, see George Ottley, *A Bibliography of British Railway History*. London: Allen and Unwin, 1965.

Adler, Dorothy R. *British Investment in American Railways, 1834-1898*. Charlottesville, Va.: University of Virginia Press, 1970.

Alderman, Geoffrey. *The Railway Interest*. Leicester: University Press, 1973.

Cort, Richard. *Railway Impositions Detected*. London: 1834.

Dauzet, Pierre. *La siècle des chemins de fer en France (1821-1938)*. Fontenay-aux-Roses: Bellenand, 1948.

Hawke, G. T. *Railways and Economic Growth in England and Wales, 1840-1870*. Oxford: Clarendon, 1970.

Lamalle, Ulysse. *Histoire des chemins de fer belges*. Bruxelles: 1943.

Lefevre, Andre. *Sous le Second Empire: chemins de fer et politique*. Paris: 1957.

Newbold, J. T. *The Railways, 1825-1925*. London: Labour Publications, 1925.

Salvago, Georges. *Le probleme de l'etatisation des chemins de fer en France depuis leur origine jusqu'en 1857*. Paris; Duchemin, 1922.

BANKING AND POLITICS

Allyn, Emily. *Lords Versus Commons*. New York: Century, 1931.

Bouvier, Jean. *Les Rothschild*. Paris: Fayard, 1967.

Dupleix. "La colosse bancaire francais. . . *Cahiers du Bolchevisme*, I mars, I avril, I et 5 mai, 1925, pp. 854-861, 1010-1024, 1162-

1167,1233-1243.

Dupont-Ferrier, P. *Le marche financier de Paris sous le second empire.* Paris: Alcan, 1925

Elwitt, Sanford. *The Making of the Third Republic: Class and Politics in France, 1868-1884.* Baton Rouge, La.: State University, 1975.

Emden, Paul N. *Money Powers of Europe in the Nineteenth and Twentieth Centuries.* New York: Appleton-Century, 1938.

Fulford, Roger. *Glyn's 1753-1953:* Six generations in Lombard Street. London:

Gille, Bertrand. "La fondation de la Societe generale." *Histoire des Entreprises* 8 (Novembre, 1961)

_____. *Histoire de la Maison Rothschild.* Geneve: Droz, 1967. 2 vols. Travaux de Droit, d'Economie, de Sociologie et de Sciences Politiques, No. 56, II, pp.

_____. "Recherches sur la formation de la grande entreprise capitaliste (1815-1848)." *Affaires et Gens d'Affaires* 17. Paris: SEVPEN, 1959.

Hunt, Bishop Carleton. *The Development of the Business Corporation in England, 1800-1867.* New York: Russell and Russell, 1969 (c. 1936).

Jenks, Leland H. *The Migration of British Capital to 1875.* New York: Harper and Row, 1928.

Loewenstein, Arthur. *Geschichte des Wuerttembergischen Kreditbankwesens und seiner Beziehungen zu Handel and Industrie.* Tubingen: Mohr, 1912. Archiv fuer Sozialwissenschaft und Socialpolitik, Ergaenzungsheft V.

Marx, Karl. *The Class Struggles in France, 1848-50.* Moscow: Cooperative Publishing Society of Foreign Workers of the U.S.S.R., 1934.

Priouret, Roger. *Origines du patronat francais.* Paris: Grasset, 1963.

Semmel, Bernard. *The Rise of Free Trade Imperialism.* Classical political economy, the empire of free trade and imperialism, 1750-1850. Cambridge: Cambridge University Press, 1970.

Thomas, J. A. *The House of Commons, 1832-1901:* A Study of Its Economic and Functional Character. Cardiff: University of Wales Press Board, 1939.

PETROLEUM AND METALLURGY _

Brackel, Oswald von u. Joseph Leis. *Der dreissigyaehrige Petroleumkrieg.* Berlin: Guttentag, 1903.

Gheciu, Basile, *La politique du petrole en France.* Paris: Jouve, 1921.

Roy, Joseph Antoine. *Histoire de la famille Schneider et du Creusot.* Paris: M. Riviere, 1962.

Seeman, E. F. *Die Monopolisierung des Petroleumhandels und der Petroleum Industrie.* Berlin: L. Simion, 1893.

Sturdza, D. *La Question du petrole en Roumaine.* Berlin: Puttenkammer u. Muehlbrecht, 1906.

Zoepfl, Gottfried. *Der Wettbewerb des russischen und amerikanischen Petroleums.* Berlin: Siemenroth, 1899.

TRANSPORT

Grahame, Thomas. *Correspondence* between the Board of Trade and T. Grahame, Esq., late chairman of the Grand Junction Canal Company on Railway and Canal Combination. London: Ridgway, 1853.

Jackman, W. T. *The Development of Transportation in Modern England.* London: Cass, 1962.

Sankey, Marjorie. *"Care of Mr. Waghorn."* Bath: Postal History Society, 1964.

Spence, Peter. *How the Railway Companies Are Crippling British Industry and Destroying the Canals,* with suggestions for reforming the whole system, of railway charges, and rescuing the waterways, permanently for the nation. Manchester: Heywood, 1882.

Toutain, J. C. *Les Transports en France de 1830 a 1965.* Cahiers de l'ISEA, No. 8. Paris: Presses Universitaire, September-October 1967.

PARLIAMENTARY PAPERS—NINETEENTH CENTURY

France. *Arrete.*
"Arrete du 20 avril 1866." Ministere de l'Agriculture, du Commerce et des Travaux Publics, F 1410.0007 (1866). Archives Nationales de France. Paris, France.

Great Britain. House of Commons. *Journals.*
_____. House of Lords. *Journals.*
_____. Parliament. *Debates and Proceedings.*

The Mirror of Parliament.

Great Britain. Parliament. *Sessional Papers.*
Report from the Select Committee appointed to inquire into the proportion of tolls which ought to be imposed upon coaches and other vehicles propelled by steam or gas, upon turnpike roads, and also to inquire into the rate of toll actually levied upon such coaches and other vehicles under an Act of Parliament now in force, and who were instructed to inquire generally into the present state and future prospects of land carriage, by means of wheeled vehicles propelled by steam or gas on common roads; with the minutes of Evidence and Appendix, 1831. Vlll.

Report from the Select Committee on Mr. Goldsworthy Gurney's Case, with the minutes of Evidence. 1834. Xl. 1835. xm

Report from the Select Committee on Turnpike Trusts and Tolls. 1836. XIX.

Report from the Select Committee on Turnpike Trusts and the Creditors of such Trusts. 1839. IX.

List of names, descriptions, and places of abode of all Persons subscribing to the Amount of £2,000 and upwards to a Railway Subscription Contract deposited in the Private Bill Of fice during the present Session of Parliament; the Amount subscribed by each Person for every Railway to which he may be a Subscriber; and the Total Amount of such Subscription by each Person. 1845. XL. 1846. XXXVIII.

Minutes of Evidence taken before the Select Comittee on the Locomotive Bill, with the Proceedings of the Committee. 1859. *Sess. 2. V.*

Report from the Select Committee on Turnpike Trusts. 1864 V.

Report from the Select Committee on Locomotives on Roads. 1873. XVI.

Report from the Standing Committee on Law and Courts of Justice and Legal Procedure on the Locomotives on Highways Bill, House of Commons. 1896. X.

Report from the Select Committee on Petroleum with proceedings, July 23, 1896. 1896. Xll.

Great Britain. House of Lords. *Papers.*

Report from the Select Committee of the House of Lords on the Locomotives on Roads Bill. 1865. XXI.

Return to an address of the House of Lords, dated 20th May 1870 for Any Reports made by officers of the War Department to the Secretary of State for War as to the applicability to Military Purposes on Mr. Thomson's Road Steamer or Locomotion for Common Roads. 1870. XIII.

Great Britain. House of Lords. *Journals.* "Appendices."

Report from the Select Committee of the House of Lords appointed to inquire whether any danger by fire is likely to arise from Locomotive Engines being used on Railroads passing through narrow Streets, with minutes of Evidence and Appendices. v. 68 (1836), App. 5.

Report from the Select Committee appointed to consider a Bill entitled, "An Act to repeal such Portions of all Acts as impose prohibitory Tolls on Steam Carriages. v. 68 (1836), App. 7.

Bills

To regulate the Turnpike Toll on Steam Carriages. Sessional Papers. 1831-32. IV. 489.

To repeal such Portions of all Acts as impose prohibitory Tolls on Steam Carriages, and to substitute other Tolls on an equitable Footing with Horse Carriages. *Sessional Papers.* 1836. Vl. 67.

Acts

Great Britain. Statutes. *Local Acts.*

"An Act for more effectively repairing and improving several Roads leading into and from the Town of Cheltenham in the County of Gloucester, and for making new Branches of Roads to communicate therewith (30th July 1831) 1& 2 Will. IV, Cap.XVI.

_____. _____. *Public Acts.*

"An Act to consolidate and amend the Laws relating to Highways in that part of Great Britain called England (31st August 1833)." 1835. 5 & 6 Will. IV, Cap.L.

"An Act for regulating the Use of Locomotives on Turnpike and other Roads, and the Tolls to be levied on such Locomotives and on the Waggons and Carriages drawn or propelled by the same (I st August 1861). " 1861. 24 & 25 Vict., Cap. LXX.

"An Act to amend the Law relating to certain Nuisances on Turnpike Roads, and to continue certain Turnpike Acts in Great Britain (29th July 1864)." 1864. 27 & 28 Vict., Cap LXXV.

"An Act for further regulating the Use of Locomotives on Turnpike and other Roads for agricultural and other Purposes (5th July 1865). " 1865. 28 & 29 Vict., Cap LXXXIII.

"An Act to amend the Law relating to Highways in England and the Acts relating to Locomotives on Roads; and for other purposes (16th August 1878)."1878. 41 & 42 Vict., Cap. LXXVII.

"An Act for further regulating the Use of Locomotives on Highways in Scotland (16th August 1878)." 1878. 41 & 42 Vict., Cap. LVIII.

"An Act to amend the Law with respect to the Use of Locomotives on Highways (14th August 1896)." 1896. 59 & 60 Vict., Cap. LVIII.

"An Act to amend the Law with respect to the Use of Locomotives on Highways, and with respect to extraordinary Traffic (2nd August 1898)." 1898. 61 & 62 Vict., Cap. XXIX.

"An Act to amend the Locomotives on Highways Act, 1896 (14th August 1903)." 1903. 3 Edw. 7, Cap. XXXVI.

MANUSCRIPT SOURCES

Brougham, Lord Henry. Collection. University College Library, London University.

Central Agricultural Society. "Papers." Ipswich Record Office. Ipswich, East Suffolk.

Downey, William. "Letters: Steam Carriage Co. of Scotland." Society of Civil Engineers, London.

Hanning, William. "Letters and Accounts: Gurney Steam Carriage Co." Taunton Record Office, Taunton, Somerset.

Parnell, Sir Henry. Account Books. c/o Lord Congleton, Salisbury, Wilts.

Richmond, 5th Duke of. "Papers." West Sussex County Council, Chichester, West Sussex.

Rothschild Bank. "Papers." Paris House. Archives Nationales, Paris. London House. Rothschilds, New Court, St. Swithins Lane, London.

Simms, Frederick. "Papers." Senate House Library. London University.

Telford, Thomas. "Letters." Ironbridge Gorge Museum Trust. Telford, Salop.

For a bibliography of works by and about Sir Goldsworthy Gurney and his other inventions, see:

Boase, G. C. *Collectanea Cornubiensia.* Truro: 1890, p. 304.

_____, and W. P. Courtney. *Bibliotheca Cornubiensis.* London: Longmans, 1874, Vol. 1, pp. 198-199; 1882, Vol. 3, pp. 1210, 1212-1213.

INDEX

171

173

174

175

180